Emma's breath caught at the way her nerves leaped beneath her skin as George rested a hand on the back of her chair.

He looked as handsome in his suit as he had in his uniform the other day. Their only meeting had been almost two years ago and had been brief, but she'd never forgotten his eyes. They'd held her attention at her aunt's house that day, and again in the hallway the day before yesterday. They were blue, a real bright blue, and twinkled like none she'd ever seen.

"I'll get you a glass of punch," he said quietly. "Unless you'd prefer something different?"

She had to swallow, hard, before she was able to say, "Punch would be lovely. Thank you."

"I'll be right back," he said.

She didn't release the air locked in her lungs until he'd walked away. Then, as her shoulders slumped, Emma questioned her sanity. As soon as she'd seen George, a hundred questions that she wanted to ask had formed in her mind. About men he'd mentioned in his letters as well as places and things that he'd seen. Most of all, she wanted to ask him how he was doing, being back home. He had to be happy about that, but it had to be different than before. So very different.

Author Note

If you're like me, as soon as there is a nip in the air, you're ready to start reading Christmas stories. Then again, I've also been known to read them in July and, well, pretty much every other month.

In *The Captain's Christmas Homecoming*, you'll be taken to a chilly, snowy upstate New York, which had been known as the Lumber Capital of the World.

The hero in this story, George Weston, comes from a family of lumber barons. He's next in line and is dedicated to using the skills he'd honed while serving in WWI to grow the entire industry.

However, while he'd been overseas, he'd received enchanting letters, and meeting the woman who had written them was his first priority.

This story was built around a single image I had one day while mowing the lawn... I saw a young solider, arriving home, stepping off a train and searching the crowd for a woman. The woman was unknown to him but was to have a flower in her hat. He saw the hat. Saw the woman, and found himself speechless because, though she was charming, the woman was also gray-haired and quite old.

I hope you enjoy reading about George, Emma and Beverly Buttons as much as I enjoyed writing their story. And I hope your Christmas wishes come true.

LAURI ROBINSON

The Captain's Christmas Homecoming

HARLEQUIN®
HISTORICAL™

Recycling programs
for this product may
not exist in your area.

ISBN-13: 978-1-335-72352-9

The Captain's Christmas Homecoming

Copyright © 2022 by Lauri Robinson

Harlequin Enterprises ULC
22 Adelaide St. West, 41st Floor
Toronto, Ontario M5H 4E3, Canada
www.Harlequin.com

Printed in U.S.A.

A lover of fairy tales and history, **Lauri Robinson** can't imagine a better profession than penning happily-ever-after stories about men and women in days gone past. Her favorite settings include World War II, the Roaring Twenties and the Old West. Lauri and her husband raised three sons in their rural Minnesota home and are now getting their just rewards by spoiling their grandchildren. Visit her at laurirobinson.blogspot.com, Facebook.com/lauri.robinson1 or Twitter.com/laurir.

Books by Lauri Robinson

Harlequin Historical

Diary of a War Bride
A Family for the Titanic Survivor
The Captain's Christmas Homecoming

The Osterlund Saga

Marriage or Ruin for the Heiress
The Heiress and the Baby Boom

Twins of the Twenties

Scandal at the Speakeasy
A Proposal for the Unwed Mother

Sisters of the Roaring Twenties

The Flapper's Fake Fiancé
The Flapper's Baby Scandal
The Flapper's Scandalous Elopement

Brides of the Roaring Twenties

Baby on His Hollywood Doorstep
Stolen Kiss with the Hollywood Starlet

Visit the Author Profile page
at Harlequin.com for more titles.

To our newest granddaughter, Avery.
You've been an adventurer, and an adventure,
since the day you were born. Papa and Drama
love you to the moon and back.

Chapter One

November 1918

It had been a long time since George Weston had felt like this—like a kid at Christmas. That's what he compared the surge of excitement that shot through him to as the screech and hiss of the train applying its brakes filled the air. Other passengers began to shift in their seats, to collect belongings or button their coats as the train rolled into town. George repositioned the hat on his head and checked the belt around his waist on the outside of his uniform jacket, then retrieved his bag from under the train seat and stood, waiting for his turn to enter the aisle and proceed to the exit.

Every life had issues. Complexities and events that brought great joys and sorrows. He'd experienced a fair share of such events the last eighteen months, while overseas, in the trenches, witnessing the death and destruction of war, but also successes and friendships. There were things he'd never forget—it would be impossible to—as well as people. Not only his own countrymen, but also those from around the world that he'd encountered and collaborated with in many circumstances.

He glanced out the windows lining the train car's wall, at the gray skies. November could bring cold and gloomy days, a precursor to winter bearing down, yet the gratefulness inside George was warm and bright. But for grace, he could be coming home in a box, or not at all, buried on the French countryside or in some other foreign land, a body too damaged to identify.

The gratitude he felt for that, for coming home, wasn't just for himself, but for his family, his parents. And one other person.

Miss Beverly Buttons.

He hadn't known her when he'd left Albany eighteen months ago, ready and willing to fulfill a duty of serving his country just as his ancestors had since the Revolutionary War. He hadn't known a lot of things, especially what to expect. He certainly hadn't expected to rise through the ranks and return home as a captain. While others attributed that to his intelligence, courage and character, he attributed it to his father. Since the age of seven, his father had allowed him to tag along and learn every aspect of the family lumber company. He'd been ten the first time he'd joined a cruiser to inspect trees to be harvested and by the time he'd been thirteen, he had been cruising on his own. Walking miles upon miles through wooded terrain and marking trees to be harvested had honed his map-reading abilities, and those abilities had played a major role in his military advancements. One look at a map and he had it memorized, both the way in and the way out. He'd taken each and every advancement of rank seriously, had worked diligently to lead his unit through battles, and ultimately, thankfully, had led them out of trouble.

There had been plenty of that. Trouble. And gas. The fear of being gassed while in the trenches filled with brackish water and rats—no one could ever forget the rats—had affected every man in his company. Luckily, his troops had never encountered gas during any of their missions. They'd moved quickly, struck their attacks and retreated, then moved on to their next assignment, which is why he was on his way home now.

His company's last mission had been completed and they'd returned to base to await their next orders. Then, because the Treaty of Versailles had been signed in June and implications of that treaty had been put in place, it had been determined he and his men would be sent home.

That had taken place so quickly, he hadn't had a chance to write a single letter to let anyone know of his return. He'd been on a ship bound for America when Germany had formally surrendered last week, officially ending the war.

He was ready to hang up his captain's hat and become a civilian again. George reached into his uniform suit pocket, felt the stack of letters bound by a broken bootlace and grinned at how his excitement grew. He had no idea what Beverly Buttons looked like, but he couldn't wait to see her because she wasn't unknown to him. Through the letters they'd shared, he felt as if he knew her better than any woman he'd ever known.

While in the trenches, he'd kept the letters he'd received from her tucked inside the lining of his trousers, hoping the wool would keep them from getting soaked through so he could read them over and over as time permitted. They'd been his lifeline, and had reinforced his goal to get home, so they could meet in person.

That would happen today. The months, weeks, days and hours he'd been waiting were now down to minutes.

Each time he'd returned to base he'd been thrilled by the letters awaiting him. There had always been one or two from family members, but it had been those from Beverly that he'd looked forward to the most and read first. Each one had been like a gift. Every line, every word, had made him smile and filled him with optimism for his life upon returning home.

Her name had been unfamiliar to him when he'd received her first letter, and he'd questioned if the letter had truly been meant for him, until he'd opened it, read how she was from his hometown of Albany, New York, and was hoping that he'd like to hear the latest happenings around town.

He hadn't been sent afield yet upon receiving that first letter and had instantly written to her in return. Those first few letters that they'd exchanged had been his rock, his connection to the outside world while traipsing the Western Front.

As soon as his ship had docked in the New York harbor, he'd sent a telegram to Miss Beverly Buttons, explaining that he'd be arriving today, on the noon train, and asked if she would meet him at the station.

Her response had come the following morning, via return telegram, telling him that she'd be there, and that she'd have a white-and-yellow flower pinned to her hat so that he'd recognize her.

He'd barely been able to think of anything else while making his way through the discharge process. More than once, he'd wondered what color her hair would be, and her eyes, and what her voice would sound like, but in all actuality, it didn't matter.

There comes a time when a man knows, just knows, deep down what he wants and that's what had happened to him. While reading her letters, he'd determined that she was the woman he would marry.

This time around, he was going to ask a woman to marry him because he wanted to, not because someone else wanted that to happen.

That's how it had been with Martha. They'd agreed to get married because it would have built their lumber companies into an empire. That's what both of their families wanted, and he would have married Martha before he'd left for the war if she hadn't wanted to wait until he returned, so they could have the wedding that society expected.

He and Martha came from two of the wealthiest families in the state, thanks to the lumber industry that their families had been a part of for generations. A merger of the two families would create one company—the largest in the nation.

He'd wanted that for his family, had promised it would happen, and had left for the war with the full understanding that they'd marry upon his return. However, the first letter he'd received after leaving home had been from Martha, telling him that she was calling off their wedding, and the second letter had come from his mother, regretfully informing him that Martha had eloped with a man he'd never heard of—Delmar Christianson.

The news had come as a surprise, but his heart hadn't been shattered, because he hadn't loved Martha. He'd never planned on loving her. Marriage had simply been the next step in his plan for Weston Lumber. His family had to be disappointed that it hadn't happened, and that was the one thing that he'd promised to never do—disappoint his parents.

He'd thought about that a lot while overseas, and had hopes of keeping his promise in another way. Perhaps two ways, due to Beverly's letters. Her first letter had arrived right after the one from Martha. Her neat, elegant handwriting hadn't mentioned people or gossip that might have been floating around about him and his broken engagement. Instead, it had been full of how the warm summer weather had allowed flowers to bloom all across the city, how children could be seen playing hopscotch on the sidewalks and swinging on swings in the city park.

All of her letters had been like that first one, full of things he'd been able to visualize throughout the seasons and months. The colors of the changing leaves, how a snowfall had made everything look fresh and clean and children could be spotted ice skating on the pond in the center of the city park and the budding of leaves in the spring. Visualizing those things had made him feel as if he was back home at times, but more than that, he could tell Beverly loved Albany as much as he did, and that gave him a real connection to her.

They'd come to know each other through their letters. She'd asked him about numerous subjects, including books, and they'd discussed more than one book in succedent letters. His favorite part of her letters had been how she'd always included a riddle or joke, with the answer near the end. Things that would make him laugh, such as: Why couldn't the pony sing? Because he was little hoarse. Or, why do fish live in salt water?

Because pepper makes them sneeze. Or what time do ducks wake up? At the quack of dawn.

George peered over the heads of those in front of him as they slowly moved forward toward the door. Beverly's jokes had kept him and the other soldiers entertained during more than one long, dark night and he couldn't wait to finally meet the woman who'd written them to him. Tell her how much her letters had meant to him, how much she meant to him.

His car would be waiting at the train station. The one he'd purchased right before leaving. A Nash. Red with a black canopy top, black fenders and interior, and a four-cylinder gas engine. He'd telephoned home from New York City and left a message for Willis, the family chauffeur, to have the car delivered to the station. He'd explained to James, the butler who had answered the phone, that he wanted his return to be a surprise to his parents, but in all actuality, he'd wanted a few hours with Beverly before making his homecoming known to his family.

He had plans of asking her to have coffee with him at a café, and truly couldn't wait to see her face, hear her voice. In his mind, he imagined she was close to his age of twenty-four, with brown hair and brown eyes. He couldn't say why he thought that—he just did. And she was pretty. Very. And soft-spoken. And thoughtful, and kind, and smart and generous. An all-around wonderful person.

It was finally his turn to exit, and he couldn't help but scan the area, looking for a hat with a flower pinned to it, even though he knew he wouldn't be able to see her from here. With over a hundred trains rolling in and out of the station on a daily basis, there were multiple tracks and long, covered embarking-and-loading islands that he'd have to walk through before entering the elaborate white brick building with arched, two-story windows that was the most modern depot in the state.

No expense had been spared. New Yorkers loved their state capital and were proud for it to hold the finest amenities in the state. Finer than those in New York City.

His family had been a part of Albany for generations and Weston Lumber had been used to build the now massive city for nearly half a century, including the impressive governor's mansion and state capital buildings.

He was proud of his heritage, of his family, and was ready to take on a larger role in the lumber company. To make it the largest company in the nation, as he'd promised.

Walking shoulder to shoulder with those leaving other trains, George crossed the crowded platform to the depot building that he knew contained several rows of benches for people to wait for departures or to greet those arriving. The entire time he was walking, he was scanning the crowd for a woman wearing a hat with a yellow-and-white flower.

There were plenty of woman wearing all styles, shapes and colors of hats. Some even had flowers on them, but none were the one he was looking for.

The crowd dispersed in all directions as they entered the spacious building. Noise echoed off the tall ceiling. George ignored the sounds of people talking, greeting each other, their footfalls clicking on the tile floors, and the louder voices announcing the incoming and departing trains as he walked toward the long benches in the center of the lobby.

His heartbeat increased at the sight of a pretty blond woman sitting alone near the end of one bench. She was not wearing a hat but was searching the crowd. He increased his speed when she stood, but then slowed his footsteps when a man hurried around him and the woman smiled, rushing forward to greet him.

As the man and woman embraced, George shifted his gaze to the rows of benches again, searching for a hat with a white-and-yellow flower.

He saw one. A white, rolled brim hat, with a white-and-yellow daisy pinned near the crown, but upon espying the woman wearing it, he continued searching, even though a tiny quiver coiled up his spine.

The woman wearing that hat couldn't be Beverly. She was elderly. Quite elderly.

His throat grew thick when he found no other white-and-yellow flowers pinned on hats and his gaze found the woman again.

She smiled at him. A soft, sweet smile that lit up her aged face. She also stood and gave him a timid wave with all four fingers of one white-gloved hand.

George wasn't sure if it was disbelief or disappointment that washed over him. Either way, he held it in and put a smile on his face as he stopped near the bench where the woman stood.

"Hello, Captain Weston," she said softly. "I saw you walk through the door and knew it was you immediately."

George set his bag on the floor. "You must be Miss Buttons." He flinched slightly, wondering if he should have said Mrs. Buttons.

"Oh, please, call me Beverly."

He held out a hand. "And you must call me George."

She laid her hand in his. "I'm so happy to meet you, and so very grateful that you made it back home. That has been my greatest wish since your first letter."

George lifted her gloved hand, kissed the back of it. "That has been my wish as well, and I've looked forward to meeting you."

"I do hope I'm not a disappointment to you," she said.

"No, I'm not disappointed." How could he be? This woman had been a light inside him when everything around him had been dark and dangerous. Her face was wrinkled, her hair a silvery gray, but he could see her beauty. Inside and out. "Not at all," he added, and gave her hand a gentle squeeze before releasing it.

"I'm grateful to hear that," she said with pinkening cheeks. "Though I wouldn't be surprised if you're disappointed that I'm not younger, prettier."

The flare of disappointment that he had felt upon realizing she was indeed Beverly was directed at him, not her. He should not have gotten his hopes up, shouldn't have hoped that he'd found a way to ease his family's disappointment in him. He'd worked his entire life to not hurt his parents, not disappoint them, and not marrying Martha had been the first time that had happened. Perhaps that had been why he'd thought, even dreamed, about marrying Beverly. Wrongly thinking that might make up for it. Marrying someone else wouldn't make up for anything, or make the merger happen.

However, above all, he should never have assumed Beverly would be anyone other than who she was, for this woman was truly a dear. He could see that by the sincerity on her face. She was the woman who had written to him and for that he was truly grateful.

"I have seen better years," she said.

His smile became even more genuine as a special warmth filled him. "My greatest wish was to meet you, here today, and you made that wish come true. Nothing could be more wonderful and you couldn't be prettier."

She covered her giggle with one hand. "Oh, dear, you are as charming as your letters."

"As are you." He picked up his bag and held out his elbow for her to take. "May I interest you in a cup of coffee at a nearby café?"

Looping an arm around his, she smiled up him. "I was hoping you'd suggest that. I truly was."

Unable to sit or even stand still, Emma Leigh Ellis paced the floor of her tiny apartment, wringing her hands together and pausing at the slightest sound coming from the hallway. Beverly should have been back from the train station by now. George's train would have arrived hours ago.

Emma's heart thudded, both at the idea of him being home and her elderly neighbor not back from the station yet. It was chilly outside and though she'd made Beverly promise that she would travel to and from the station in a taxi, Beverly could be stubborn and may have chosen to walk. Despite the fact that their apartment building was downtown, miles from the station.

Regret, along with frustration and worry, had Emma opening the door again, peering into the hallway of the second floor. The walls were white, the floor brown, and both had deep nicks and dark scratches from years of people moving possessions in and out. The hall was also empty.

Emma closed the door, leaned against it and pressed both hands to her cheeks. Why had she involved Beverly in all of this? Why had she written to George in the first place?

Because she'd had to.

If she hadn't left New York City, hadn't moved to Albany, Delmar would have never come here, never have met Martha, and therefore, Martha would have married George as planned instead of eloping with Delmar.

George had expected to come home from the war and marry the woman he loved. Knowing that wasn't going to happen is why she'd written to him, and why she'd asked Beverly if she could use her name on the letters, so he wouldn't know whom the letters had really come from.

The guilt and remorse filling her was overwhelming. She had once been so proud of herself for changing her life, turning it into one she loved, and had never meant to hurt anyone in the process. But she had and if anyone ever learned the truth, it would be awful. Truly awful.

Beverly not being home yet was also truly awful! Now, because of Emma, there was a woman who was almost seventy years old walking home from the train station, and it was cold out. Nearly freezing.

Emma glanced at the clock. She'd been home from school for almost half an hour. Pushing off the door, she retrieved her coat. She had to go find Beverly. Now, before it got any later.

She buttoned her coat all the way up to the collar, pulled the triangle-folded scarf from a pocket and tied it tightly beneath her chin before opening the door and hurrying down the hallway and the stairway.

What had she expected? That George wouldn't want to meet the woman writing to him all these months? Of course, he would! Why hadn't she thought of that?

Because she hadn't been thinking! That's why.

She opened the door. The chilling breeze nearly took her breath away as she stepped out of the apartment building and she shoved her hands in her pockets, digging for her gloves. The wind had grown colder during the time she'd been inside and she became even more concerned over Beverly being outside, walking home in this weather.

Emma increased her pace, hurrying along the sidewalk while scanning the cars at the intersection for a taxi that might, just might, be bringing Beverly home.

For years, automobiles had shared the streets with horse-drawn wagons, but lately, the number of automobiles had grown, and not a one of them in sight was a taxi. However, the number of automobiles rolling up and down the streets said she'd be at the corner for an extended length of time before she'd be able to cross the street. As a milk truck drove past, she couldn't help but wonder if her father would still be alive today if he'd been in an automobile instead of the horse-drawn milk wagon. That had been six years ago. All the milkmen in New York City had used horse-drawn wagons then.

Stepping from foot to foot to try to stay warm while waiting on the traffic, Emma squeezed her eyes shut. Filled with overwhelming remorse and guilt, she whispered, "I know you're up there watching me, Dad, and you know the mess I've made. I hate to ask, but if you could finagle just a little miracle, I promise I'll never ask again."

She opened her eyes and glanced around to make sure no one had heard her, but was more surprised by the lack of traffic than by the other people waiting to cross the street beside her. There was only one car advancing toward the corner. Letting out a groan, she said, "I didn't mean the traffic."

"Excuse me?" a man who stood next to her asked.

He was tall, with a flat-brimmed hat and a heavy wool coat, and unfamiliar—which wasn't unusual. Albany was a very large city, however, unlike New York City, Albany was a friendly city. People often spoke to each other at street corners. "I'm sorry," Emma said, trying to explain herself. "It was nothing, I was just— just—" Talking to angels? Though she did that often enough, she doubted that others did and shook her head. "It was just nothing." Totally flustered, she stepped forward, ready to cross the street as soon as the automobile rolled past.

The black-and-red vehicle didn't go straight. Instead it turned, taking the corner where she was, and the sight of the woman sitting in the passenger seat had Emma pressing her hands over her heart. "Beverly!"

"Excuse me?" the man said again. "Your name is Beverly?"

His frown had grown…and so had her embarrassment. "No."

"Are you lost?" he asked. "Do you need assistance?"

"No." Any further explanation would be useless, not to mention that she couldn't think of one. She spun around to hurry toward the car that was pulling up to the curb in front of her and Beverly's apartment building at the end of the block.

She was about halfway there when she noticed the driver. A man in uniform. Emma's heart hit the back of her throat so fast her breath stalled. But her mind didn't. She couldn't let George see her. He might recognize her. They had only met one time, but still, he might remember that she was Martha's cousin.

She pivoted, took a step back toward the corner, but the man who'd asked if she needed help was still there, looking at her as if he questioned if she was lost or something. She'd already made a big enough fool of herself and made a half turn, toward the buildings lining the sidewalk, and hurried to the closest door.

"Good day, Miss Ellis."

"Hello, Mr. Martin," she greeted the man behind the counter as she entered the shop.

"Is there something I can help you with today?"

Emma twisted to look out the glass window in the door. "No, thank you. I'm just browsing," she replied while watching as George climbed out of the car.

"Browsing?"

"Yes." Emma's gaze remained out the window. George looked overly handsome in his uniform. Fit and well. Her heart nearly beat its way right out of her chest. She'd been so proud of him when he'd written to say he'd been promoted to a captain. She'd been proud of all of his promotions and was very grateful that he'd made it home safe and sound. She should have known that he would escort Beverly home. He was a true gentleman. She'd recognized that the one and only time she'd met him, but the letters they'd shared had truly confirmed it. A somewhat winsome sigh filled her chest. Each one of his letters had been a joy. His humor and charm had come across in each line and had filled her heart. Relief had also filled her when each letter had arrived. The time between his letters had sometimes caused her worry, even though he'd forewarned her that his replies could be delayed by his assignments.

"We don't have anything to browse," Mr. Martin said.

Emma flinched inside. She knew that. Knew she'd entered the laundry. The air around the building always smelled clean and she liked that. Especially in the summer, when the clean, fresh scent floated inside her apartment windows. It was so much better than the smells that had filled the air near her old apartment in New York City. Her entire apartment building here was so much better than the one in New York City. It was larger, nicer and well-maintained. The entire city of Albany was nicer as well.

Even the streets were cleaner.

There were some nice parts of New York City, or so she'd heard. She'd never seen them. Perhaps she had, when she'd been younger, and just couldn't remember any of it. Or perhaps her memories of New York were tainted by the time she'd lived there. Either way, she'd wanted to move, and had, and now loved Albany.

"Did you mean our used clothing?" Mr. Martin asked. "I can fetch my wife."

Eyes still out the window, Emma watched the wind catch Beverly's hat, and how the elderly woman quickly held it in place as George opened her car door. "No, there's no need for that. I just thought I'd step inside for a moment."

If Mr. Martin thought that odd, especially since her apartment was only two doors down, he didn't voice it. Not wanting him to think she was as crazy as the man on the street corner most likely did, she turned about. "To say hello."

With his frown deepening, Mr. Martin asked, "Is this about the children? An issue with them. They are very excited to be back at school."

"Oh, no, of course not! Your children are very well-behaved. Please don't be concerned," she replied. Mr. Martin had four children who attended the school where she worked in the library. They were dears, and like them, she was glad that schools had reopened.

The flu that had swept across the country, and the world, had done more than close schools and businesses—it had taken lives. So had the war. So many lives had been lost. Everyone was anxious for things to get back to normal, but normal had changed, and her heart ached for the children and families who had lost fathers and mothers, brothers and sisters, to both the flu and the war.

"You're sure?" he asked, walking around the counter.

"Yes, very sure." She rubbed her hands together as if warming them, and twisted, glancing out the window again. Once more, her heart leaped, then began to pound as she watched George holding on to Beverly's arm as he escorted her toward their apartment building.

"Are you looking for someone?" Mr. Martin asked.

Her gaze was still on George and Beverly, and she didn't have time to answer before Mr. Martin arrived at her side.

Gazing out the same the window, he said, "It's good to see him home."

"Do you know—" She stopped herself before saying "George." "Him?" she asked.

"No, but it's good to see every soldier lucky enough to return."

Her stomach knotted with trepidation. "Yes, it is."

She was glad for George and every soldier who returned home; she just couldn't let anyone ever find out what she'd done.

Not ever.

"That's Mrs. Buttons with him," Mr. Martin said.

She felt her shoulders slump clear to her hips. "Yes, it is."

"That's who you were waiting for, isn't it? And here I am keeping you talking. I'm sorry. Here, let me get the door for you."

Knowing she had no choice, she nodded, thanked him and stepped out the door he held open.

Then, she walked toward her apartment building, knowing Beverly and George couldn't be upstairs yet, but with Mr. Martin watching her every step—she was sure he was watching—she had to keep walking, all the way to the door.

Holding her breath, she opened the door, and upon seeing their backs on the staircase, she shot inside, around the stairwell and into the phone booth. She'd only used it a time or two, but Beverly used it weekly, to talk to her daughter, Mary, in Florida.

With her heart pounding, she listened to their footfalls, the murmur of their voices. She couldn't hear their conversation but heard one word: coffee. Beverly always invited everyone in for coffee, therefore, as soon as she heard a door close, she shot out of the booth and up the stairs.

At the top of the steps, she turned the corner, and hit something solid.

Not the wall.

Him.

George.

Momentarily stunned, she couldn't do anything but stare at him, until her senses returned.

"My apologies," he said.

She couldn't answer. All she could do was duck her head and run down the hallway, to her apartment.

Luckily, she'd dug the key from her pocket while downstairs and though her fingers trembled, she unlocked the door and shot inside.

Chapter Two

In the two days since he'd returned home, George had been implanted back into the life he'd left. Oddly, though, he felt like an outsider. Not because things here had changed, but because he had, and he was grappling with that.

The home that had been commonplace, natural, when he'd left, was now a glaring reminder of who he was, and the expectations he was expected to fulfill. While in the army, he'd been exactly like everyone else. A soldier. He'd liked that.

Here, he wasn't like anyone else.

Thoughts of home had always been on his mind, but the pressures hadn't been.

Those pressures were back now.

Tenfold.

His father had said that Weston Lumber and North Country Logging would continue to work together just as they had for years and years, but George couldn't help but question if that was the best thing for Weston Lumber. After he'd known the merger with North Country Logging wouldn't happen, he'd come up with a new plan for Weston Lumber but needed to do some background work before discussing it with his father.

That, too—his new plan—he credited to Beverly's letters.

His plan of marrying her was no longer an option—he couldn't marry a woman three times his age—but he now considered that a blessing in disguise.

He also understood how that had come about.

While overseas, bunking with men who had married women they loved and couldn't wait to return home to, he'd begun to think about Beverly along those lines… due to her letters. He'd created a woman who didn't exist, except in his mind, and had decided to marry her. An act that would have been nothing more than a means to the end.

The exact same thing that his marriage to Martha would have been.

That was definite proof that he was incapable of loving anything except his family and Weston Lumber.

Even though he'd created a dream woman, he hadn't wanted her to love him. He had known the pain of loving someone only to lose them and didn't wish that upon anyone. Not even himself. He'd been young, but the event was unforgettable.

Furthermore, he'd witnessed more of that than he'd ever want anyone to experience while in the army. How death devastated loved ones.

Therefore, he was glad that Beverly turned out to be exactly who she was—a dear old lady who had brightened his world at a time when he'd needed it the most.

He sat down on the bed to pull on his socks and shoes, because some things would never change. In her usual fashion, his mother had already thrown together a party to celebrate his return home.

He'd protested, insisted that there were plenty of other men from Albany who had, or would be, returning, and so many who wouldn't ever be returning home, and that there was no need to celebrate his return. It wasn't special. He wasn't special.

Of course, his protests had fallen on deaf ears. She had responded, "You're a Weston. The only Weston of the next generation, and that makes you special. Makes your return special."

She didn't need to remind him, though. He knew he was the only Weston of his generation. It had been that way since Robert had died.

George pushed out a sigh as he rose and glanced in the mirror to check that his tie was straight. Robert had been seven years older than him, age fourteen when he died. He'd been sick for a few months. Cancer is what the doctors had said. That there was nothing they could do for him. George remembered a lot about his brother, even though he'd only been seven, but most of all, he remembered how Robert's death had hurt. Hurt everyone.

Robert hadn't meant to die, hadn't meant to hurt any of them, but that is what happens when someone you love dies.

With a shake of his head, George cleared his mind, grabbed his suit coat and left his bedroom. His mother had asked if there was anyone specific that he wanted invited to the party tonight. He'd told her no, but there was, and thinking of how Beverly's appearance might surprise people made him smile.

Beverly was a delightful person. In a different way than she had been in her letters, but that could be expected because of the images he'd mistakenly created about her. Nonetheless, if there was anyone deserving of celebrating his return, it was her.

Within the hour, he knocked on Beverly's door with a bouquet of greenhouse flowers in one hand that he quickly tucked behind his back.

As he waited for the door to be answered, he glanced down the hallway, in the direction that the young woman had run when they'd bumped into each other at the top of the stairs. He hadn't meant to frighten her, but she clearly had been scared out of her wits by running into a strange man in the hallway.

The door opened and Beverly's green eyes brightened. "Oh, George. It's so lovely to see you again."

Tiny, short, the top of her silver head barely reached his chest, but her personality made up for her stature. He pulled the flowers from behind his back and presented them to her. "For you."

"Flowers." She covered her giggle with one hand as she took the bouquet with the other hand. "It's been years since someone has given me flowers." Her eyes closed as she sniffed the petals. "Heavenly. Simply heavenly," she said with a sigh. "Can you come in for a moment? I have some fresh-baked ginger bars."

He nodded. "I would appreciate a moment or two of your time."

Her lifting giggle floated into the hallway as she stepped over the threshold to allow him to enter the apartment ahead of her. "I have more than a minute or two to share with you, George."

He paused at how she'd nearly shouted the words, especially his name, down the hallway.

As if her actions hadn't been out of the ordinary, she smiled and waved for him to enter.

He'd merely walked her to her door after giving her a ride home the other day, and as he stepped inside her apartment now, he noted it was small, yet, like her, it was charming and quaint. The seat cushions were all covered in the same flowery pink, red and white print as the window curtains and tablecloth, and white lacy doilies were draped over the backs of the chairs, including the rocking chair and sofa in the small sitting area near the windows.

"Let me just put these in some water so they don't droop, and I'll make coffee to go with the ginger bars." Beverly hurried past him with quick, short footsteps to the kitchen area. "Please, just have a seat anywhere."

George walked to the table and sat on one of the two chairs flanking it. "I am here to ask a favor of you, Beverly."

"Oh?" She filled a green porcelain vase with water and proceeded to place the bouquet in it, then set the vase in the center of the table. "There. They look so pretty, don't they?"

"They do," he agreed.

Smiling, she eyed him. "Tell me, what is the favor?"

"There is an event that I must attend tonight, and I was hoping that you would be interested in accompanying me."

The smile slipped from her mouth, but not her eyes. "Your welcome-home party?"

Of course, she'd have heard about it. His mother's goal was for the entire town to hear about it, and attend. "Yes."

She moved to the sink and turned on the tap to fill

the coffeepot. "Oh, George, dear, you don't want to take me to your party. I'm an old lady."

"You are young at heart."

She chuckled while scooping ground coffee into the pot. "And you are too charming for your own good."

"I really would like for you to attend. It's at seven tonight, at the State Hotel. I could pick you up, or send a car for you, if you'd prefer."

After lighting the flame on the stove burner and setting the coffeepot atop it, she turned about. "Send a car for me? The State Hotel? You'll make me blush making it sound so elegant."

Even though elegance was what his mother liked and sought, he most certainly didn't want Beverly to be intimidated by that. "It's just a simple party, and I'd truly like for you to be there. Your letters were what I looked forward to the most during every mission. During my entire time away."

"Oh, George. Your letters were received with great joy, here, too. Never doubt that." She looked at the door of her apartment for a moment. "Each and every one of them."

"Will you attend?"

She let out a long breath and shook her head. "I would like to say yes, but…"

He truly wanted her to attend but wouldn't press her into doing something she didn't want to do, because in all truth, there was no reason for her to want to attend. "I understand. Thank you for hearing my request."

"I'm sure it will be a wonderful party. Truly lovely. And you deserve such a homecoming, you truly do."

He didn't respond, because he didn't believe he de-

served a party any more than any other soldier returning home.

With a pensive gaze, she looked at the door again.
"I'm so glad you stopped by this morning."

She sounded almost forlorn. Her gaze on the door
looked forlorn, too. "Are you expecting someone? I
didn't mean to interrupt. I'll leave—"

"No, you absolutely cannot leave yet. I can't drink a
whole pot of coffee by myself, and the ginger bars are
quite delicious. I've already eaten two today and it's not
even lunchtime yet. I declare they are one of my favor-
ites." She moved to the cupboard and lifted out cups.
"What is your favorite dessert?"

"I'm not sure, but if I had to guess, I'd say apple pie."

"Oh, yes, apple pie. That was one of Alvin's favor-
ites. He was my husband. Been gone over twenty years
now..."

She had told him about her husband the other day,
and their daughter, who had moved to Florida after
getting married and Beverly hadn't seen her in almost
thirty years. He did wonder why she'd never told him
any of that in her letters but didn't stop her from telling him all about them again as the coffee perked and
they ate ginger bars once the coffee was done. He did
agree with her that the bars were delicious. Especially
the thin vanilla frosting.

As he finished his second one, he said, "Thank you
for the coffee and bars. They are very good."

"I agree." She patted the corners of her mouth with
her napkin. "My neighbor made them. The same neighbor who stops by every night to make sure I go to my
bed rather than sleep all night in the rocking chair."

He was glad to hear that there was someone looking out for her. "That sounds like a very good neighbor."

She nodded and while glancing at the door again, asked, "If I were to go to your party this evening, could someone come with me?"

A wave of happiness filled him. "Your neighbor?"

She nodded.

He momentarily thought about the young woman he'd run into but figured the neighbor Beverly referred to would be closer to her age, not his. "Of course. I can send a car to pick both of you up and bring you back home before it grows too late."

She tapped one wrinkled cheek with a finger for a moment, then her smile filled her face. "What time should we be ready for this car?"

"Beverly, I can't." Emma pressed a hand to her forehead. "I just can't."

"He doesn't know you wrote the letters," Beverly insisted. "I didn't tell him that, but it's his party, and he wants the person who wrote to him to be there. I could tell that by the look on his face. I tried telling him no, but it nearly broke my heart. I was hoping that you'd come over and say hello."

Emma had heard Beverly shout his name in the hallway earlier and had instantly locked her door, afraid Beverly might bring him to her apartment. Every time she entered the hallway, she remembered running into him. "I couldn't. He might recognize me."

"He might not."

That was true, but if he learned who she was, he wouldn't like her. No one at the party would. And only the good Lord knew what might happen if she encountered her aunt Jill.

The thought of her aunt discovering the truth made her quiver from head to toe.

"You didn't do anything wrong. Your cousin is the one who married someone else." Beverly shook her head. "Foolish woman."

Emma wasn't going to pass judgment on Martha's choices and she knew it was her own actions that had put her in this pickle. "I should never have written to him."

"What's done is done."

"Yes, it is, and I—"

"I couldn't say no to him," Beverly interrupted. "Just like I hadn't been able to say no to meeting him at the train station and no to you when you asked if you could use my name while writing to him."

The guilt inside Emma was so huge and dark it made her feel as if she weighed a thousand pounds. She'd wished she'd never asked that of Beverly, and should never have continued writing to him, but each time a letter arrived from him, she'd responded, because not doing so had filled her with another form of guilt.

She hadn't wanted to let him down. No, in truth, it had been more than that. She'd wanted to write to him, and she'd wanted to receive another letter in return. Through their letters she'd felt a connection to him that was unlike anything she'd ever known. Though Beverly's name was on the letters, the other woman had never read a letter from George, nor composed one to him. She'd said they were private, though she would listen intently any time Emma offered to read the letters aloud.

Beverly had also fretted, worried and feared something had happened to George between the lapses in his letter writing. Just as Emma had. One of her greatest fears had been that something would happen to him, and that had made her fearful to read the newspaper, afraid she'd learn devastating news.

Emma was extremely grateful that had never happened, but she truly had created a mess, a terrible one, and had to figure out a way out of it that wouldn't cause even more of a mess. Now, before it was too late.

Her heart sank. It was already too late. *Oh, Dad, I really could use a miracle. A big one right about now!*

Asking her father for help was all she could think to do. That's what she'd always done—when she'd wanted to move away from New York, but had needed a job, and once she'd arrived here and needed a reference to rent her apartment—and each time when things had worked out, she'd believed it had been because of his help from heaven. He'd taught her how to do that. Her and her sister, after their mother had died, and each time something good had happened, he'd said it had been their mother, watching out for them from heaven.

Her father had also known the wrath of Aunt Jill, as he'd been the one to protect both her and her sister, Sharon, from Aunt Jill after their mother had died, when their aunt had tried to take them away from him. That in itself should have been enough for her to have moved to anywhere except Albany, but this is where she'd found a job. A job she loved.

"A car will be here to pick us up a little before seven," Beverly said.

Emma hung her head, feeling more hopeless than she had after her father's death. "If my aunt discovers that I wrote to George, she'll—"

"Hate you?" Beverly sighed heavily as she reached over and wrapped her fingers around Emma's hand. "Darling, she already does. Has since you were born."

The air shook as it left Emma's lungs. That was true. She had told Beverly all about Aunt Jill and how her aunt had always hated her and her sister because they were their father's daughters. Aunt Jill had claimed that their mother had married beneath her, that their father had ruined their mother by forcing her to move from Albany to New York City, and that he'd killed her by forcing her to live in the slums of the city.

And that, because he was their father, she and Sharon had bad blood running through them.

The anger and hate in her aunt's words to her father at her mother's funeral still echoed inside Emma's head. She'd been nine and had known that her aunt didn't like any of them, but that day she'd felt true hatred. She'd felt it again the day she'd gone to her aunt's house, shortly after moving here, to ask for a letter of recommendation in order to rent an apartment.

"I should never have moved to Albany," Emma said. She'd known Aunt Jill lived here, but that hadn't seemed like an issue at the time. In truth, moving had felt like a miracle. Being left alone upon the death of their father, both she and Sharon had found jobs in order to make enough money to pay the rent on the apartment they'd lived in their entire lives. They'd managed to get by for over four years, then Sharon had married Eddie Warren.

Emma had been happy for her sister, still was happy for Sharon, but had known that there had been no way she'd ever be able to pay the rent alone. Rolling cigars didn't pay enough for that and she'd hated the job, anyway.

Sharon and Eddie had said that she could live with them, but she couldn't do that. They were moving in with his parents until they could afford their own place, which they had now, and again, she was happy for them. Sharon had said that marrying Eddie was her dream come true.

Emma's dream had always been to move to Albany. Her mother had talked fondly about growing up here, and wanting that—wanting out of New York City, out of the life she'd always known—she had prayed, asked her father for a miracle.

That had happened when Eddie, a teacher, had told her about a job working in the library at a school in Albany. She'd packed her bags that day and taken the train north, knowing it was her miracle.

"You did move here," Beverly said. "And your aunt's behavior is a demonstration of her character, not yours. Your character is of the utmost. Unflawed in any way. You are compassionate and caring, even to those you don't know. That is why you wrote to George."

Emma shook her head. That, how she'd written to him, was proof that her character was indeed flawed. She should have minded her own business.

"Yes," Beverly said, nodding. "You wrote to him because you were concerned, cared about him, and that's why you continued writing. I became concerned about him, too, and I care about him, which is why I don't want to let him down by not attending his party tonight. Now, if you will allow me, I believe we have a way that not even your aunt would recognize you."

The enormity of the weight on her shoulders made Emma's entire body ache. "I can't—"

"Yes, you can," Beverly insisted.

* * *

Several hours later, as Emma stared in the mirror, she believed there was a possibility that her aunt wouldn't recognize her. No one would. She barely recognized herself. If not for the pure fact that she still felt the same way on the inside as she had earlier—utterly despondent—she would have believed that the person in the mirror was a woman without a care in the world except for the party she was about to attend.

The smooth silk of the dress brushed against her shins and ankles, as well as her arms, as she shifted, looking at herself from different angles. She'd never felt anything so soft, so luxurious. Pink with black stripes, it had an ankle-length underskirt, covered by a knee-length tunic with long sleeves and white cuffs, and a silk black belt tied around her waist. There was a row of black silk-covered buttons down the front of the tunic and it had a crisp white collar.

It just might be the prettiest dress she'd ever seen, and the matching, short-brimmed hat, trimmed with a short, white veil that stopped at eye level, was the most fashionable hat she'd ever worn.

Both the gown and hat had come from the laundry next door. Mrs. Martin often created new clothes from those that the owners no longer wanted because they were damaged or stained beyond repair. Emma had purchased several items from the laundry since moving to Albany, but never anything this elegant.

She truly didn't look like herself, and it wasn't just because of the dress. Instead of pinning up her hair as she normally did, Beverly had insisted that she put it in a black hairnet. Tied atop her head beneath the hat and filled with her hair, the net hung down her back between her shoulders, and the tight weave of the netting made her hair look black instead of its normal dull brown.

"One final thing." One at a time, Beverly reached up and clipped teardrop-shaped pearl earbobs onto both of Emma's lobes. "There."

A shattering of nerves rippled through Emma. "I still don't know about this, Beverly."

"I do. You look beautiful."

Emma twisted away from the mirror and couldn't help but smile at the older woman, who was wearing a pale blue dress with a stiff, white eyelet collar that framed her face in an enchanting way. The eyelet also trimmed the cuffs and the hem of her dress, and her hat was the white crocheted one that she'd worn to the train station the other day, with the white-and-yellow silk daisy still pinned on one side.

"You are the one who looks beautiful," Emma said.

Beverly shrugged one shoulder while glancing in the mirror. "I'm just an old lady, but I do like how this dress looks on me and I thought I better wear the hat so George recognizes me."

"He may not recognize you without it," Emma said. Though that was doubtful. She still wasn't comfortable with the idea of going, but she couldn't disappoint Beverly. It was clear the other woman truly wanted to attend the party.

Beverly lifted a metal container off the dressing table in her bedroom and opened it. While watching herself in the mirror, she applied red lipstick with the tip of one pinkie finger. She then held out the opened container.

"I've never worn lipstick," Emma said, shaking her head.

"Which is why you must tonight. Just dab on enough

for color—you don't want it to look like frosting on a cake," Beverly said.

Emma took the container and copied what Beverly had done, dabbing a small amount of color on her lips, and again, was surprised by how much she didn't look like herself.

But if she wasn't herself, then who was she?

"Come," Beverly said. "The car will be here any minute."

They both had just put on their coats and were about to exit Beverly's apartment to wait downstairs when a knock sounded on the door.

An older man, with dark hair that was speckled with gray and wearing a long, wool evening coat, bowed slightly as Beverly opened the door.

"Mrs. Buttons?" he asked.

He had a kind face, with shimmering green eyes surrounded by tiny wrinkles formed by his smile.

"Yes," Beverly said.

"My name is Willis. I will be your chauffeur for the evening."

The nod Beverly gave him was so elegant that Emma had to pinch her lips to keep her grin from growing. The older woman was in her glory, and Emma was glad for that, despite her own reservations.

"Thank you, Willis," Beverly said. "Allow me to introduce you to my friend Emma, who will be accompanying me this evening."

Chapter Three

"A merger had never been our only option," his father said. "I've thought about a buyout for years."

With one foot on the brass footrail that ran the length of the bar, George spun his glass around on the varnished bar top as his father spoke. There was always one thing on Craig Weston's mind. Business. This evening was no different. Nor was the conversation. His father had already mentioned a buyout twice in the last couple of days.

George had taken in of all his father had said with deep thoughtfulness. Like him, Martha was an only child and next in line to inherit North Country Logging, but from what his father had said, her new husband had his own business and was not interested in taking over the logging company, which was troubling Roy King, Martha's father, and infuriating her mother.

While George listened to his father's remarks, his eyes were on the door of the massive room, watching the first few guests—his aunt, uncle and cousin—walk through the double set of mahogany doors and into the banquet hall with its darkly painted scrollwork-patterned walls and bronze inlaid ceiling tiles.

The guests would mainly be friends and business associates of the family. Due to the war having only ended ten days ago, many of his friends were still overseas, and he'd been surprised and saddened by the number of names his mother had told him that wouldn't ever be coming home. He'd also been shocked by the number of people who had perished from influenza. The news reinforced all that he had to be grateful for, and that he should be nothing but happy to be home. Happy to be able to resume the life he'd left.

"Roy is considering it," his father continued. "It's Jill who refuses to contemplate selling as an option."

Of course, she wasn't. Jill King was headstrong, opinionated and ruthless. He knew from experience.

George took a sip of his drink. "If you want my opinion, I say a buyout isn't necessary. It's time we start our own logging company."

His father frowned. "Of course, I want your opinion. Now that you're home, we're partners. You have as much say in the company as I do, but are you considering cutting ties with them because of what happened with Martha?"

He now considered what had *happened* with Martha as a blessing but didn't voice that. A marriage just to grow the company was not needed, and he'd prove it.

This was his opportunity to put all his focus on the company, which suited him. Thrilled him in ways he hadn't expected. "I'm saying that because we own the timberland, and we own the mills. I know North Country Logging has always harvested our lumber, but it's never made sense for us to rely on a middleman for the logging and transportation of the logs when we could be doing it ourselves. Not to mention the list of other loggers we could be working with rather than just one."

"We've always done that because my father and Jill King's father formed the partnership to corner the market and build up both companies, which they did."

"I am fully aware of that." George finished his drink and set down his glass. "But the industry has grown exponentially, and as the next generation of Westons, my loyalties lie with Weston Lumber, not North Country Logging. I believe starting our own logging company would be more beneficial than buying theirs. I'd also like to see us collaborating with several other companies."

His father stared at him for a long moment before his gaze shifted and he straightened his stance. After emptying his glass in one swallow, he set it on the bar. "We'll discuss this later. Your mother is heading our way."

George bit back a smile. There was only one person who could make his father stop talking about business, and that was his mother. She'd already warned that there would be no business talk tonight and wouldn't be happy to hear that there had been.

"The guests are arriving," she said while approaching them.

His father slapped his shoulder. "Let's go greet them."

Walking beside his parents, George proceeded across the thick carpet to the double doors. Once stationed there, he acknowledged each guest as they entered. He was glad to see some that he hadn't expected, men who had already returned home from the war, or who hadn't gone for one reason or another.

He was in the midst of joking with Tad Myers and Sam Brown, two men he'd grown up with, when he caught sight of a hat. A white one with a daisy pinned on the side. That made him grin. "Excuse me, fellas, there is someone I need to greet."

Obligated to say hello to others, he was slightly stalled en route. When he managed to arrive at the door, his feet nearly glued themselves to the carpet as a strange shiver rippled over his entire body. It wasn't a chill, more of an awakening, and was caused by the woman standing next to Beverly.

It was her. The young woman he'd met in the hallway. He knew by her eyes. Dark brown and thickly lashed, they were enchanting. She was enchanting. More than that, something about her drew him to her. Or maybe it was something inside him.

Either way, it took concentrated effort to pull his eyes off the young woman and look at Beverly. "I'm honored you were able to attend. I hope the car ride was satisfactory."

"Oh, heavens, yes," Beverly replied. "Willis is an excellent driver." She looped her arm through the younger woman's. "And we are delighted, simply delighted to be here. This, George, dear, is my friend, Emma."

His heart was pounding inside his chest. He could only contribute it to the loveliness of the young woman. Besides her memorable dark brown eyes, her face was striking, with high cheekbones that were slightly flushed from the cold ride. Her pert lips had a thin coat of red lipstick, and her earbobs enhanced her elegant and slender neck. "Does your friend have a last name?" he asked Beverly. "So I can greet her appropriately."

"Oh, just call her Emma," Beverly said.

He looked at the young woman.

Her smile wobbled slightly as she glanced from Beverly to him. "Hello, Captain Weston," she said softly.

She had the cutest little mole above her upper lip on the left side of her mouth, and noting that, his mouth went dry. So dry he had to peel his tongue off the roof of his mouth. "Hello, Emma, but please, it's George. I'm once again a civilian."

"Welcome home," she said. "Thank you for your service to our country."

"Thank you, and thank you for attending this evening. It's a pleasure to have you both here." He held out an elbow for Beverly. "May I escort you ladies to a table?"

Beverly laid a hand on his arm. "That would be lovely."

Emma gently laid a hand atop Beverly's. "It would be lovely, but you have more guests to greet, and we wouldn't want to keep you from that." She smiled at Beverly. "We will find a table."

Beverly slowly, almost reluctantly, removed her hand from his arm. "Yes, we will."

George could have agreed that he should continue to greet guests but chose not to. "I have all evening to greet guests. I want to make sure you find the right table."

"Is there a difference?" Beverly asked as she hooked a hand beneath his elbow.

"Not in size or shape." They were all round, covered with white cloths and surrounded by chairs. "But you will be seated at my table. The meal will be served at seven thirty. I do hope you like roast beef."

"Oh, my, we are so honored," Beverly said, with a twinkle in her eyes that emphasized she was thrilled by the seating arrangement.

However, the way Emma closed her eyes for a brief moment told him she wasn't nearly as happy as Beverly about being at his table. Could he blame her? Coming to a party for someone she didn't know. He wondered if Beverly had told her about their letters. Knowing Beverly, he assumed she had, and he held a fondness that a woman so young and pretty would give up her Saturday evening to accompany Beverly tonight.

Suddenly, he wanted to know what she might have given up. "I do hope this event didn't interrupt other plans."

"Oh, heavens no," Beverly said.

He let his gaze travel to Emma for her answer.

Walking on the other side of Beverly, she smiled shyly and shook her head.

"How long have the two of you been neighbors?" he asked while guiding them around tables to the one near the front of the room, where his mother had indicated the family would be sitting.

"Almost two years," Beverly replied. She then waved a hand to where the small band was set up near the wooden dance floor. "Will there be dancing?"

"There will be," he replied. "Do you dance?"

Her giggle was as adorable as the silver curls poking out from beneath her daisy hat. Yet, on her other side, he once again noticed a reluctance or distress from Emma.

"Not anymore," Beverly said. "But I used to, and, of course, Emma dances."

Once again, the younger woman closed her eyes, and this time, pinched her lips together to keep from speaking.

Beverly's smile increased as she looked up at him.

He gave her a nod as they arrived at the table.

His mother's sister, her husband and their daughter were already seated, and he made introductions. "This is my aunt Adelle, my uncle Walt and their daughter, my cousin Janice." To his family, he said, "This is Beverly Buttons and Emma, friends of mine."

As they greeted each other, Aunt Adelle shared how happy they were that he'd come home and that Janice's husband, Bill, was still overseas, but would be home in time for Christmas, which would make Christmas extra special, especially for Janice and Bill's two young children.

During that exchange, George assisted Beverly onto a chair.

"I knew an Alvin Buttons," Uncle Walt said. "He owned the shoemaking shop on the north end of town years ago."

"Yes." Beverly pressed a hand to her bosom. "That was my Alvin. My husband. When he passed on, I couldn't run the shop by myself. I never learned a thing about making shoes."

"But the shop is still there," Walt said.

"It is," Beverly replied. "Silas Nelson runs it now. I sold him the business, all the supplies and tools, but I still own the building."

As Beverly continued to explain how Silas rented from her, George stepped closer to the chair Emma sat upon. A soft, subtle scent instantly filled his senses.

The familiarity of it was instantly recognized. All of Beverly's letters had held that same scent.

Emma's breath caught at the way her nerves leaped beneath her skin as George rested a hand on the back of her chair. It wasn't just her nerves. Her heart was pounding so hard it echoed in her ears. He looked as handsome in his suit as he had in his uniform the other day. Their only meeting had been almost two years ago and had been brief, but she'd never forgotten his eyes. They'd held her attention at her aunt's house that day, and again in the hallway the day before yesterday. They were blue, a real bright blue, and twinkled like none she'd ever seen.

"I'll get you each a glass of punch," he said quietly. "Unless you'd prefer something different?"

Her voice felt as if it didn't want to work, and she had to swallow, hard, before she was able to reply. "Punch would be lovely. Thank you."

"I'll be right back," he said.

She didn't release the air locked in her lungs until he'd walked away. Then, as her shoulders slumped, Emma questioned her sanity. As soon as she'd seen George, a hundred questions that she wanted to ask had formed in her mind. About men he'd mentioned in his letters as well as places and things that he'd seen. Most of all, she wanted to ask him how he was doing, being back home. He had to be happy about that, but it had to be different than before. So very different.

He'd never mentioned Martha in his letters, not once, nor had she, but that had to be first on his mind.

Martha wasn't one of the topics she wanted to ask about, but unfortunately, she couldn't ask him any questions of any kind, and that saddened her. She'd enjoyed hearing about the men he'd served with and about those he'd met overseas, and the things he'd seen. He'd never mentioned the war itself, and neither had she. Their letters had been about the good things in the world. For almost two years, he and his letters had become an important part of her life. That was now over.

Over for good.

Emma's chest tightened, stung. She should be glad, grateful that it was over. She'd started writing to him because of her own guilt over Martha marrying Delmar. Delmar had been pursuing her for over a year before she'd moved to Albany, but she hadn't wanted anything to do with him, even when he'd said he could make her life so much better. She'd wanted that, of course, but knew there was a better way to achieve it than giving him what he wanted from her.

Working for his family's company had been the only job she'd been able to obtain after her father's death, and she'd hated it. Hated the hours she had to spend rolling cigars at her kitchen table and how the tobacco had made the entire apartment stink. Each month, the first thing she'd purchased when she got paid was a new bottle of vanilla so she could put drops of it on the light bulb to hide the tobacco scent. She still did that. She'd grown used to the warm vanilla scent and still liked it.

Her move to Albany had not only been a dream come true. It had also been an escape from that awful job and from Delmar. Men like him were not in her future. Nor was marriage. Her parents had loved each other, she had no doubt about that, but she also knew that when two people get married, they brought things with them. Their families, and the baggage of that, the hatefulness of that, can ruin even the strongest love because it wears a person out.

Since she'd moved here and began working at the school, she'd found a wonderful life. One that proved she didn't need a man or marriage. She enjoyed the life she had right now. Enjoyed it very much.

A heavy sigh built inside her. At least, she had enjoyed it until George had returned. Now she may have to escape again, and this time it wouldn't also fulfill a dream.

Emma twisted in her seat to gaze around the room in an attempt to relieve the pressure inside her.

Beverly was fully engaged in a conversation with George's aunt and uncle, and his cousin was talking to a man who had asked about her husband.

Emma tried to change her thoughts by admiring the elegance of the room. She had never seen anything like it. The numerous tiny lights on the crystal chandeliers were like stars in the sky as they reflected off the bronze tiled ceiling and made the entire room shimmer and sparkle.

The tables were draped with creamy white linen cloths, while the metal chairs were a glossy black and had thick padded seats upholstered with plush gold brocade material. The tall—well over ten feet—wooden walls had sections that held intricate scrollwork and other areas where large landscape paintings hung inside gold frames, and there were people everywhere. Seated at the tables, standing in clusters, talking and laughing, while others continued to flow through the double doorway, filling up the room. She was grateful for the dress from Mrs. Martin. Nothing in her wardrobe would have fit in with the fashionable gowns the women were wearing, or the men in their spiffy suits.

The sounds of laughter and greetings filled the room with a sense of gaiety, and she wished she, too, could take part. For she was glad the war was over, that George was home. It did fill her with happiness—it was just a happiness that she couldn't share, not even privately because of her deceitfulness.

Her heart stalled midbeat as she caught sight of a man with a mustache that curled up on both sides walking through the doorway, and the woman at the man's side, wearing a shimmering black dress.

For a brief moment, she couldn't help but stare at her aunt because there were true similarities to her mother. The same shade of brown hair, the same oval-shaped face and high cheekbones. Other features were also similar, except that she remembered her mother's eyes and mouth being soft, full of tender expressions. Aunt Jill's were firm, as if full of harsh criticism.

After her aunt had refused to give her a recommendation and told her to go back to New York, Emma had become even more determined to stay. To live the life she wanted. To no longer even think about the hatred of Aunt Jill.

She could be stubborn that way. Leastwise, that's what she'd been told.

She'd even felt proud of herself for staying here, right up until it hit her that if her aunt ever discovered she'd written to George, Jill would take that as retaliation for Martha's actions and react.

Emma pulled her eyes away from her aunt and pressed a hand to her mouth, covering how heavy her breathing had become. This was exactly what she'd feared knowing that the King family and the Weston family were well acquainted through their businesses.

Emma's heart kicked in and began to race as her aunt and uncle walked toward the tables that filled the room.

She couldn't take the chance that Aunt Jill would recognize her, and quickly pushed her chair away from the table, leaped to her feet.

Turning, about to make an escape, she bumped into something, someone. It was only a matter of seconds before she realized it was George, with a cup of punch in each hand. She tried to catch a cup, or do something to stop the punch from spilling, but it was already too late. He'd pulled the cups toward him to keep them from spilling on her and now he had red punch with orange pulp trickling down the front of his gray suit coat.

"Oh, no. No. I'm so sorry!" She looked for a napkin, or anything to wipe the punch from his coat, but there was nothing, other than the tablecloth, which she couldn't pull off the table, so she used her hands. "I'm so sorry. So sorry."

"It's just a little punch." He set both cups on the table and grasped her wrists. "Where were you going in such a hurry?"

Her face felt like it was on fire. "The um, um…"

"Powder room?" he asked.

Anywhere away from this table was where she'd been headed, therefore the powder room sounded like a plausible place to hide. "Yes."

"I'll show you where it's at."

She didn't dare turn around to see how close her aunt was to the table now, and the urgency to move, go anywhere, had her shifting from foot to foot. "That's all right, you can just tell me."

"No, I'll show you." He released her wrists. "I need to wash the punch off my hands."

Her wrists felt as if they were on fire, but she had no time to worry about that and as he took a step in the opposite direction from where her aunt was approaching, she quickly shot forward. "I'm so sorry about spilling the punch. I truly am." She waved toward a doorway leading into a hallway and hoped that was the direction of the powder room. "Through there?"

His long strides were easily keeping up with her hurried steps. "Yes, and to the right."

Thank goodness! The farther away from her aunt, the better, but she wouldn't be able to hide out in the powder room all evening. Why on earth had she agreed to come here tonight? Why did nothing ever go her way?

"It appears as if we are creating a habit of running into each other," he said.

Heat filled her cheeks.

"That was you in the hallway at the apartment building, wasn't it?"

"Yes. I'm sorry about that, too."

"Don't be. I'm didn't mean to startle you that day, or just now."

She nodded but said nothing as they walked down the hallway.

"Here we are." George gestured to a door. "I'll wait for you."

She shook her head. "That's not necessary." Not wanting to sound ungrateful, she continued, "You have guests to see to."

He stepped closer to the door and turned the knob. "You are a guest. I'll be here when you exit."

She wanted to dart into the room and hide, forever,

but couldn't do that with him waiting in the hallway. "Really, I—"

"I'll be here."

As if it might help, she held her breath and tried to think of a likely excuse or reason for him to return to the other room without her.

He lifted an eyebrow. "Or we can stand here all evening. Arguing."

Embarrassment heated her face, but it was mixed with something else because of the smile on his face. He made her want to smile, despite nothing about any of this being funny. Shaking her head, then nodding it because she was utterly confused, she said, "I'm not arguing, I'm just—"

"Arguing," he said, with a chuckle.

With extremely heated cheeks, she said, "I'll be right out."

The slight nod he gave was charming—*he* was charming, but she'd already known that from his letters. She stepped around him into the powder room, where she had to take several deep breaths to make her heart stop racing. George was not only charming, but also handsome, with his hair combed neatly to one side and the collar of his white shirt pressed stiff, he was… Perfect. There was no other word. He was the perfect gentleman in so many ways.

That was the reason she was here, too. Beverly hadn't been the only one who'd wanted to attend. She had. She'd wanted to see him, talk to him in person, not just through letters, and that had been foolish. So incredibly foolish.

After a moment of hanging her head, of badgering herself for being so stupid, she lifted her head to examine herself in the mirror. She hated this. Hated being so upset with herself. For being such a ninny. What she needed to do was stand up to her aunt. Tell her she could write to anyone she wanted to, whenever she wanted.

That's what she'd done to Delmar. Told him she could live wherever she wanted.

She hung her head again at how well that had worked out for her.

What she needed was a miracle. A true miracle.

Something along the lines of being able to disappear into thin air would work. Or even a window to climb out of, which caused her to lift her head again and look around. There was no window available in the fancy room, with its red-and-gold wallpaper, sparkling porcelain sink and fluffy white hand towels hanging on the bar beneath the mirror.

Letting out a sigh, she quickly washed the stickiness off her hands from brushing the punch off George's suit jacket. Then she wet one of the white hand towels and carried it into the hallway.

George was there, but no longer wearing his suit coat. The muscles of his upper arms and shoulders stretched the material of his starched white shirt, which was now covered by just his blue corduroy vest. One that made his blue eyes all the brighter. The smile was still on his face; a gentle, sweet smile. All in all, it reminded her of the only other time they'd met.

Her fingers shook, causing the wet towel to slip from her hold. She managed to catch it before it dropped to the floor as she recalled how her aunt had told her to leave and never come back, that she never wanted to see her. Ever. That's what she'd been doing—leaving—

when she'd encountered him and Martha in the hallway of her aunt's house.

He took the towel from her hand. "Are you all right?"

She pushed the memory away and nodded. "Yes. Yes. I, uh, wet the towel to wipe off your suit coat."

"Thank you. That was thoughtful." He set the towel on the edge of a hall table. "But a waiter is seeing to my coat."

"Oh, that's very kind." It sure would be nice if she could just disappear right now. Or maybe sprout wings, fly away. Or something similar. She shouldn't be here, no matter how badly she'd wanted to see him.

He tilted his head slightly to the left and looked at her quizzically. "Forgive me for asking, or forgetting if that is the case, but did you and I meet before I left for the war?"

Her heart felt as if it had suddenly grown arms and crawled up into her throat. He couldn't remember her. Their meeting had been brief. A mere passing in the hallway. Yes, she remembered him, but he was unforgettable. She wasn't. There was nothing memorable about her.

"Something about you is familiar to me," he said.

Not sure if her voice would work or not, because she'd never been good at lying, rarely even tried, she pressed a hand to her throat. "Perhaps I look—"

"Like someone I know?" he said, finishing for her.

She nodded, having been about to say something to that effect, with an oddly squeaky sounding voice.

"Perhaps, but..." He shook his head. "Were you in a grade, or a couple of grades, below me in school?"

She shook her head. "No." Flustered, because she was younger than him, she tried again. "I mean—"

"You didn't go to school in Albany?"

"Yes... I mean, no, I didn't."

He grinned, nodded, then lifted an eyebrow. "College?"

"No."

After what felt like a very long stretch of silence, he gently wrapped a hand around her elbow. "Shall we return to our table?"

She had no idea if Aunt Jill and Uncle Roy would be near the table or not and wasn't ready to find out. "Don't you...?" She had to clear her throat because she still didn't sound like herself. How could she with her own heart trying to strangle her? "Need to wait for your suit coat?"

"No. He'll deliver it to the table."

"Oh."

He held out an elbow and, grasping her hand, hooked it beneath it. "Believe me, if there was a way to escape, I would, but, as my mother pointed out, it's my party."

"You don't want to be here?" she asked as they began walking.

"It's nice to see everyone, but I'm not the only soldier returning home. I'm no one special and shouldn't be treated any different than anyone else."

He was special to her. Knowing she couldn't say that, she said, "You're special to Beverly."

He grinned. "She is special to me, too."

Something inside her felt as if it was melting and her nerves were playing hopscotch beneath her skin at the way she could feel the warmth of his arm through the sleeve of his shirt.

"How about we try getting her a cup of punch again?" he asked as they entered the room.

Emma's first glance went to the punch table, and seeing no sign of her aunt or uncle, she then glanced at the table where Beverly sat. A small amount of relief washed over her because her aunt and uncle weren't near that table, either. She wanted to scan the rest of the room but was afraid of making eye contact with her aunt.

"Okay."

At the punch table, he filled two cups, gave one to her and carried one for Beverly.

"This must be Emma," a woman said as they arrived at the table where Beverly was seated.

"Yes, it is," George replied as he set a cup of punch on the table near Beverly. "Emma, allow me to introduce you to my parents. My mother, Amy, and my father, Craig."

"We just met Beverly." Trim, with short blond hair and twinkling blue eyes, his mother glanced at the table. "And learned how she wrote to George the entire time he was overseas. That was so wonderful."

Emma shot a quick glance at Beverly, who was grinning from ear to ear, before she nodded to his parents. "Mr. and Mrs. Weston. It's nice to meet you."

"Oh, please, call us Craig and Amy." His father was as tall as George, and though his hair was gray, he looked like an older version of his son, except that George had clearly inherited his twinkling blue eyes from his mother. "We are delighted to meet both you and Beverly," his father said. "And to have you join us tonight."

"Indeed we are, and yes, dear, do call us by our given names," his mother said. "You've already met the rest of the family, so let's be seated." With a wave of one hand, his mother turned her smile on George. "Your father will make a quick speech before the meal is served. You sit right here, and Emma, you sit right there next to him."

Chapter Four

His father's speech was short and to the point as he thanked everyone for joining the family in welcoming him home, the meal that was served was delicious and plentiful and the sounds filling the room told him that people were enjoying the opportunity to get together. George was fully aware of all this, even while his mind and a large portion of his attention was focused on Emma.

He had this deep gut feeling that he'd met her before. When she'd walked out of the bathroom and their gazes had locked, he'd had a distinct feeling of déjà vu. As if he'd seen those exact same thickly lashed brown eyes looking up at him before today, and before the other day in the apartment-building hallway.

Her voice wasn't familiar, nor were her mannerisms, and he couldn't remember ever meeting a woman named Emma, but his instincts were too strong to ignore, which made him search his mind more thoroughly.

"George?"

He turned to his left, where his mother sat. Emma was on his right.

"I said it's really a nice turnout, don't you think?" his mother asked.

His mother thrived on planning and executing parties and community events, and for her sake, he nodded. "Yes, it is. Thank you for all your work in planning it."

"This? It was nothing. A few phone calls and it was all set, but you're welcome." She patted his arm. "I'm so glad you invited Beverly and Emma. I didn't know you'd been exchanging letters with them."

He almost corrected her by saying it had only been Beverly that he'd exchanged letters with, but the tingling sensation rippling over his shoulders made him question if that was true. The warm vanilla scent that had been on those letters was still filling his nose, and it was coming from Emma, not Beverly. Perhaps she had assisted Beverly in writing the letters.

Less than a minute later, that idea become even more imbedded in him because of his uncle Walt.

Known for his jokes, Uncle Walt asked, "Anyone know what the tablecloth said to the table?"

As others shook their heads or rolled their eyes—that was Aunt Adelle and Janice, who were exposed to Walt's jokes all the time—Beverly spoke up.

"Oh, I'm sure Emma knows," she said, with adoration in her eyes and voice. "She knows all sorts of jokes and riddles. It's because she works with children. That's what she does. Works in the library at the elementary school on Washington Street."

All eyes turned to Emma. A protectiveness arose in George, and he wanted to touch her hand, tell her she didn't have to answer.

With her cheeks flushed, she gently shook her head. "I don't believe I know that one."

"I've got you covered!" Uncle Walt answered, laughing harder than anyone else.

"We'll have to write that one down," Beverly said to Emma.

Emma nodded, but George sensed that she'd known the answer and hadn't wanted to intrude on Walt's enjoyment of sharing the answer. He questioned if she had supplied Beverly with the jokes and riddles in the letters.

"Tell them one of your riddles," Beverly encouraged Emma.

Emma bowed her head shyly.

George knew the feeling of being put on the spot and pushed his chair back from the table. The meal had ended, and others were moving to the dance floor. He tapped Emma's shoulder. "Would you care to dance?"

Disappointment rose inside him at her hesitancy as she glanced across the room, towards the dance floor, but then, to his surprise, she turned to him and nodded.

He wondered if he should question the excitement that her response created inside him, but chose not to as he rose to his feet and assisted her from her chair. Taking her elbow, he guided her left, around their table, mainly because of the couple approaching their table from the right. He'd spoken to Roy and Jill King on his first night home. They'd came over to the house and assured him that they hadn't known anything about Martha breaking their engagement until she'd already eloped.

Their attitude had created nothing but sympathy for Martha, mixed with a bit of happiness because of her courage. From what her parents had said, they hadn't seen her since her elopement, as she hadn't come back to Albany since then.

That didn't surprise him. Martha had often talked of moving to New York City, and it was clear her parents were still upset over the elopement. Especially Jill. She obviously cared more about the future of North Country Logging than about her daughter's happiness.

That hadn't surprised him, either. She'd been the one to suggest the marriage, the merger. It had been shortly after Robert had died, and Jill had been at their house. He remembered it plainly, because he'd told her that he'd take over the company someday and make it the biggest and best in the nation.

She'd scowled at him and said the only way he'd ever do that was to marry Martha and merge their two companies.

He'd only been a kid, a little kid, and she'd scared the dickens out of him, and in his attempt to be brave, to be older, he'd told her that he would do that, and he'd told his parents, too.

Over the years, they had questioned him about his childhood decision, but when he'd continued to state that's what he'd wanted, they'd agreed.

Glancing at Emma walking beside him, he asked, "You work at the elementary school library?"

"Yes."

"For how long?" he asked while guiding them around tables.

"Almost two years."

"Is that when you moved to Albany?"

"Yes."

"From where?" He clamped his teeth together, feeling as if he was drilling her for answers. He was curious to know more about her but hadn't meant for it to sound like an inquiry.

For the first time since they'd left the table, she glanced up at him. "New York City."

He smiled at her, hoping that would make his list of questions appear less intrusive. "How does Albany compare?"

A hint of a shimmer flashed in her eyes. "Albany is wonderful. It's still a large city, but so much friendlier, and cleaner."

"I agree. I've always thought that New York City would be a fine place to be from, but not to live in."

A tiny frown formed between her eyebrows. "You have?"

"Yes. I've lived in Albany my entire life, but I've been to New York City often enough to know I'm not a fan of their politics. The problem is, the city has been corrupted for so long, it's become commonplace." Understanding his own biases were coming through, he paused his steps as they arrived at the wooden dance-floor area. "I apologize for speaking unkindly about your hometown. Albany and New York City have had a rivalry since Albany became the state capitol. There's been a push to change the capitol location ever since and that has never set well with the residents here."

Her smile was kind and understanding. "There is no reason to apologize, you're simply being honest, and I agree about the politics in New York City. Having lived there, I know how it affects certain residents more than others."

Sensing a sadness in her, he gave her a nod and held out a hand to take hers. She laid her other hand on his shoulder, and he rested his other one lightly on her waist, and then took the lead.

She was a natural dancer, her steps flawless as they made their way around the floor. Dancing with her was enchanting, and a little bit nerve-racking at the same time. The nerve-racking part was because of the way he felt a connection to her that went beyond their hands casually touching each other as they danced. The soft scent of warm vanilla had a strong effect on him, too.

All in all, the sensations inside him were uncanny, yet George allowed himself to bring their bodies closer, in part because he didn't have much choice. The dance floor was crowded.

She bit her bottom lip and her gaze flitted around the area before coming back to him, as if unsure they should be dancing so close.

"Do you enjoy working at the school?" he asked, wanting to ease her concern.

Once again, her eyes took on a shimmer. "Yes, very much."

"Is that what you did in New York City as well?"

"No. My brother-in-law assisted me in finding the job here." She sighed softly. "I'm just an assistant to the librarian, but it's wonderful to see children excited about literature. I love reading to them and suggesting books for them to check out and read on their own."

Her face had taken on a glow. "I can tell that you enjoy it," he said. "And I'm sure you are very good at it. Have you always enjoyed literature?"

"Yes. My father enjoyed reading and used to tell me that I could visit every country in the world by simply reading about them."

Once again, there was an odd little hitch inside him,

like two links clicking together. Beverly's letters often referenced different landmarks and she'd ask if he'd seen them. If he had, he'd describe what he'd seen to her in a return letter. It wouldn't have been unusual for her to assist Beverly, would it? Furthermore, why did it matter?

As if reading his thoughts, she added, "Beverly loves to read, too. We often share books that I check out from the library."

That could explain it, and he didn't feel the need to push it further right now. "Does your father still live in New York City?"

The twinkle in her eyes faded. "No, he passed away a few years ago."

"I'm sorry for your loss," he said, sincerely, because he did know the pain of losing a family member. "What about your mother?"

"She died several years ago."

"My sincere condolences again."

She gave a small nod. "Thank you. My sister and brother-in-law live in New York City. He's a teacher and they are expecting a baby next spring."

He had an urge to ask if that's what she wanted, to be married, have children, which was a very personal thing to ask someone he'd just met. Furthermore, her answer shouldn't matter one way or the other. Marriage was no longer in his future. He'd been cut free from that path and wasn't looking to repeat it. Right now, he had the opportunity to make significant changes in the lumber world and that would be his focus. His only focus.

The song ended and he took a step back to release her, but paused because her upper teeth were buried in her bottom lip so deeply it was turning it white. She was gazing toward their table. Being shorter than him, she wouldn't be able to see over the heads of the other dancers, but he could, and noting that Roy and Jill King were still at the table, he asked, "Would you care to dance again?"

She nodded as if relieved to a somewhat minimal degree.

As the music started up again, they stepped closer, and the warm vanilla scent turned his mind back to Beverly's letters. It had been foolish of him to think of marriage just because of a few letters. Beverly was a dear, but she hadn't been the woman he'd created in his mind, and neither was Emma, if that's what he was trying to convince himself of. For all he knew, she could be married herself. Perhaps that was why she said he could call her Emma. Maybe he even knew her husband.

Searching for what he thought might be a less direct way of enquiring if she was married, he asked, "Was your husband unable to attend this evening?"

Frowning, she shook her head. "I didn't mean to make it sound that way. I'm not married. My sister is. I have no interest in getting married."

Curious, he continued, "May I ask why?"

A faraway and thoughtful gaze filled her eyes as she said, "My mother's family didn't care much for my father and it made our lives difficult, for both of them and for my sister and I, though my parents tried hard to not let it affect us, especially my father after my mother died." A glimmer of a smile returned to her lips, "And because I like how things are now. My job at the school and living here in Albany."

"I'm glad you found happiness here," he replied in earnest. "And I understand family interference. I, too, have no interest in marriage."

"Understandably, after—" She clamped her lips together and bowed her head, eyes closed. Her feet also lost the rhythm of the music, which she quickly, and awkwardly, tried to regain.

He increased the pressure of his hand on her side and guided her back into the rhythm of the steps.

"I'm sorry," she said. "I had two left feet there for a moment."

"It's all right," he said. "No harm done." He waited until she nodded before he added, "It's all right to mention my broken engagement. It's well in my past."

The light of the overhead chandelier enhanced the blush on her cheeks. "It is?"

"Yes. I'm sure it was the talk of the town when it first happened, but by now, it's old news and there is no reason for anyone to feel they need to skip around it. I wish Martha and her husband all the happiness they deserve."

"You do?"

She looked and sounded flabbergasted. He grinned at that. At her. "Yes, I do."

"That…that's very generous of you."

"No, just honest. I said that I understand family interference. I'm also fully aware that marriage isn't just between two people, it includes families." That had been something he'd thought about for years and so he was doubly glad that he wouldn't be related to Jill King through marriage.

"Surely Martha's family liked you," she said.

He laughed. Jill King didn't like anyone.

Emma questioned if George was one more thing that she'd wonder about in perpetuity. There were other things that one couldn't help but wonder about forever, for there were no defined answers, and he could very well be one of those.

Not even Aunt Jill could find something not to like about him. Emma was sure of that. She was also sure that with his looks and charm, women would line up to marry him.

They were probably lining up to dance with him, too. He was an exceptional dancer who made her feel as if she was floating around the room, even when she'd stumbled after bringing up his broken engagement. A slip of the tongue like that was exactly what she'd feared might happen tonight. Second only to coming face-to-face with Aunt Jill.

Her gaze crossed the room and relief filled her when she saw her aunt and uncle were no longer at the table. Heaven above, but she hoped that Beverly hadn't said anything. She trusted her not to, but like her, Beverly could easily have had a slip of the tongue.

Was he really fine with Martha being married to someone else? And wished them well?

He didn't seem upset.

In fact, he seemed perfectly fine. Smiling and laughing.

She certainly wasn't fine, though it was difficult not to smile.

Dancing with him was doing all sorts of things to her. Not only did she feel like she was floating on air, but dancing with him was also dreamlike. She had the desire to lean her head on his shoulder and close her eyes. Dream that there was nothing wrong with her dancing with him.

That this life that she'd come to love could continue, and include him.

It couldn't, and that solidified what needed to happen as the music ended. "Thank you for the dance. Both dances," she said while removing one hand from his shoulder and slipping the other from his hold.

"It was my pleasure."

Nervousness was overcoming her as she made a quick scan of the room, looking for her aunt and uncle. "Beverly tires easily."

"Does she?"

There was humor on his face, and in his tone, which only added to the emotions that were battling over what she should feel and think. It had been that way all night, but after dancing with him, her heart was truly trying to beat its way out of her chest. She was breathless, too, and couldn't pull her gaze off him. He had the best smile she'd ever seen. The absolute best. "Yes, she does," she said, trying hard to keep her wits about her. "I should see her home now."

He took a gentle hold on her elbow to escort her off the floor. "Shall we ask her?"

"No!" She sucked in air at how fast she'd answered, how nervous she'd sounded even to her own ears. "No. We don't want her to feel bad."

"No, we don't."

They walked in silence to the table, and upon arrival Emma leaned down and whispered that it was time to leave in Beverly's ear.

The older woman glanced at her and then at George.

Emma was once again praying for a miracle. One that included Beverly not insisting that they stay longer, for it appeared that's what she was considering.

Thankfully, Beverly smiled and nodded.

They included another thank-you to the hosts for the

invitation and the wonderful meal before making their departure. As they made their way across the room to the doorway, Emma continuously scanned for her aunt. For the first time since meeting Beverly, she wished the old woman's bones would allow her to move faster because when a person was making an escape, the need to hurry was foremost. That is what she was doing again. Escaping. Like she had earlier, to the powder room, and when George had suggested they dance—she had considered declining his offer until seeing Jill and Roy approaching the table. She'd also escaped into the laundry the other day when she'd seen him give Beverly a ride home, and into the phone booth. Her move to Albany had been an escape, too. It appeared as if escaping was what she'd been doing for a long time.

She was growing tired of it, but couldn't stop now.

They reached the entrance without encountering her aunt or uncle and were in the midst of collecting their coats when Willis appeared.

Buttoning his long coat, Willis gave a slight bow. "It will only take me a moment to bring the car around."

"Thank you," Emma replied, accepting Beverly's coat from the attendant so she could help Beverly put it on.

"Here, allow me."

Emma spun about, and if he'd had cups of punch in his hands, George would have been wearing it again. She hadn't realized he'd followed them. With little choice, because he already had a hold of Beverly coat, she released it to him.

"Here, dear, hold this for me, will you?" Beverly asked, holding out her white handbag.

Emma took it, which meant she'd have to wait to put

on her own coat because she was also holding her own purse. She gave the attendant an apologetic smile. The man nodded and smiled in return as if there was no issue in him waiting to hand over her coat.

Emma kept one eye on the door leading into the party, fully prepared to make a dash for the outside door if either her aunt or uncle walked past. As soon as Beverly had her coat on, Emma handed over the handbag and then turned to collect her coat, but once again, George was there. This time holding her coat.

As graceful as possible, which wasn't overly graceful with the way she was trembling, she allowed him to assist her putting it on.

"You ladies wait here where it's warm," George said. "I'll step outside to see if Willis is here yet."

"No." Emma stepped in front of him. "That's not necessary. Beverly can wait here. I'll step outside. You have guests to see to. Thank you again for a lovely party."

The cold air made her eyes sting as she walked out the door that a man opened for her, but that didn't stop her from taking the first deep breath she'd taken since entering the building hours before. She was so thankful, so very thankful that Aunt Jill hadn't recognized her.

"That's the car right there."

The air gushed out of her lungs at the sound of George's voice. He was standing right next to her.

Of course, he was. He had more manners than any man she'd ever known. Not as if she'd known many.

He assisted both her and Beverly into the back seat of the car and thanked them again for coming.

While Beverly gushed over how enjoyable their evening had been, Emma remained quiet, merely smiling and nodding, but she did bid George farewell as he closed the door. Then she kept her gaze averted from the window because he remained there, watching them as the car pulled away.

The ride home was chilly, even with the blanket over their legs and their coats wrapped tight around them, and their breathing made the car windows fog on the inside. Yet, Emma felt a warm glow inside as she thought about the evening. She was still eternally grateful that she hadn't run into Aunt Jill, but dancing with George was what was filling her mind now.

She hadn't danced in a very long time and never with anyone as handsome as him. He'd smelled good, too. Nothing particular, just clean and fresh, with a hint of spice. It truly had been dreamlike, so very dreamlike.

A hint of chagrin washed over her as she recalled telling him about not wanting to get married, about her mother's family. She'd never told anyone that, even though it was true.

She'd told Beverly some things, but had never said that she didn't want to get married, probably because she knew how Beverly would react to that. She was still in love with her husband, all these years after he'd died, and would never understand.

Beverly probably had never had someone look at her like they wanted to spit on her.

That's how Aunt Jill had always looked at her and her sister, and when she'd spoken of her father, she'd looked downright evil.

Emma's stomach churned, remembering how Aunt Jill had made a point of coming to see them once a year. Not to their apartment. She would always stay at a hotel and tell their mother to come there. Their father was never invited. He was always at work when her mother would take her and Sharon to the hotel, where Aunt Jill would click her tongue and announce that it was a good thing that she'd packed up some of Martha's old clothes for the *girls*. That's what she'd always called her and Sharon. The *girls*. In a tone that made it sound like a bad word. She'd never used their names. Ever.

Both she and Sharon had hated the visits because most of the time was spent with Aunt Jill saying bad things about their father and how her mother should come back home to Albany. She'd say that the *girls* could stay in New York with their father. Aunt Jill never used his name, either, but would talk about how his bad blood ran in their veins and say that they'd never amount to anything. Just like him. And she'd remind their mother that she would be better off without any of them.

Emma could recall being so mad she'd shook all over and how she'd wanted to say that her father's name was William. William Ellis and that he wasn't a bad man with bad blood. He was a wonderful man. A wonderful father. Mother had said that many times, but eventually quit trying to explain anything to Aunt Jill. She must have known that it wouldn't do any good. She'd also quit telling Aunt Jill that she'd never leave her children and husband, but as soon as they left the hotel, their mother would assure her and Sharon that she'd never leave them. Any of them. That she loved them all dearly, and she'd asked them to say a special prayer for Aunt Jill, and to forgive her for the things she'd said.

Emma hadn't wanted to forgive her; she hadn't wanted the clothes, either.

She'd hated them—every dress, nightgown and pair

of shoes that they'd haul home from those visits. So had Sharon. But Martha was three years older than Emma, and one year older than Sharon, so the clothes had always fit one or the other of them, and in the end, they'd worn them because they'd never been wasteful people.

Thinking about her childhood reminded her that what George had said about the corruption in New York City was very true. She'd lived it her entire life. People in her neighborhood had earned enough money just to get by. Never enough to get ahead, because if that happened, the employers of the area would lose their workforce and the landlords their tenants, and none of them had wanted that to happen. It was a trap. The politicians knew all of that. They'd come to the neighborhoods spouting promises, telling the men if they voted for them, they'd see that changes were made.

That never happened and she doubted that it ever would.

After their father had died, both she and Sharon vowed to get out. To move away as soon as possible.

Sharon had known Eddie from school. They had graduated the same year and he'd promised that as soon as he completed college, they'd get married. Eddie hadn't lived in their neighborhood and he'd gone to a different high school than they had, but he and Sharon had met at a school event when they'd been seniors and taken a shine to each other.

Sure enough, the day he'd graduated from college, Eddie had shown up at their apartment, ready to marry Sharon, just like he'd promised.

Sharon had said it was a good thing that she loved Eddie, because love him or not, she would have to marry a man who kept a promise like that.

Emma sighed. No one had promised to come get her. She'd had to get out on her own.

There had never been a boy in school or anywhere else that she'd taken a shine to, either. Rightfully so, because even back then, she'd had no intention of getting married. She'd been hated her entire life and wasn't about to take the chance of that happening all over again. Of being hated by her husband's family like her mother's family had hated her father.

Her shifting thoughts returned to George, and she wondered why he'd laughed and hadn't answered if Martha's family had liked him. Nor had he explained if that was why he no longer wanted to get married.

"I'll get the door for you ladies," Willis said.

Emma glanced out the window, not having realized the car had stopped at their apartment building.

A few moments later, after Willis had walked them to Beverly's apartment, with Beverly gushing over him and the party the entire time, Emma closed the door behind him.

"Oh, my, wasn't that just the most delightful party?" Beverly asked while removing her coat. "The roast beef was so tender, it just melted in your mouth, and I'm sure they used both butter and cream in those whipped potatoes. Had to have. They were so creamy. Don't you agree?"

"Yes." Emma took Beverly's coat to hang it on the hook near the door, as well as her hat with the daisy still pinned on it. "The meal was delicious."

"You and George certainly made a lovely couple on the dance floor."

Emma flinched slightly at the way her breath caught and had to wait until it was ready to leave her lungs before she hung up the coat and hat and turned about. "I had no choice but to dance with him. My aunt and uncle were approaching the table."

"Yes, well, about that. I now know why you're so afraid of that woman. Your aunt Jill is a spiteful broad if I ever met one. Rude and spiteful!"

A shiver rippled her spine. "You didn't say anything to her, did you?"

"Of course, I did." Beverly plopped down in her rocking chair. "When she finally stopped waggling her tongue."

Emma had never felt faint in her life but did at that moment. She was so light-headed she had to grasp ahold of the chair in front of her. Terrified to ask, yet knowing she had to, she muttered, "Oh, Beverly, what did you say?"

"I didn't tell her who you were." Beverly set her chair rocking with a kick of one foot while simultaneously picking up her knitting needles from the basket beside her chair. "But I wanted to. I really wanted to. Wanted to say a whole lot more than, that, too, but I held my tongue. Mostly."

Chapter Five

George wasted no time in getting to work on creating a logging division for Weston Lumber. It was time. Beyond time. There was no reason for their company or the Kings to depend so heavily upon one another. Especially when working with other companies would be good for many others.

He'd thought of little else after Emma had left the party the other night, especially due to the way Jill King had drilled him as to who he'd been dancing with and where he'd met her. His replies had been vague, which irritated Jill even more. He'd also laughed when he learned about how Beverly had quite abruptly put a stop to Jill's questions about Emma while the two of them had been dancing. Per his cousin Janice, Beverly had told Jill that she was a snoop and should mind her own business.

He hadn't danced with anyone else because he'd known he'd have compared the experience to dancing with Emma, and truthfully, he'd have found anyone else lacking.

If it had been possible, he'd have left the party when

she had, then he wouldn't have had to listen to Jill telling him that he needed to go to New York, find Martha and bring her home.

He wasn't about to do that. Early the next morning, he'd packed a suitcase and headed north, out of the city. Jake Turner had been a logger all his life and George had found him exactly where he'd thought. Deep in the woods, felling trees, limbing and bucking them, and hauling them into camp.

George had expected to be put to work and began helping limb trees upon arrival.

Loggers worked from sunup to sundown, and it was hard work, physically and mentally, because they had to be aware of his surroundings at all times. George didn't mind any of that.

The long hours and hard work aided him in getting Emma off his mind. Keeping her off was another issue. Thoughts of dancing with her filtered into his dreams as soon as he'd fallen asleep in a spare bunk that first night, and each night since.

He'd dreamed of a woman before, while overseas and exchanging letters with Beverly. That's who he'd dreamed of then. Beverly. Before he'd met her. Ironically, Emma had fit the image of the woman he'd dreamed about, and try as he might, he couldn't change that. She was there, every night.

She was there during the days, too, but he still managed to make his waking hours productive. Jake Turner was interested in partnering with Weston Lumber and George considered that the win he'd needed to get things started.

Convincing his father would take work, but with Jake willing to come aboard immediately, his father would understand how seriously he was in putting changes in place.

Taller and broader than any other man George had ever met, Jake had worked for logging companies from the west coast to the east. The fact that the Adirondack area of New York State had been labeled the lumber capital of the world years ago, had produced more lumber than any other state, is what had drawn Jake into the area a few years ago, and kept him here.

Lumbermen were a rare breed, and George had instantly recognized Jake as a master of his trade upon meeting him back then, and had encouraged him to go to work for North Country Logging. Jake had considered it and visited a North Country Logging camp, but ultimately declined working for them. Jake had never shared why, but George knew that lumbermen could be superstitious and set in their ways, and figured Jake had seen something he didn't like at North Country.

It hadn't stopped the two of them from becoming friends, and George was even more thankful for that now. Jake had started his own company, but it was small, and he wanted to make it bigger, and recognized what George was offering would do that.

Four days after arriving, with the key to making his plan work in place, George was ready to head back to the city.

Just in time, because he'd promised his mother that he'd be home for Thanksgiving when he'd left the morning after his party.

It was well over a four-hour drive, and George knew he'd be cutting it close to be home by noon due to the winding, twisting and rutted roads, but he'd been too tired to start the drive after working all day yesterday.

"I'll be in touch within a couple of weeks," George told Jake as he carried his suitcase to his truck, one of several trucks that Weston Lumber owned. The sun was just starting to rise, and the air had a cold bite to it along with a few tiny snowflakes.

"Good. Very good," Jake replied with his deep northern brogue. "I like your plan."

"Our plan," George said. "You'll talk to the others?"

"Yah, yah, I will. They will agree with me." Jake pulled his thick stocking cap down over his ears. "It will be good for all of us."

"It will be." George climbed into the truck. "Thanks for letting me bunk here for a few days."

Jake let out a belly laugh. "Yah. That was good. You can work for me anytime."

George chuckled. "We'll be working together soon."

"That will be good."

They said goodbye as George closed the truck door, then started the engine and gave a final wave to Jake as the other man walked back to the long bunkhouse building. Letting the motor warm up, George stared at the building. Built of logs, it was crude, but sturdy. As were the cook shack and the stables for the horses. He'd been in several North Country Logging camps, and those building were canvas shanties that had been nearly impossible to heat, which was critical because the men worked for five months straight, in the dead of winter.

The bunkhouse he'd slept in had been warm enough, and he knew he'd miss that warmth as he shifted the truck into gear and steered toward the road to start his long, cold ride home.

Bringing Jake onboard right from the start would be

a signal to other logging companies and mills that working together would be good for everyone. There was room for growth in the industry and that was needed now more than ever. Wood for bridges and buildings, furniture and homes, and everything in between would always be important, as would pulp wood for paper products, and with the war over, the entire world would be looking to move forward.

George spent some time thinking about all of that, but it wasn't long before his line of thought went down another route that had nothing to do with logging, lumber, the winding road, or the snowflakes that were growing larger and falling faster.

Emma.

He just couldn't get her off his mind. It was as if he had a unique connection to her that he didn't quite understand. She could have assisted Beverly in writing to him, but there was nothing significant about that.

He tried to think about other things. Weston Lumber, the trees lining the winding road, the snow that was starting to stick to the ground, if he would make it home in time for Thanksgiving dinner.

That was his goal for the day.

And that made him wonder where Emma was having Thanksgiving.

Or if she had thought about dancing with him as much as he'd thought about dancing with her.

He wondered if she'd thought of him at all. She didn't have much reason to. It wasn't as if they knew each other, or were even likely to see each other again.

That thought didn't settle well, and he wondered if he might need to make a reason to see her again.

* * *

Hours later, as he arrived home, he still hadn't come up with a good reason, but it was no longer snowing and though Uncle Walt's car was in the driveway, there almost an hour before the meal would be served.

Carrying his bag, George made his way to the front door of the massive three-story home. Built on the banks of the Mohawk River, his grandfather had purchased the house and property after marrying his grandmother and with the idea of filling it with family. Sadly, his grandmother had died shortly after his father had been born, and his grandfather never remarried, and had died before George had been born.

Someday, that conversation would come up. Of how he was expected to marry, produce the next generation. Another way marriage was simply a means to an end. Nothing about that encouraged him to change his mind about going down that road again. He felt free, having had that weight lifted from him for now, and wasn't interested in changing that, and couldn't imagine that anything would change his mind. Not for a long time.

He was still climbing the steps when the front door opened and James, tall, thin and impeccably dressed in an all-black suit, gave a customary bow.

"Good day, sir," James said. "Happy to have you home."

George laughed as he stepped inside. "I'm sure you mean relieved, James. I know my mother, and she's been fretting all morning that I wouldn't arrive in time."

James cracked a smile as he closed the door. "She has."

The butler had been with his family since before George had been born and probably knew more family secrets than anyone else ever would. "I will go say hello and then get cleaned up with plenty of time to spare."

"Very well. Everyone is in the front room." With a wide smile, James held out a hand. "I'll take your luggage and lay out clean clothes for you."

"Thank you." George handed over his bag, hat and coat, and while James headed for the curving staircase off the entranceway, George made his way down the long, wide hallway, pausing for a moment near one of the radiators to warm his hands.

The front room, as it was called, was on the far side of the house with a row of tall windows that faced the river. When the house had been built, years and years ago, it had been miles from town and the river had been used for traveling more than roads. Since then, Albany had grown a considerable amount, and their large acreage was now part of the city limits, though it still held a privacy that he'd always found tranquil.

The tantalizing smell of roasting turkey filled the air. He left the radiator and as he passed the doorway to the kitchen, his stomach growled. The food at the lumber camp had been plentiful but had taken a good portion of salt and pepper to make it edible, much like the meals he'd had in the army. Miss Maybelle's cooking had been one of the top things he'd missed during his time away from home.

Like James, Maybelle had been with the family since before George, and few could hold a candle to her meals and pastries.

Other than those ginger bars he'd eaten at Beverly's house the day he'd invited her to the party. As that thought settled, he recalled that Beverly had said her neighbor had made them, and he had to conclude that neighbor was Emma.

As if his mind had conjured her up, she—Emma— was the first person he saw as he approached the wide archway leading into the front room. He paused, blinking to check his eyesight, but it was her. Sitting on the green sofa that was near the fireplace that took up a large portion of the north wall, she had a child on each side of her—Janice's children—and was reading a story to them.

They were all so engrossed they didn't see him, and he stood there, staring, wondering if Emma had grown prettier during his absence. Her brown hair was pinned up, with a few loose tendrils framing her face as she read, smiling, and glanced between the storybook and Nate and Nellie.

"George!"

He stepped into the room at the sound of his mother's voice.

"I was starting to question if you'd keep your promise," she said, raising from her chair to greet him.

He noted how Emma's head snapped up, and he gave her a nod before turning his attention to his mother. "I always keep my promises," he replied, meeting his mother in the center of the room and kissing her cheek.

"I know you do, but I was still worried. That's what mothers do." She looped an arm through his. "Come say hello to everyone, then you'll have just enough time to get out of those lumberman clothes before we eat."

"That was my plan," he said, unable to stop his gaze from going to the sofa, now questioning why Emma was here.

* * *

Emma had lost her place in the book and was quickly scanning the paragraphs so she could pick up again before the children noticed. She'd been pleasantly surprised to learn that Nathaniel and Nellie Cramer were Janice's children. Both children had instantly recognized her from school, and it hadn't taken long before they'd appeared before her with a book. Several, actually, which she hadn't minded.

Truth was, she was slightly miffed at Beverly for tricking her. The two of them had spent every holiday together since she'd moved into the building, and she'd assumed this year would be no different. She should have questioned why Beverly hadn't insisted a trip to the market was in order yesterday.

It hadn't been until this morning, when Beverly had declared that Willis would be there to pick them up at eleven, that Emma had learned Beverly had accepted an invitation to spend Thanksgiving with George's family.

For both of them.

Emma had declined, insisting that she'd stay home, but then Beverly had shown her the written invitation, which had included both of their names and had been delivered by Willis, days before. Beverly had also assured her that her Aunt Jill and Uncle Roy would not be there; that it would only be family, besides them.

That had made Emma question their attendance even more, but Beverly had claimed it was too late to declare a change of plans, so they had arrived here, at George's home, over half an hour ago.

His parents, Amy and Craig, were very nice people and seemed genuinely pleased to have her and Beverly join them for the holiday.

Amy had also explained that George had gone north, to visit a logging camp, but had promised that he'd be home by the time Thanksgiving dinner was served at one.

Her scanning of sentences had brought her back to the place in their story, but neither child was interested. They'd both jumped off the sofa to race across the room, where George had lifted them one at time to give them a playful toss in the air, making them squeal with joy.

After he'd said hello to the others, he then approached her, with a child tugging on each arm, and she had no choice but to set aside the book and rise to her feet.

"Hello," he said, with that one-of-a-kind, best-in-the-world smile. "How are you?"

"Fine, thank you," she said even though her breath was caught somewhere between her lungs and mouth. Why did it feel like she hadn't seen him in years? Moreover, why did she wish she could give him a hug like all the others in the room had? Pushing the air from her lungs, she added, "And you?"

He gestured to his black-and-red plaid shirt, dark wool pants held up by suspenders over his shoulders and brown work boots. "Other than in need of a few minutes to become more presentable, I'm well, thank you."

Emma thought he looked very presentable, and handsome. More so than she remembered.

Nellie released his hand, grasped hers and looked up at her with a glow on her face that made the tiny row of freckles across her nose shimmer. "Miss Ellis works in the library in our school."

The children had been as surprised as she had been when she and Beverly had arrived at the house. She had thought that she'd been prepared to see him when they'd arrived, but the way her heart was pounding right now, said she hadn't been prepared, then or now. She pressed her heels deeper into the thick rug in front of the sofa to stay put. Thoughts of escaping, or hugging him, were intermingling in her mind.

George tugged on one of Nellie's long, rust-colored braids. "Does she?"

"Yes, she does, and she was reading to us," Nathaniel replied. He was six, two years younger than his sister, and had his own set of freckles over the bridge of his nose.

"I saw she was reading to you." George ruffled Nathaniel's thick, curly rust-colored hair. "You three can finish the story while I go change my clothes." He kneeled in front of Nathaniel. "But you have to promise to set up the checkerboard so we can play a game before we eat."

Excitement made Nathaniel jump up and down. "I promise! I promise! But you have to promise to be fast!"

"All right then." George nodded at Emma. "I'll be back in a wink and a nod. I promise."

Emma's knees felt so weak, she lowered herself onto the sofa as soon as his back was turned, and attempted to draw in a deep, stabilizing breath. She knew he wasn't promising her anything, yet she had to wonder, if they'd have met under different circumstances, would they have taken a shine to each other? Which was the silliest thought she'd ever had. He had no reason to take a shine to her, and the circumstances couldn't be different. Ever.

"Can you read faster?" Nathaniel asked while climbing up on the sofa beside her.

His honesty made her chuckle. She picked up the book. "I will try."

* * *

The story was completed and the checkerboard set out on a small table by the time George returned wearing a light gray suit, white shirt and black tie. His hair was still damp from being washed and the stubble that had been on his cheeks and chin was gone. Emma couldn't stop herself from looking at him and tried to do so unnoticed. His smile never faded—in fact, it grew when they made eye contact, which caused her to quickly look away.

She sincerely hoped he didn't think that she had finagled an invitation to his family's Thanksgiving, even though she wasn't overly confident that Beverly hadn't done exactly that. Beverly claimed the invitation had shown up out of the blue, but that was a little unbelievable. There was no reason for his family to invite her and Beverly to the meal. No reason at all.

Right from the start of the checkers game, it was evident who would win. However, George wasn't just letting Nathaniel win, he was teaching him how to win. With each move he'd point out how Nathaniel needed to examine the pieces around the one he was about to move, both the red and black pieces and how each move would change the pathway to the other side of the board. She was impressed with George's patience and by how he explained everything in a way that Nathaniel, only six, could understand, his excitement and pride growing with each move.

There was a round of applause by all over Nathaniel's win at the end of the game, which was quickly followed by the announcement that the meal was ready to be served.

Emma wasn't sure if it was by chance or direction

that George ended up at her side, to escort her to the dining room. Either way, he gently held her elbow as they followed the rest of the group out of the room.

The home was the largest and most beautiful one she'd seen. The soles of her shoes sank into the deep, lush carpet that covered the glossy floors at intervals in the large front room. The windows, with lacy, sheer curtains that were pulled back, filled the entire room with bright sunshine and provided a view of a yard that sloped down to the Mohawk River. Clusters of large hardwood and fir trees, along with several flowerbeds, were also visible out the windows. An old and deep longing had filled her as soon as she'd gotten her first glance out the windows. It had always been her deepest wish to live in a house, with grass and trees and flowers she could tend. Her entire life, all that had ever been outside of her windows had been buildings and streets. And people. The streets had always been full of people, day and night.

"I'm glad you and Beverly were able to join us today," George said as they entered the long, wide hallway that had tall wooden walls and numerous doors, some open, some closed. "But I do hope you weren't coerced into being here."

"I hope your family wasn't coerced into inviting us," she said, looking at the back of Beverly's head. Her friend was walking with George's parents several steps ahead of everyone else.

He chuckled. "Beverly endeared herself to my mother at the party, and knowing my mother as I do, she willingly sent the invite and wouldn't have taken no for an answer."

"Beverly can be an endearing soul."

"Yes, she can, and seeing both of you here was a very pleasant surprise to me."

Why did everything he said or did make her breathless? "Your—" She forced herself to breathe. "Your mother mentioned you were out of town."

"Yes, investigating options for expanding our lumber company," he replied. "I'd promised I'd be home for dinner today, but had I known you and Beverly would be here, I would have come home last night so I was here when you arrived."

"There would have been no need for that." A wave of frustration washed over her. Beverly had said that she needed to tell him the truth about the letters, and she'd said she couldn't. That she couldn't ever explain why she'd written to him. It would cause even more problems.

"It sounds like your attendance was a wonderful surprise for Nellie and Nathaniel," he said.

"It was for me, too," she admitted. "They are adorable, and very well behaved."

"They are, and they grew a lot while I was overseas." He chuckled. "The first thing Nathaniel told me when I got home that first night was that he'd quit biting the checker pieces."

His expression was filled with humor, and she covered her giggle with one hand. "Biting the checker pieces?"

"Yes. If you don't believe me, look at them. Every wooden disc has his teeth marks on them. He just couldn't seem to help himself."

"I believe you, and you did a very good job teaching him how to play."

"Well, I had a very smart teacher who taught me."

She assumed he meant his father and wanted to ask why he'd never mentioned any of them in his letters, yet couldn't. Actually, neither of them had mentioned family in their letters.

"I hope you're hungry," he said as they approached the long table surrounded by chairs and laden with food, including a golden-brown turkey. "Miss Maybelle is an outstanding cook, and I swear, she outdoes herself each and every year."

"It certainly smells and looks delicious."

He pulled out a chair for her to sit. "I'd tell you to leave room for dessert, but there's no reason to. We'll have that later this afternoon, after the meal settles, and then this evening, we'll have leftovers."

Emma held her response as he sat in the chair next to her, for no other reason than she planned on leaving right after dinner. She'd made Beverly promise that they would.

Chapter Six

The conversation around the dinner table was lively and joyful. His father's prayer of thanks had included his homecoming and the impending return of Bill, Janice's husband, before Christmas. It also included having Beverly and Emma join them for the day. George wholeheartedly agreed with each part.

Before he'd gone upstairs to quickly bathe, shave and put on clean clothes, his mother had explained that she'd invited Beverly and Emma, knowing that he wouldn't mind.

He had wondered if he should mind, considering he'd worked so hard to get Emma off his mind the last several days, but figured he would simply enjoy her company instead. Her participation in the conversations that flowed as they ate demonstrated that she was far more comfortable today than she had been at his party. She'd been quiet and subdued then, but today her laughter was light and lifting, and to everyone's delight, she knew the answers to several of Uncle Walt's jokes but would whisper the answer to Nellie, who sat on her other side and would promptly announce it, overly excited to have an answer for her grandfather.

That thrilled Walt and made him work harder at coming up with jokes and riddles that no one would know the answers to, which kept everyone laughing.

When the meal ended, George knew what would happen next. Although he'd been gone for Thanksgiving last year, things hadn't changed all that much. The entire family would move back to the front room, where his father and uncle would soon fall asleep in the armed chairs and his mother, Aunt Adelle and Janice would sit together to discuss what the children would like for Christmas and who would buy what so that there weren't any duplicates.

In the past, he and Bill had taken the children outside so they could burn off some energy and not hear the conversation about Christmas gifts. With Bill still overseas, he would take that job on himself.

Or perhaps not entirely by himself...

"Would you care to walk down to the river?" he asked Emma as they exited the dining room.

Her hesitation had him nodding toward the children, who stood in the hallway with Janice and were looking at him expectantly. "It's tradition."

Janice, knowing full well what the children expected, shook her head. "George, please don't feel obligated to—"

"Take these carpet crawlers outside?" he interrupted. "That's the best part of Thanksgiving."

"Yippie!" Nate exclaimed, right before he frowned. "Why do you call us carpet crawlers?"

"Because that's what you did when you were babies—crawled across the carpets—and you still do."

George tickled his tummy then patted his head. "Go get your coats."

The kids shot down the hallway and Janice stepped closer. "Really, you don't have to keep them entertained."

"I don't mind," he said. "Besides, the older they get, the bigger their ears get."

Beverly was making her way out of the dining room with his mother, and said, "Emma, dear, I must sit down and rest my stomach for a while. I haven't eaten that much in ages."

George took advantage of that to ask her again. This time he said, "Would you care to join the children and me?"

Emma watched Beverly walk down the hall in the opposite direction before she turned to him. "Yes, I would."

"Thank you both," Janice said sincerely. "Last year was so hard without—" She pinched her lips together and shook her head.

A head shorter than him, and like his mother and hers, Janice had blond hair and blue eyes, and was as close to him as any sister ever would have been. He gave her a tight hug and kissed the top of her head. "Bill will be home soon, and everything will be back to normal."

She nodded and patted his back before tightening the hug again. "I know. It's just—" She sniffled. "The waiting is so hard. It was so hard with both of you gone."

"I know," he whispered and kissed the top of her head again before stepping back and releasing her. "Go help your carpet crawlers put on their coats so they are buttoned straight."

Smiling softly, Janice quietly thanked both him and Emma before heading down the hallway.

"I hope you don't mind," he said to Emma.

She studied him thoughtfully for a moment and then shook her head. "No, I don't mind. You are a very nice person."

"I'm sure there are people who wouldn't agree with you." He winked at her. "But I'm glad you think so, and I think you are a very nice person, too."

She grinned. "I'm sure there are others who wouldn't agree with you."

"Tell me who and I'll tell them they are wrong."

A flash of seriousness crossed her face. "They wouldn't believe you."

At that moment he wanted to know whom she was referring to, because he would tell them, and not be overly kind because someone hadn't been kind to her, his gut told him that.

James appeared in the hallway, with coats for both of them, and within minutes, the four of them were outside, with Nellie and Nate running down the hill toward the river. He and Emma weren't running, but they weren't strolling, either.

Although he was still thinking about their hallway exchange, he explained the children's speed, "There's a sandy area along the bank where the children like to search for treasures."

"Treasures?"

"Yep. The flatter, the better."

The scarf over her head and tied beneath her chin was blue, the same shade of blue as her wool coat, and it framed her face perfectly, making her look of confusion all the more apparent. "Flat treasures?"

Teasingly, he shook his head at her. "Please don't tell me you've never searched for flat treasures?"

Her dark eyes were shimmering in the sunlight as she shrugged. "Considering I don't know what they are, I have to admit that I've never searched for flat treasures."

"Does that mean you've never skipped a rock?"

Her smile was captivating as it slowly grew broader. "No, I haven't."

He grasped her hand. "Everyone needs to skip rocks at least once in their life." Then he led her down the hill to where the children were already searching for rocks.

Once on the shoreline, he kneeled and picked up a rock. A nice flat one. "This is a flat treasure. They can't be too little, or too big. This is the perfect size. And you hold it like this." He folded one finger and his thumb around the outer circumference of the rock. "Then pull back and pitch it forward with a sidearm throw, keeping it flat so it'll skip across the water before sinking." He released the rock, waited as it flew toward the river, then skipped across the top of the water four times before disappearing. "Your turn."

Her smile was bright as she nodded, then scanned the ground near her feet. She kneeled and picked up a flat rock. "Will this one work?"

"Yes, that's a good one."

Carefully following the instructions he'd given her, she gripped the rock and gave it a good sidearm toss at the river. Whether it was beginner's luck or natural skill, her throw was a success. The rock skipped across the water three times before it sank.

"Oh, my goodness! I did it! Did you see that?"

Excitement echoed in her voice and glowed on her

face, and one thought flashed across his mind—kiss her. He'd dreamed about that and imagined kissing her would be as unforgettable as dancing had been.

She was looking at him with an expression that made him wonder if she was thinking the same thing, and that caused his heart to skip more beats than her rocked had skipped over the water.

It felt as if time was standing still, and the only way to make it start up again was to move, so he did, taking a step forward.

Her gaze flitted downward, to his mouth, then back up to his eyes.

Whatever connection was between them was real. More real than anything he'd ever felt before, even though it was also nonexistent. Or should be, because they didn't know each other well enough for anything to be between them. He'd known Martha his entire life, had known they would marry for years, yet she had never filled his mind like Emma had since the moment they'd met, and that left him questioning reality in ways he never had.

He reached out, touched her hand. "Emma—"

Shouts from the children interrupted whatever he'd been about to say as they arrived, clapping and congratulating her on her throw.

It was probably best, because he wasn't sure what had been about to leave his mouth. His brain was in some sort of early morning fog, like he'd just woken up and wasn't sure where he'd spent the night.

He did know that he was touching her hand and gave it a slight squeeze before releasing it. "I agree." He glanced at Nellie and Nate before turning to Emma again. "That was a perfect toss."

She blinked and took a step back before looking at the children. "Thank you. I believe it was beginner's luck."

George scanned the ground and found another rock. He picked it up and held it out to her. "The only way to know for sure is to throw another one."

She glanced at the rock as if not sure if she should take it.

"It's why we are here," he said. "To skip rocks."

"Throw another one, Miss Ellis," Nate said. "I bet you'll make it skip again."

With a grin that appeared and disappeared as quick as lightning, she took the rock and stepped closer to the water, giving herself room to throw it sidearm.

It skipped twice before sinking, and they all clapped, congratulating her again before the search for the perfect rock continued and pitching them began in earnest.

The wind was blowing, causing waves in the water, and he was sure the storm that he'd driven through this morning would arrive soon, but he wasn't about to let any of that stop the children, or Emma, from throwing a number of rocks. Each of them had several successes with their rocks, as well as a few failures.

"It's easier when there aren't any waves," Nellie told Emma after another rock sank without skipping. "We'll come back another day when the wind's not blowing, then you'll see. Right, George?"

"You are right as rain, Nellie jelly," he said.

Giggling, she told Emma, "He always calls me that."

"He calls me Nate bait," Nate said. "What does he call you?"

George looked at her, waiting for her answer. He could be wrong because her cheeks and nose were red from the weather, but he could have sworn a blush covered her face.

"Emma," she said. "He calls me Emma."

"Not Miss Ellis?" Nate asked.

"Of course not, silly," Nellie said. "She's not his teacher."

"Yeah, well, he taught her how to throw rocks," Nate argued.

"That's not the same thing as being a schoolteacher," Nellie said.

George held back his grin as he watched Emma glance between the children, and then stepped between them.

"You are both right," she said, "We aren't in school, but George did teach me how to skip rocks."

That seemed like a good enough explanation to Nate, yet he had more to say. "George is really good at skipping rocks, but Dad is better. Isn't he, George?"

Every child should believe their father is best at everything, and George patted Nate's shoulder. "Yes, he is."

Satisfied with that answer as well, Nate then asked, "Can we go see the bear cave now?"

They had been outside for over an hour, so instead of answering, George asked, "You aren't cold yet?"

"No," Nate replied.

"How about you girls?" George asked Emma and Nellie.

"No," Nellie answered him as she looked up at Emma. "You'll like the bear cave. Don't worry, we can't get close enough to see any bears."

George was again watching Emma, waiting for her answer.

She kept her gaze on Nellie. "That's good to know."

The children took that as her answer, and with whoops and giggles, they took off up the bank, to where a large grove of trees grew along the riverbank.

"Stay on the trail!" George yelled in their wake, then said to Emma, "It's not far, but if you'd prefer, I can tell them to wait until I walk you back up to the house."

Another one of her lightning smiles flashed as she shook her head. "I couldn't do that to them. Besides, I'd like to see a bear cave."

They began following the children. "Well, in that case, it's only fair to warn you that it sounds more exciting that it is."

She giggled slightly. "I'd say that to some people, it's as exciting as flat treasures."

George nodded and was fully aware of Emma walking at his side, from the tips of his toes to the top of his head and everywhere in between. Her glowing, cold-nipped skin and her windswept hair, which was fluttering around the edges of her scarf, were adorable, and even in the cold, he could smell the subtle warm vanilla scent that floated around her.

"This is all so beautiful. The river and trees, the grass and fresh air—it's as if we aren't in the city." Looking up at him, she asked, "Have you always lived here?"

"Yes, my entire life. The house was built by a general in the Continental Army who was also one of the first US senators. My grandfather bought it after Weston Lumber became profitable and lived here until he died." He had no idea why he told her all that, and added, "That's probably more than you wanted to know."

"Not at all. It's amazing to have such history, and it's a very beautiful home, beautiful property."

He held a tree branch out of the way so she wouldn't have to duck. "My grandfather added on what is referred to as the east wing so my parents would have their privacy after they got married."

"Is this where you and Marth—" She quickly glanced away as if embarrassed. "I mean, will you always live here?"

"More than likely," he said, ignoring her slip, both because he didn't want to embarrass her and because he had no desire to even remember how Martha had insisted that they'd build their own house. "Between the two wings there are eight bedrooms. I plan on traveling a lot, though, far more than my father has for the company."

"Does your mother know that?"

He laughed at how well she already knew his mother. "Not yet."

"Dare I say, I'd like to be a mouse in the corner when that happens?"

Enjoying her sense of humor, he laughed harder. "Her bark is worse than her bite."

Her smile included her eyes. "For her sake, I was very happy when you arrived in time for dinner."

He had a great desire to ask if she'd been happy for her own sake, but instead, for whatever reason, he explained, "I once promised to never hurt them, to never disappoint them, and I've worked hard to fulfill that promise."

Her smile softened, became even more endearing. "That's quite a promise to fulfill."

"I'm an only child," he said, as if that explained it all.

Emma nodded as if she understood, and they walked a short distance before she asked, "Why will you be traveling?"

"Because the world will always need lumber, and though Weston Lumber is known as one of the largest companies in the states, I plan on making it larger. Making the entire industry larger. We own timberland from New York to Maine, but have focused logging the land in New York. I plan on changing that."

As she had before, she eyed him thoughtfully before nodding. "I believe you will."

"Hurry up!" Nate shouted while waving from the top of the small knoll ahead of them.

"Ready to see a bear cave?" he asked.

"Ready or not, I believe it's about to happen."

She didn't act scared, just slightly wary, and he took ahold of her hand. "I've never seen a bear here, and I've been up here a million times."

"There's a first time for everything."

"That there is." He tugged her forward.

They reached the top of the knoll, where the children stood looking across the river, and Nate quickly pointed at the hole in the side of the bank on the opposite side of the river. "See that. That hole? It's a cave. A bear cave! Uncle Craig saw a bear there when he was a little boy. Didn't he, George?"

"That's what I've always been told," he answered.

"But we won't see one today, 'cause they're hibin—hiber—hi—"

"Hibernating," Emma said, supplying the word for him.

"Yeah! It's means they're sleeping. All winter." Nate never took his eyes off the cave. "Right there in that cave. When I get bigger, I'm going to take a boat across the river, climb up the bank and take a look in there."

"No, you're not," Nellie said. "You'd get in trouble."

"Not if Dad comes with me," Nate argued. "He said he would. When I get bigger. He promised." Needing confirmation, he added, "Didn't he, George? And you're going with us, aren't you? And Dad's going to take pictures."

Before he'd left for the service, he and Bill and Nate had walked up here, and Bill had promised they would. "That's correct." George turned to Emma and explained, "Bill is a photographer. He turns his pictures into postcards and sells them."

"Janice told me about that," she said. "It was exciting to learn that some of the postcards I've sent my sister of Albany were Bill's pictures."

He'd never thought about it before, but for a moment, George felt a hint of envy toward Janice and Bill. They'd gotten married for no other reason than because they'd wanted to, chose to. Bill had chosen his profession as well. George couldn't help but wonder if he'd think about things differently if everything wasn't a means to an end, an expectation.

Chasing away those thoughts, he considered explaining that the river would soon be frozen, so the trip wouldn't happen until next spring, but it wasn't necessary because Nate was too busy boasting his correctness to his sister, to which Nellie was insisting that she didn't want to see a bear.

"You're just mad that I'm right," Nate said.

"No, I'm not," Nellie said. "I'm cold. I'm going back to the house."

"It's time we all go back to the house." George held out a hand to catch a snowflake. "It's starting to snow."

Nate let out a squeal. "That means Christmas will be here soon! I told Grammy that I want a train that runs on tracks and a wagon and a goldfish in a bowl and…"

George shook his head at Emma as they started down the trail, following the children, with Nate still listing things he wanted for Christmas.

"You are a brave woman," George said.

"Excuse me?"

He gestured to Nellie and Nate, who were now in a race to see who could get to the house first. "Working at the school, with children every day."

She shook her head. "I'm not brave, I'm lucky."

At that moment, he felt lucky. Lucky in a way he hadn't ever felt. In all the years of Martha being at his house, he could count on one hand the number of times she'd walked down to the river with him, and never with Nellie and Nate in tow. He wasn't interested in aligning himself with any one woman like that again, but he liked the connection he felt toward Emma. He still couldn't explain it, nor could he deny that he wanted to see more of her.

From the moment she'd been hired at the school, Emma had felt lucky. Lucky to have a job, let alone such a wonderful one. Lucky that she'd found a way to move out of the slums of New York City. Lucky to live in a wonderful apartment, with Beverly just down the hall. She couldn't deny that she was lucky today, too, having had what could very well be her best Thanksgiving ever. She had memories of Thanksgivings when her mother was alive, but she'd been too small to understand thankfulness. Now, looking back, she was thankful to have memories of her family, her parents and sister, together, and memories after that, when it had just been her father and Sharon and her.

Her father had tried hard to make holidays memorable, but after he'd died, it had just been her and Sharon, and they'd worked through the holidays, because they hadn't been able to afford to take a day off. They had stopped rolling cigars long enough to cook and eat, and to give thanks, but today had been truly joyful and fun. She hadn't had such fun in a very long time.

The changes to her life that had happened since she'd moved to Albany were monumental, and she didn't want to do anything that might change that. At the same time, she knew she didn't belong here. At this house, with George. Not only because of her secret letter writing, but also because of who she was. Despite Aunt Jill's claims, she knew her father hadn't had bad blood—he'd been a good person, but they had been poor. She wasn't of the same class as George and his family, and there was nothing that would ever change that.

She and Beverly needed to leave as soon as she returned to the house. Due to all of that, but also for another reason. Ever since George had shown her how to throw a rock, she'd been wondering what it would be like to kiss him.

Never in her life had she wondered what it would be like to kiss a man, but she had today.

All in all, that scared her.

The door opened as they neared the house, and Janice stepped outside. She was very nice, and very pretty with short blond hair that had been elegantly styled with a curling iron in soft waves. Emma had tried using Beverly's iron, but her hair was too long and it just ended up in ringlets rather than soft waves. She could have her hair cut, but the only people who had ever cut her hair had been her mother and Sharon. She hadn't seen her sister since moving to Albany. They wrote regularly and she had already purchased a ticket so she could go to New York after the baby was born. She'd only stay a weekend, because of school. Maybe she'd have Sharon cut it then, if she was up to doing so after giving birth.

Janice shooed the children inside and then said, "Thank you both for entertaining them. That was very kind, and I appreciate it."

"I hope you left something on their lists for me to buy them for Christmas," George said.

"Your mother laid claim to a new wagon and doll, and that is more than enough from all of you," Janice said. "Having you and Bill home will be the best Christmas present of all. Now, I'll leave you two for a few moments of peace. Dessert won't be served for a while yet. Dad and Uncle Craig are still napping. Thank you again for keeping the children occupied."

Janice included her in her thank-you and Emma smiled in return. "It was fun—they showed me the bear cave and how to skip rocks."

"Oh, goodness, all I can say to that is *brrr*." Janice rubbed her arms as she laughed and turned about to hurry inside.

"Are you cold?" George asked. "We can go inside, or I can show you one more thing."

A deep division formed inside her. She'd barely noticed the cold due to an inner warmth that had been with her since they'd walked out of the house well over an hour ago. Prior to that, seeing him had filled her with a nervous excitement and her heart hadn't stopped thudding since then. A part of her wanted to say that she wanted to see whatever else he wanted to show her, because she truly did, but she knew she couldn't. Half afraid that her voice would crack, she shook her head.

"No to going inside or to seeing my special place?" he asked.

Special place? He was making this so difficult. She held in a sigh. "It…it's time for Beverly and me to leave."

"Oh." He frowned slightly. "Before dessert?"

"Beverly tires easily." She flinched inwardly, hoping lightning wouldn't suddenly appear and strike her for not telling the truth. Beverly had the energy of someone half her age.

Lightning didn't strike, but guilt for blaming things on Beverly did. "I have a lot to do yet today."

"On Thanksgiving?"

"Yes." Her mouth had gone dry and she licked her lips, tried to swallow, but there wasn't anything to swallow. "Well, you see, I'd planned on spending the day knitting."

"Knitting?"

It was the truth, but certainly sounded like an excuse. If she wasn't so fickle when it came to him, it wouldn't be so hard to talk. Drawing in a breath, she nodded. "Yes. The flu took a lot of lives, left many children orphaned. Several that used to attend school no longer do because they live at the orphanage now. I'm making scarves for all of them and Beverly is making mittens for them." Explaining that she'd just recently learned how to knit so the straight back-and-forth pattern for a scarf was all she had mastered, whereas Beverly could knit a pair of mittens with ribbed cuffs and perfect thumbs in a single evening, would take too much breath. She was already having a hard enough time talking, breathing, thinking.

"Well, now, that is very generous of you."

Her heart ached for all the children who hadn't returned to school when it had reopened. "I just don't want them to not to have something to open Christmas morning." Wanting him to understand that she wasn't making an excuse, she added, "I have a lot of scarves to knit between now and then."

He gave her a slight nod. "I'm sure you do. I'll get my car and give you a ride home."

Her mind didn't seem to be working, as all she said was, "Willis…"

"I already have my coat on," he said.

Chapter Seven

Thank goodness Beverly didn't question their leaving. Then again, the large basket of desserts and leftover food that George's mother insisted they take with them helped with that. So did the snowflakes that had started to fall, but nothing helped with the large amount of guilt that had taken residence inside Emma.

She sat in the front seat as George drove and Beverly sat in the back with the basket of food. Snow swirled around them, making it hard to see at times, and though it was less than ten miles from his countryside home to her apartment building downtown, it felt as if it was taking hours to get there.

When they finally arrived, and he carried the basket upstairs to Beverly's door, Emma quickly thanked him and took the basket from his hand.

"Thank you both for attending dinner today," he replied.

"It was our pleasure," Beverly said. "Your family is so wonderful, and it was so kind of all of you to include us today. You drive careful on your way home, now."

Emma found herself momentarily stunned. The way

Beverly wasn't attempting to make him stay longer certainly could qualify as a miracle. A little one, and certainly not one that would change anything, but a miracle for sure.

"I will," he said.

Beverly stepped farther into her apartment and as Emma followed, George touched her arm, causing her heart to skip yet another beat. She doubted it would ever find its normal pace again.

"Would you care to join me for dinner some evening?" he asked.

Every part of her sank, except for her heart—it pounded harder and once again rose into her throat, where it threatened to strangle her. There was no sense wishing things could be different because they couldn't. "I'm sorry, but I can't."

He released his hold and nodded. "No, I'm sorry. I was assuming there wasn't someone—"

"No. It's not that." She bit her lips together at how her tongue had betrayed her. "I just have a lot to do."

He nodded again and gave a slight wave. "All right, then. Well, goodbye, Emma."

"Goodbye, George," she said, feeling as if she was saying goodbye forever. That should be what she wanted. To never see him again.

Her entire being felt sick, truly sick, as she watched him walk down the hall and enter the stairway that would take him downstairs.

The hold that grasped her arm was firmer than a woman of half of Beverly's age. So was the yank that pulled her into the apartment.

"You most certainly have time to go out to dinner with him," Beverly said while closing the door.

Emma walked over and set the basket on the table. "Time or not, I can't, and you know why."

Beverly hung her coat on the hook. "Just tell him you were the one to write to him, not me."

"It's more than that." So much more.

"You are putting too much emphasis on your aunt." Beverly walked to the table. "Some people are simply not nice people, but they can't hurt you unless you let them."

Emma took the cloth off the top of the basket in order to put the food away. "It's more than my aunt." The pumpkin pie she was lifting out of the basket grew blurry from the tears welling in her eyes. "It's me."

"You?"

"Yes. Aunt Jill can hate me all she wants. She has my entire life, and nothing will change that." She set the pie on the table. "But I can't have her hating someone else the way she did my father. It was awful and it terrifies me that she—" She had to draw in a deep breath to combat the heaviness inside her and chose not to say George's name. "Could hate someone else because of me. She's always hated anything to do with my family. Everyone. The way she would talk about my father was awful, and about Sharon and me. She said we were just like our father and tried everything to make my mother leave us."

Beverly laid a hand on her arm. "That's why you've never made friends with anyone here?"

Other than Beverly, she hadn't attempted to make friends, just merely acquaintances. "Yes."

"Oh, sweetie, you can't let the past control your life."

"I don't have a choice." Anguish filled her. "I am who I am." Her throat began to burn, her eyes, too. She may have moved out of the slum that she grew up in, but that is who she would always be. Delmar had said as much when he'd thought she should be willing to give him what he'd wanted.

"Go take your coat off and collect your knitting," Beverly said. "I'll put on the teakettle, and we'll have a piece of pie before we get to work on those scarves and mittens. I'll have everything ready by the time you get back. Hurry along now."

George had just topped the stairway when he heard a door close and he rounded the corner in time to watch Emma walk down the hall and unlock the door across the hall. The one to her apartment. He glanced at the glove in his hand. He'd found it on the front seat of his car and had known it was hers. She'd played with her gloves, taking them off and putting them back on, nearly the entire way home.

He'd also sat in his car wondering if he should bring the glove up to her or pretend that he hadn't noticed it until arriving home and then request that Willis deliver it to her tomorrow.

The weather was what had changed his mind. It was snowing, and if she went outside for any reason, she would need her glove.

He waited until she entered her apartment and then walked down the hall. It so happened that he arrived at her doorway just as she was about to close the door. Despite how disappointed he'd been over her response to going out to dinner with him, the wide-eyed shock on her face made him smile.

And apologize. "I didn't mean to startle you." He held up the glove. "You left this in the car."

"Oh." She didn't move. Just stood there staring at him.

He wasn't much better, the way he simply stood there, staring back. There was no reason to hang around. It wasn't as if she would change her mind about going out with him. He should be glad she'd said no. He wasn't looking for a means to an end or anything else. Seeing a desk of sorts right next to the door, he leaned inside the apartment to set the glove on it.

As he was about to drop the glove, his breath caught at what was lying on the desktop. There were thousands of cream-colored, rectangular envelopes just like it in the world, but the handwriting on this one had been on each and every letter delivered to him. The slanted writing was neat and precise, elegant, especially the way the *W* was written. That's what held his eye. The *W*. It was exactly like the ones on his letters, with a curlicue shape at the top.

"Thank you," she said.

Yes, he was being nosy, but so be it. He set down the glove and picked up the envelope. It was addressed to Mrs. Eddie Warren in New York City, and the return address was Miss Emma Ellis. "A letter to your sister?"

With that wide-eyed look still on her face, she nodded.

"There's no stamp on it," he said, while his mind was whirling.

"I need to go to the post office."

Suspicions about Beverly's letters had been teasing him since his return, and either way, he had to know the truth. She stepped back as he stepped forward and closed the door behind him. The scent of warm vanilla filled the air. Neat and uncluttered, the apartment was similar to Beverly's, with an icebox, cookstove, cupboard on the wall and a cabinet with a sink. A small, round wooden table with two chairs sat next to a small sitting area with the smallest sofa he'd ever seen and a single armchair, both covered in brown upholstery. The only interior door was open, showing a made bed, dresser and another door that he assumed led to the bathroom.

The woodwork was painted white, the walls were papered with a floral print of white and gold, and the floors were hardwood and covered with two small braided rugs. One he stood upon, the other was in front of the sofa. The only sound in the room was the hissing of the cast-iron radiator in front of the window near the sofa, until he spoke. "Why does it smell like vanilla in here?"

She bit down on her bottom lip as she glanced up at the single light hanging overhead. "I put a drop on the light bulb."

"Never heard of that," he admitted.

"It…it's a habit I learned from my mother." She gestured toward the small writing desk next to him. "I'm sorry, I hadn't realized I'd dropped a glove."

"Probably because you leaped out of the car like it was on fire as soon as I pulled up next to the curb."

Her only response was the blush that covered her cheeks.

He hadn't tried to embarrass her, but she had shot out of the car earlier, and he was pretty certain he knew why. With his free hand, he unbuttoned his coat. "We need to talk."

She gasped, or coughed—it was so soft he wasn't sure which.

"About what?" she asked.

He held up the letter, then laid it on the desk next to her glove. "I think you know."

She spun about and grasped the back of one of the chairs pushed up to the table.

George glanced in the direction of the sofa, mainly to take his gaze off her and the way her shoulders were shaking. There was a wicker basket holding yarn next to the sofa, and what could be folded scarves. He could just leave. Forget about the letters and her. Yet, he couldn't. He had to know the truth. "You wrote those letters to me, not Beverly."

Her shoulders drooped a bit more.

Still, he couldn't let her off the hook. "She had me convinced that she had," he said. "Right up until I met you."

Twisting slightly, she glanced over her shoulder at him.

Reading the question in her eyes, he said, "You, and your apartment, smell just like all the letters had." He lifted an eyebrow. "Like warm vanilla. I know the smell from my younger days of sitting in the kitchen while Miss Maybelle cooked. She always let me lick the icing bowl. Vanilla icing was my favorite."

She closed her eyes and shook her head with what looked like disbelief.

He could tell her other things, like the jokes, the books they'd discussed and how his own instincts kept pointing at her, like she was the red X on a map he was following. Done with the buttons, he removed his coat, hung it on a hook on the back of the door. "I've always been a good listener, and patient, so take your time, but I'm not leaving until I know why you didn't want me to know it was you writing to me."

She straightened her stance, released the chair and fully turned about. "I need to put my coat in the bedroom."

It was her home, but still he gestured with one hand, giving her permission.

While crossing the small room, she removed her long coat, revealing the light green dress with its wide white collar that he'd admired earlier. He'd admired everything about her; how pretty she'd looked when he'd seen her sitting on the sofa with Nellie and Nate.

She returned momentarily. "Would you care for some coffee, or a glass of water?"

"No, thank you, I'm fine." Stepping forward, he pulled a chair out from the table, gestured to it. "Shall we sit?"

With a nod, she sat in the chair, and he walked around the table to sit in the chair across from her. There was a small plate in the center of the table, holding a single apple and an orange. For a moment, he considered the life of abundance that he'd lived until going to war, of how he'd never wanted for anything. There never had been a need to think ahead; his entire life had been laid out for him—still was. It hadn't been that way for her, he was certain of that.

"I'm sorry," she said. "I truly am."

"I'm not. I enjoyed your letters very much and looked forward to meeting you."

He couldn't put his finger on what he saw in her eyes at that moment, perhaps because there was a mixture of things glistening in them.

"You looked forward to meeting Beverly Buttons, not me."

He nodded. "That was the name, but from the moment I met her, I wasn't convinced that she was the one who had penned those letters. She was convincing, knew about many of the things we'd written about, but I just couldn't completely believe it had been her."

"Why? Because of her age?"

"No, I don't think so."

"You don't think so?"

He shook his head. "I can't tell you why because I don't know myself. It was just a feeling I had."

Both of her hands were on the table, and she was tracing a line of gold stitching on the white tablecloth with one finger.

He wanted to reach out and place a hand on her hand, but didn't. He waited, and when the silence felt too lengthy, he asked, "How did you choose me to write to? Did you see a list of men deployed in the newspaper or something?"

"No."

Silence again, but this time, he told himself to wait it out.

"I had—" she swallowed visibly and lifted her chin slightly "—learned about Martha's elopement."

He wasn't surprised about that. It probably had been the talk of the town. It was how she'd taken pity upon him that made his jaw tighten. He didn't need pity. Not from her or anyone else. "And you pitied me."

Her eyes widened. "No. I felt guilty."

"Guilty? Why? Do you know Martha?"

She nodded, then sighed. "But I don't know where she's at now, if that's what you're asking."

"No, it's not. If I wanted to know that, all I would have to do is ask her mother."

Her hands balled into fists and she set them in her lap.

"As I said before," he continued, "I wish Martha and Delmar the best, wherever they are." He talked as if he knew Delmar, only because he'd heard the name so often since returning home, but he wasn't here to talk about Delmar or Martha. "What I do want to know is why you wrote the letters in Beverly's name."

Since his return home, it had seemed fictional that Beverly had been the one to write to him, like it just couldn't be true, but in all honesty, so did this, that Emma had been the one to write to him, in Beverly's name. Fictional, or like some kind of riddle he needed to know the answer to.

Emma questioned why she wasn't shaking from head to toe. Probably because her heart was pounding so hard, her body couldn't muster up another reaction.

Oh, where was a miracle when she needed one? One that could just make her disappear or turn back time? Either of those would be true miracles right now. Neither of them was about to happen, either. "She was the only person I could ask."

His frown seemed to grow with each of her answers. She couldn't blame him. It was confusing.

"I suspect asking someone to use their name is a bit unusual," he said.

"Very."

"Why couldn't you use your own name?"

Oh, fiddlesticks! How could she tell him the truth, without telling him the truth? That's what she had to do, and while in the midst of pondering that, the door to her apartment opened and Beverly appeared in the doorway. Wide-eyed, she stared at them sitting at the table.

"Oh. Oh—oh, my," Beverly sputtered before finding her tongue. "Hello, George. Nice to see you. Don't mind me. I don't need anything. Not a thing. Not at all. You two just stay right there. Right where you are. Emma, we'll knit later. Yes, we'll knit later." She was pulling the door closed again. "Just forget you saw me. Forget all about me."

The door clicked shut and the scampering of feet quickly faded.

George chuckled slightly. "It wasn't hard to convince her, was it?"

Emma felt a smile growing and couldn't stop it. "No, it wasn't."

"Does she know Martha, too?"

"No."

He frowned again. "Did you meet Martha here, or after she moved to New York?"

She didn't know when or where she'd first met Martha, considering she would have been a baby. If she said New York, which was the most probable, he might ask where in New York, probably assuming it had been after the elopement. Therefore, she said, "Here." That, too, was a possibility. Her mother had traveled to Albany with them when her grandmother had died, and again when her grandfather had died a few months later. She'd been a baby both times, so didn't remember her grandparents or the trips here, but her mother must have told her about attending the funerals.

"When?"

The trouble with lying, or even simply stretching the truth, was how it had to keep being stretched, and then having to remember all that stretching. She'd be far better off to simply state the truth and face the consequences.

Her entire being was trembling now, and the pounding of her heart had become irregular enough to hurt. She squeezed her hands together, hard. "The truth is…" Oh, heavens this was hard. "I'm the reason Martha eloped."

"You?"

"Yes." She pressed a hand to her forehead, wondering if a person could run a fever from making themselves sick. She certainly felt overheated.

"How?"

"I'm the reason she met Delmar. Not on purpose. I knew him in New York, and he'd found out that I'd moved here, I'm not sure how, but he showed up one day, and Martha just so happened to stop by while he was here." The one and only time her cousin had stopped by, claiming that she needed to know if the landlord had gotten her reference. That had been a surprise, knowing that Martha had vouched for her. It had also irritated Delmar, and he and Martha had shared cross words with each other before they'd left. "They both left after I told Delmar that I had a job here and wouldn't be returning to New York. That I could live wherever I wanted to live."

"Why did he want you to return to New York?"

"Because I'd worked for him. For his family's company."

"Doing what?"

"Rolling cigars. Both my sister and I did that after our father died." Quickly changing the subject, she continued, "I never imagined that Delmar and Martha would elope." A feather could have knocked her over when Martha had pulled up next to her in a car one day while she'd been walking home from school and told her that she was on her way to New York, to marry Delmar, and that no one was to know. No one was to know that she'd given her a reference, either, or how she'd met Delmar.

Emma hadn't told anyone about any of that, until this very moment. Martha had also said that she'd write to her mother when the time was right, but if her mother asked her, she was to say that she didn't know anything, especially not Delmar's name. She'd been shocked, overly shocked, because Delmar and Martha hadn't appeared to have liked each other at all when they'd left her apartment.

They must have, though, and the time had to have been right for Martha to write to her mother sooner than later, because within no time, the entire town had been talking about the elopement. Beverly had told her all about it one evening. The next day, the teachers were talking about it at school. That's all they talked about the rest of the week, and beyond. And George, of course, how he was off fighting in the war.

A somewhat secretive grin was on his face, and for the life of her, she couldn't figure out why.

It disappeared when he asked, "So when they eloped, you felt guilty and sorry for me and decided to write."

"It was my fault, and I thought maybe if you received a letter from someone in your hometown, telling you about the things happening here, it might make you feel better." That sounded silly to her own ears, let alone his, and she felt mortified all over again. "Or maybe I thought it would make me feel better."

He didn't say anything. Just looked at her.

She let the air out of her lungs. "I didn't know what

to do. People were talking about what a nice man you were and how you were overseas and—"

"You never once mentioned Martha or her elopement in your letters."

"Of course not. I didn't want to remind you of it. I wanted you to think about other things."

"You certainly did that. Not just me. Many of the men in my troop enjoyed your jokes."

"My father used to tease us with riddles and jokes, much like your uncle Walt. Beverly suggested that I not put the answer in the letter. Make you wait until the next letter, but I thought that would be mean." Actually, the idea of him never receiving a letter with the answer had frightened her, because that would have meant something had happened to him.

"And you don't have a mean bone in your body," he said.

Guilt welled inside her. "Yes, I do," she admitted. "I lied to you, and I'm very sorry about that. I should never have done that."

His smile was truly genuine. It was one of his best-in-the-world ones. "I forgive you." He let out a low chuckle. "At least now I know the answer."

Confused, she asked, "Answer to what?"

"Discovering who actually wrote the letters." He pointed a finger at her. "It felt like a riddle, one I needed to find the answer to."

It had never felt like a riddle in her mind. Far from that, because it hadn't been meant as a joke and things went far deeper, but she couldn't tell him all of that.

"Now that we know the truth, we can move forward."

She froze, as if her blood had suddenly turned cold. "What do you mean 'move forward'?"

"We can be friends, can't we? I know you're busy making scarves, but surely you have time for friends."

Chapter Eight

George hadn't felt so light inside for a long time. His suspicions had been proven correct. Emma had been the one writing to him all along, and somehow, that felt right. So very right.

"No."

He glanced up at her response.

She was shaking her head. "I'm mean we can't tell anyone that it was me and not Beverly who wrote to you. Your parents and family and others—others who were at your party believe it was her."

That was true.

"No one can know otherwise," she said.

He wasn't sure why she was so adamant about that, other than for Beverly's sake. "Beverly did appear to enjoy having everyone believe it was her."

"Yes." She let out a sigh. "Beverly is lonely. Very lonely—she doesn't get very many visitors."

"Other than you."

She nodded.

He pondered that for a moment. "All right, we won't tell anyone." Truth was, no one else needed to know.

She was nibbling on her bottom lip, which by now he took to mean she needed to say something but didn't want to.

"We won't tell anyone about Beverly not writing the letters, or about…" She bit her lip again.

"About you introducing Martha and Delmar?" Feeling sympathy for her, he shook his head. "No one needs to know about that, either."

Her relief was visible.

"Thank you. I appreciate that."

This time he didn't hold back the want to reach across the table and lie his hand upon hers. "I hadn't planned on telling anyone." He'd wanted to know. Now he did, and that was enough. Or almost enough. "Now that we both know the truth, would you be interested in going out to dinner sometime?" He quickly added, "As friends." That felt important to him because Beverly wasn't the only one who was lonely. His instincts said Emma was, too.

The hand beneath his began to tremble and he could tell by her expression exactly what her forthcoming answer would be. Was he a glutton for punishment? Why? And why couldn't he accept her refusal She'd already voiced it once. Did he truly need to hear it a second time? Was it for her sake, or was it for his?

"Never mind." He pulled his hand off hers. "I know you're busy." He stood. "It's getting late. I need to get back home."

She rose as he walked around the table. "George, I—" She fell silent as if she'd changed her mind about whatever she'd been about to say.

If only he'd been that smart. Stayed silent instead of

asking her to go out to dinner with him again. He picked up his coat and opened the door. "Goodbye, Emma."

Her face held a pained expression as she barely whispered, "I'm sorry, George. I'm normally not a deceitful person. Truly, I'm not."

He didn't doubt that and gave a nod of acknowledgment. She was being completely honest right now. She didn't want to go out with him. To be a friend or anything else. He should be completely fine with that. "Goodbye."

Her faint goodbye met his ears as he closed the door.

He pulled on his coat as he walked down the hallway. As expected, Beverly's door was cracked open and one eyeball could be detected peeking out. Forcing himself to sound chipper, he said, "Have a good evening, Beverly."

She pulled the door open. "You, too, George."

He didn't reply because he knew that wasn't about to happen. Why did he feel so hurt inside, so disappointed? He knew the truth. Never in her letters or since meeting her had Emma given him any reason to...

What?

Fall in love with her?

Love was the last thing he wanted. He'd been willing to marry a woman that he'd merely tolerated—a feat that had been difficult at times—for the sake of his family's business. A man who wanted love would never have done that.

Furthermore, a woman like Emma needed love. Lots of love.

She deserved that, too.

A man who would love her beyond all else.

A man who would never look at marriage as a means to an end.

* * *

The snow had continued to fall the rest of that evening, and by the following morning there was a thick blanket of white covering everything in sight, making his drive to the lumber company longer than necessary.

That irritated him. So did the fact that Emma was still on his mind hours later as he walked up the steps that led to his father's office. Just as she'd been all of last evening, as well as penetrating his dreams again. He had to find a way to stop that. Stop her from being on his mind all the time.

He had work to do, things that needed to be done. Things that would affect his future as well as many others'.

Purposefully focusing on that, he knocked and then pushed open the door.

"Good morning," his father greeted from where he sat at his desk with a row of second-story windows behind him. "We missed you at breakfast."

George crossed the room and laid a rolled-up map on his father's desk before he took a seat in one of the wooden chairs facing the big desk. "I had things I wanted to get started on here."

They had discussed his trip briefly last evening before his mother had given them the look that said business wasn't an appropriate subject for Thanksgiving.

Unrolling the map, his father's eyes widened at the markings on various sections of Weston land throughout the northeast. "That's quite an ambitious number of logging camps, all the way up into Maine."

"I don't think so." George stood and walked around the desk to glance out the window at the massive acreage full of lumber at different stages, from raw logs to planked boards ready to be shipped to building sites and manufacturers. "I know that I will someday take over the reins of Weston Lumber, but it's not that time yet. You have a good number of years to sit in that chair, and you don't need me."

"Yes, I do. I hope to be in this chair for years yet, but I also need you. Your help. Your ideas. Your support to keep Weston Lumber at the top."

George watched the men below, dressed in their winter gear, moving logs to be debarked and put on the conveyor to be cut and then milled into perfect dimensions of boards. "I've worked in every department of this company, Dad. I'm not completely proficient in any of them, but I have an understanding of each of them, and I know something else."

"What is that?"

This self-awareness that had manifested itself deep in the night wasn't totally unfamiliar. He'd found it while serving overseas and hadn't realized he'd brought it home with him, but it fit. "I want to do more than just keep Weston Lumber at the top."

"Meaning?"

Pivoting so his backside was against the windowsill, George half sat on the edge. "While in the army, we all fought for the same purpose. It wasn't just to keep ourselves alive—it was to keep our troops alive. All of them, those beside us whom we knew well, and those we'd never met. We fought for our country, for all the people back home, not just a select few."

"You want to return to the army?"

"No, but I want to apply those principles to my life here." He pointed a thumb behind him, at the window and the lumberyard. "To Weston Lumber."

"I'm listening."

George had known that his father would listen, but it was convincing him that might take more time. "There are small lumberjack companies and sawmills all over the northeast." He pushed off the windowsill and crossed the room to where a map, much like the one unrolled atop his father's desk, hung in a frame. "With a little help, those small companies could be larger. Much larger."

"Are you suggesting that we help our competitors?"

"Can we really consider them competitors?" George asked. "Weston Lumber produces more finished product in one day than many of those companies do in a month."

His father leaned back farther in his chair. "You think we need to help them produce more?"

"I think we need to look at the future, which is coming quickly. The supply and demand. Now that the war is over, lumber is going to be in demand. Great demand. A demand so vast that Weston Lumber, as we operate today, won't be able to meet."

"That could be true," his father said.

"I believe it will be true, and that we have the ability for our industry as a whole to make sure the demand is met, thanks to Weston Lumber."

"Tell me more."

George pointed to the map. "We have thousands of acres of standing timber. Far more than North Country Logging could ever cut and that we could ever mill. Men are going to be coming home from the war throughout the next few months, and they'll need jobs. By partnering with the smaller companies, we can make a greater impact in the supply and demand for lumber and for jobs."

Rubbing his chin, his father asked, "You have specifics for these partnerships?"

George walked to the desk and sat in a chair. "The largest obstacles for the smaller logging companies are the costs of standing timber and finding mills to take the logs in the spring. The mills have their own issues, everything from not enough equipment and men to process the wood, to getting it to larger markets. There are ways that we could help them that would be profitable for us and them."

"You've put a lot of thought into this, haven't you?"

"Yes, sir." George didn't elaborate on how he'd needed something to take his mind off Emma, and to keep it off her. "Jake Turner is already willing to come aboard and is willing to talk to others. I plan on traveling to logging camps and lumber mills the next few weeks, gathering specifics, so by the New Year we could have a complete plan in place. I envision a commission made up of representatives from large and small operations, setting baselines and regulations for us to work together, logging and milling enough lumber so every demand is instantly met."

His father rubbed his chin. "Like a strategic line of attack."

George nodded. "That's one way of looking at it."

Looking at the map again, his father nodded. "I like it. You, and men like you, soldiers of all ranks and divisions, were there for us when we needed you, and now it's time for us to be there for them with jobs and materials to get this country rolling again."

"Exactly."

His father grinned. "Your mother has always said that we are too much alike."

"She has."

"I'm proud of you, son, and I'm behind you. Whatever you need." His father sat back in his chair and his expression turned serious. "There are going to be some that won't agree with this immediately."

George knew the *some* his father was referring to, but Jill King was the least of his worries.

Unable to concentrate on the stiches, Emma set the knitting needles on her lap. The entire last two rows were so uneven she'd have to rip them out. Beverly, however, could knit through every topic of conversation. She'd already completed a stack of fifty mittens— twenty-five identical pairs—and was now making matching adorable hats, complete with a fluffy ball on top.

"Well, don't give up hope," Beverly said. "I'm sure he'll be back. George isn't the type of man to not pursue what he wants."

Emma withheld the want to sigh. "I'm hoping he doesn't come back." The sigh was too heavy to keep inside. After a deep exhale, she continued, "Because if he does, I'd have to refuse to have dinner with him again." That had nearly gutted her twice and she didn't know if she could live through a third time.

With her needles clicking away with the precision of a clock, Beverly clicked her tongue. "I know you think you have good reason for that, but I don't."

"I don't want to see him hurt, and to me, that is a very good reason." Emma set her knitting on the sofa beside her with more force than necessary and picked her empty teacup off the table. "Would you like some more tea?"

"Yes, please, along with another one of those cinnamon cookies," Beverly replied. "I bet George would like your cookies as much as he liked your ginger bars."

Emma bit her tongue to maintain silence as she carried both of their cups and walked into Beverly's kitchen to reheat the teakettle. It had been over two weeks since Thanksgiving and she was thoroughly frustrated with the way every red-and-black car caught her attention and held it until she saw that it wasn't George's. And how she kept checking the mail for a letter, even though she knew he was no longer overseas and had absolutely no reason to send her one. She had no reason to want one, yet she did. She missed those letters, which ultimately meant she missed him.

She was just going to have to learn to live with that.

Emma hoped the silence that ensued meant any conversation about George was finally over, and once the tea was ready, she filled the cups and carried Beverly's to her, along with the cookies, before returning to collect her cup.

"Have you decided what your Christmas wish is this year?" Beverly asked.

Emma sat on the sofa and took a sip of tea as she shook her head. "I'm too old for Christmas wishes."

"Oh, posh. No one is ever too old for Christmas wishes." Beverly let out an extravagant sigh, then lifted a cookie off the plate on the table beside her rocking chair. "Mine is for this lovely pair of slippers at Ricker's Department Store. They have soft leather soles that remind me of Alvin. He was so good with leather. The shoes he made were so pliable, no one ever got a blister from a pair of his shoes. No sirree. Not ever."

"What color are the slippers?" Emma had been trying to think of something she could get Beverly for Christmas and was trying hard to remember if she'd seen Beverly eyeing any slippers the last time they had been at Ricker's. They had been there shortly after Thanksgiving, when they'd purchased more yarn.

"Dove-gray, with a single silver button on the top of each one." Beverly held her cookie near her mouth for another bite. "But don't go thinking I want you to buy them for me. That's not why I'm telling you that I want them."

"Oh?"

Beverly shook her head as she chewed. "No. Furthermore, you can't buy them."

Price could be the reason, yet Emma asked, "Why can't I?"

"Because they are no longer at the store." Beverly's eyes shone mischievously. "They are under my bed. Wrapped it the prettiest silver paper with a big blue bow and a tag with my name on them. Come Christmas morning, I will open them and be so happy."

Curious as to how the slippers ended up under Beverly's bed, Emma asked, "Did you tell your daughter about them?"

"No, Mary's too far away. They most likely don't even have slippers like that down in Florida. I told her that I needed a few more handkerchiefs. Like the ones she mailed me a couple of years ago."

Emma nodded, knowing the handkerchiefs Beverly was referring to that had different flowers embroidered in each corner.

"I told the clerk to wrap the slippers and have them delivered here when I paid for them," Beverly said. "They arrived yesterday, while you were at school."

"You bought them for yourself?"

Beverly picked the needles off her lap and began knitting again, flipping the yarn over the pointed tips with quick, smooth movements that matched the speed of the needles. "Yes, I did. Do you think that's odd?"

Even if she did think it a bit unusual, Emma would never want to hurt Beverly's feelings. "No, you can buy whatever you want for yourself."

"Yes, I can, and as soon as I spotted them, I decided I would wish for those slippers for Christmas." With her hands still moving, still making perfect stitches, Beverly looked over and smiled as their gazes met. "Do you think that there is something wrong with that?"

Emma grinned. "No, there's not."

"I'm glad you agree. That's why I told you about my slippers. No matter what anyone else thinks, there is nothing wrong with having wishes and making them come true. Especially at Christmastime. All sorts of wishes come true at Christmas. I'd bet my new slippers that I know George's Christmas wish. He was so disappointed when it was me at the train station. Though I'd never tell him that. He hid it quite well. Better than most men would have. Perhaps any other man. Rightfully so—no young man would want to discover a woman old enough to be his granny, mayhap, great granny, instead of a pretty young woman. I imagine he was overjoyed when you told him the truth."

Emma had told Beverly everything about Thanksgiving night, about telling George it had been her writing the letters, and she should have known Beverly's slippers story would lead right back to him. He'd been the only topic of conversation lately.

"His wish is to take you out to dinner," Beverly said. "That's a simple enough wish if you ask me."

Emma considered picking up her teacup, but her hands were shaking, and she didn't want to spill tea on the yarn. "I can't make his wish come true."

Beverly lifted an eyebrow. "Why?"

Frustration filled Emma and she stood, trying to walk it off. "Imagine how disappointed he'd be to learn that Martha's my cousin. That Aunt Jill and my mother were sisters. He might think that I'd lied again, that I'd introduced Martha and Delmar on purpose."

"I doubt that, and I doubt that he'd be disappointed. Either way, you could make that your Christmas wish."

Walking wasn't helping her frustration, so Emma sat in the closet chair, one next to the kitchen table. "I don't need a Christmas wish. I need a miracle."

"What's the difference?"

"A miracle is…" Emma had to pause in order to come up with the right words.

"A want, a desire," Beverly said. "Like a wish."

"Yes, but more and people can't make miracles happen."

"Are you sure?"

Emma opened her mouth to reply but was interrupted by a knock on the door.

Beverly shrugged and nodded, making a silent request for Emma to answer the door.

Emma wanted to make sure their conversation was over, so on the way to the door, she replied, "Yes, I'm sure people can't make miracles happen." That took angels and she was beginning to believe that what she needed was too hard for even them.

Willis, with snowflakes on the shoulders of his dark coat, smiled broadly and he performed a slight bow when she pulled open the door.

"Good evening, miss. Please excuse the lateness. I have an invite for you and Mrs. Buttons." He held out two envelopes.

As if she had wings rather than legs, Beverly appeared at Emma's side. "Willis, it's so good to see you again." Beverly quickly took both envelopes from his hand. "Would you care for a cup of tea and a cookie? Fresh-baked."

"That does sounds delightful, Mrs. Buttons, but regretfully, I'm only here to deliver the invites, and perhaps return with your response?"

"Oh, well, let's see here." Beverly quickly opened the envelope with her name on it and held out the other one.

Emma took it and opened it more slowly.

"Saturday," Beverly said. "Why, yes, I believe we are free, aren't we, Emma?"

The invitations were handwritten and from Amy Weston, inviting them for brunch at ten on Saturday morning. "No," Emma said, biting down on her lip so hard it stung. "I'm busy." She shifted her gaze to Willis. "I'm terribly sorry."

"Understandably, miss," Willis said. "I will give Mrs. Weston your regrets."

"Please give her my acceptance," Beverly said.

Emma had no right to say that Beverly couldn't go and closed her eyes at the other woman's positive response.

"Wonderful," Willis replied. "I shall pick you up at nine thirty if that is satisfactory."

"Very satisfactory," Beverly said. "Thank you, and please give our regards to the entire Weston family." As if an afterthought, Beverly then said, "But wait one minute while Emma gets you a couple of cookies to munch on while driving home."

Emma collected the cookies, gave them to Willis and bid him farewell. Upon closing the door, she walked back over to the sofa. "I have to go shopping on Saturday," she said. "Gifts for Sharon and Eddie, but I hope you have a lovely time."

Sitting down in her rocking chair, Beverly nodded.

"It's less than two weeks until Christmas," Emma further explained, trying her best to sound convincing. "I need to get their gifts in the post."

Beverly set her invite on the table beside her chair and gave it a little pat. "You know, dear, miracles come in all shapes and forms."

Chapter Nine

Emma left the apartment before Willis arrived to pick up Beverly on Saturday morning but saw the black car as it pulled up to the curb from the street corner. She quickly looked away. There was so much confusion inside her. So much regret and guilt, and she wished... What? That she hadn't started all this in the first place? That she'd never moved to Albany?

She'd already wished all those things, and more, and could continue to wish all she wanted, but changing any of it was impossible. No one can change the past. No one could change who she was, either.

The traffic cleared enough to cross the street, and as she stepped off the curb, a grin almost formed as she thought of Beverly and her slippers. The grin didn't form all the way, though, because her thoughts went further into that subject. Of making wishes come true. Certain wishes. Slippers was a little wish—hers were all big wishes.

Shining down as if all was well in the world, the sun reflected off the snow that had fallen several times over the last weeks and made everything overly bright and relatively warm. There were several piles of snow left by people who had shoveled the sidewalk that she had to walk around—or in some cases, through—and paths made by others. Her splattering of thoughts about wishes continued as she walked toward downtown. Ricker's Department Store was her destination, and she hoped to find a sweater for Sharon and a pair of gloves for Eddie.

Suddenly, as if the ideas for gifts connected to her thoughts about wishes, Emma knew what she had to do.

Return to New York City. If she made that her wish, she could make it come true. She already had a train ticket.

The idea was so unwanted her feet stumbled, and she barely caught herself before losing her balance and ending up in one of the snowbanks. She loved living in Albany, loved her job working at the school. Loved living next door to Beverly. However, that would be a way to put an end to the mess she'd made.

The only way.

The hard knot that had taken residency in her stomach grew larger and heavier. Many people thought New York City was the ultimate city, full of glamour and opportunity. To some it was, but it had never been that way for her. Nor for many others. The number of people she had known while living there who had perished during the pandemic was astounding, yet, not unbelievable. The building they'd lived in, the very one she'd lived it her entire life before coming here, had very few windows, and even when they were open, the air that had entered hadn't been fresh. Identical buildings were built so close that a breeze couldn't flow between them, and when it did, it was filled with smoke from the nearby manufacturers. Furthermore, the sanitary conditions there were inconceivable to her now that she had her own bathroom in her apartment. Where she'd grown up, there had been just one for three stories of apartments.

She didn't ever want to move back, but, want it or not, that's what she would do. She would not move back to that neighborhood, though. She would find a better one. Rent was far more expensive there than in Albany, and she'd have to find a job, but the savings she'd acquired since moving here would help tremendously. The money certainly wasn't all that much and wouldn't last long, but it would help.

Actually, she didn't have to move to New York City specifically. With her savings, she could move to another town, or another state, where no one knew her and she'd never have to worry about George finding out that Jill was her aunt, never have to worry about a lot of things, including seeing him again,

Which was an incredibly sad thought, even though she knew she shouldn't feel that way.

It wasn't *if* she should make moving her wish, it was when. It didn't matter where she moved, either—she just had to do it, sooner than later. The ultimate truth was that she would miss George no matter where she lived. For over a year and a half, she'd fallen to sleep thinking about him, and woken up thinking about him; that wasn't likely to change anytime soon. She knew she couldn't get him out of her mind because she had tried that, harder than ever, over the last two weeks.

So lost in thought, she may have walked right past Ricker's if her name hadn't rung out in the air. She turned, looked across the street to where the shout had come from, and could do nothing but stare, wondering if she was seeing things.

The unexpected bout of happiness that filled her was enough to convince her that she wasn't seeing things. It was also enough to confirm that she had to make moving back to New York City, or somewhere else, far, far away, her wish as soon as possible, and make it come true.

She considered pivoting about and rushing into the store but was glued to the spot by the way George dodged through the two lanes of traffic to cross the street. Filled with concern for his safety, she nearly hugged him when he finally arrived at her side.

Half scared out of her wits, she said, "You can't run through traffic like that! What if you'd have slipped and fallen? You'd have gotten run over!"

He laughed. "I've dodged worse things than a few cars."

One of his best-in-the-world smiles was on his face and she couldn't pull her eyes off it, or him. Never seeing that smile again would be such a sad thing.

"How are you?" he asked.

Shaking her head in an attempt to dispel her thoughts, she answered, "Fine. How are you?"

"Fine." He nodded, glanced around. "Imagine running into you today."

Suddenly skeptical, she couldn't hold back her question. "Did Beverly tell you I was going shopping here today?"

"Beverly?" He shook his head. "No. I haven't seen her since Thanksgiving. I've been out of town. Just got home last night, and this morning, when I learned my mother was hosting a brunch for some of her lady friends, I decided it was the perfect time for me to do some Christmas shopping. I know what I'm getting Nate, but I'm not so sure about Nellie." Giving her a hope-filled look, he added, "Would you mind helping me out?"

There was no reason for her to not believe his reasons for being at Ricker's, but she knew the children had created lists of things they wanted for Christmas. "Didn't Janice inform you of what's on Nellie's list?"

"Yes, she did. Nate's list is practically never-ending, and I've decided upon Lincoln Logs for him. Janice made me promise I wouldn't buy him a goldfish."

The grin on his face made it hard not to smile, because she could believe he'd been ready to buy Nate a goldfish and a bowl.

"But Nellie," he continued, "is mainly asking for books, and I can't imagine anyone better than someone who works at a school library to help me pick one to buy for her."

She had to say no. She really did, but was having a very hard time with the ability to voice it. Never before had she missed someone like she had him. While he'd been overseas, she'd had his letters to look forward to, but since he'd returned home, she didn't have that, and it had felt like as if a part of her had been missing. It was unexplainable, and she'd tried, hard, but she just couldn't help feeling the way she did.

People were stepping around them and he set a hand on her back. "We are blocking the sidewalk—shall we go inside? I won't take up much of your time, I promise."

"I have plenty of time." As soon as the words were

out, she bit her tongue for opposing her. She should have said no.

"Wonderful. I do, too," he said. "I have no desire to return home until the brunch is over."

He turned to escort her into the store. Though she knew in her core that she shouldn't let him, she walked beside him through the big glass door. The store was one of the largest in the city and filled with customers wandering around large displays of toys, gifts and decorations set up throughout the entire two stories, including a large Christmas tree with gaily wrapped packages beneath it.

In awe because the store hadn't looked this way the last time she'd been shopping, she couldn't stop from turning in a full circle to take everything in, including the red ribbon wrapped around the banister of the staircase leading to the second floor. "This is all so beautiful, and festive."

"It is," George agreed. "It's been a difficult couple of years, especially this past one, and people need the hope and joy of Christmas more than ever."

Sincerity filled his words and she understood why. His letters had often mentioned the things he'd missed. "You are happy to be home."

"I am, but this—" he gestured with one hand randomly at all the decorations "—is for everyone." He looked at her. "Everyone deserves to be happy, and despite what's happened the past several months, or years, or however long, they need to know it's okay to be happy, to embrace life, to forge ahead, because they aren't alone. We are all in this together." He tugged her toward the stairs. "Shall we start upstairs?"

She nodded, because that was where the toy section was located, but also because she wanted to spend time with him, despite telling herself she shouldn't. As they walked up the steps, she couldn't help but look at him, at the smile on his face. His letters had always been optimistic, and it had been through that optimism that she'd felt she'd gotten to know him, but there was something different about him today. Maybe she hadn't noticed it since meeting him in person, or maybe that change had come about in the last two weeks. He just seemed so happy. So alive.

Maybe that was it, and she wanted to be that happy, if only for a short time. Not wanting to focus on whether that was right or wrong, she asked, "Where have you been traveling?"

"Over the river and through the woods," he said in a singsong way, and with a wink.

There was no stopping, or denying how at that moment happiness filled her, and she didn't attempt to stop it as she half sang, half said, "To grandmother's house we go."

He chuckled. "Very good. Actually, I went to logging camps and sawmills. Small ones north and east of here. I've met some remarkable people. Some who have experienced great losses and difficult times and I'm working on a plan to help them." Glancing at her, he continued, "Do you remember the name Dan Stark from my letters?"

"Yes. He returned home last spring. To Vermont."

"That's right. I looked him up, met his wife and sons. My plan includes working with a lumber company in his area, which could result in a better paying job for him."

That didn't surprise her. His letters had often mentioned how the soldiers had helped each other and she'd known he was the leader of many good deeds. "What kind of plan are you working on?"

His hand was still on her back and he steered her around the top of the staircase on the second floor, toward the toy area. "Ways for Weston Lumber to collaborate with others to grow their operations. President Wilson's Thanksgiving Day proclamation put hope in people's hearts. With the war over and hopefully the worst parts of the pandemic behind us, I envision a growth in the United States. Lumber is going to be needed from the Atlantic to the Pacific, and we are living in the lumber capital of the world." His grin grew. "You knew that, didn't you?"

"Yes, I did." She also knew that Weston Lumber was the largest lumber company in the state and that they worked closely with North Country Logging, which had been started by her mother's family years ago and was currently run by Aunt Jill and Uncle Roy. The knot in her stomach returned and she glanced around, looking for an escape route. She shouldn't be here with him. Whether he needed help picking out a book or not. Whether she wanted to be happy or not.

"Excuse me? May I help you find something?"

"Yes, ma'am," George answered the clerk that approached them. "We are looking for Lincoln Logs and books for a girl. She's eight."

"Right this way," the clerk replied. "Lincoln Logs are very popular this year."

Emma fell in step beside George as he followed the clerk, who was wearing a dark blue dress and black shoes, through various departments, all the while searching her brain for an excuse for her to make an exit. A quick one.

* * *

There was no visible change in her, but George didn't need to see the change in Emma, he could sense it. She'd been hesitant when they'd met on the sidewalk, an event he practically considered a miracle. It had been as if he'd conjured her up out of thin air due to how his mind had been on her. He'd had a successful trip visiting loggers and mill workers, and she was the reason. He'd been excited to tell her that, but as soon as he'd mentioned it, she'd changed. It had felt as if a cold shiver had rippled between them.

He'd just wanted her to know what her letters had initiated, but now was questioning why that mattered so much to him.

"Here are the Lincoln Logs," the clerk said. "And the books are on the next aisle over, along the wall."

"Thanks," George said. "We'll look around and let you know if we need any additional help."

"Very well, I'll be over there, at the counter, where we offer gift wrapping for all purchases."

He thanked her again, then picked up a box of the log toys and held it out for Emma to see. "Have you heard of these?"

"No, I haven't."

"From my understanding, in this box is everything Nate needs to build a log cabin."

She peered closely at the drawing on the box of a boy building with the miniature notched logs. Her features were so delicate and enchanting. Everything about her was enchanting, pretty, and he regretted mentioning where he'd been because he'd liked the way her eyes had shone and the way she'd smiled when she'd responded to his over-the-river comment.

He'd spent his entire life believing he'd wanted one thing, believing that's all his life was about—Weston Lumber. It still was, but now he wanted what he had to become more for others. It was her letters that had instilled that in him, and the army had given him the skills to get it done.

"It looks like it would be fun," she said, referring to the box in his hand.

"Janice said that a friend of Nate's got a set for his birthday a month ago and he's been wishing for his own set ever since."

She lifted her gaze to meet his and smiled. "Well, then, you'll be making his wish come true."

While writing to her, he'd been able to ask her anything. She had answered every question in his letters, but he wasn't so sure that she would in person. It was as if she was afraid of something. Maybe that something was him. Perhaps she thought he wanted something from her. He didn't. Other than friendship. He'd have to convince her of that. "Do you have a wish?"

She sighed and pulled her gaze away.

"You can't share it?"

She shook her head.

"Because it might not come true?"

"Yes," she answered so quietly he barely heard it.

He considered telling her that if she told him her wish, he'd try his best to help her make it come true. That's what he would have done in a letter. He'd also considered writing to her several times the last couple of weeks. Deciding not to had been tough. He'd once considered marrying the woman he'd been writing to for months and months and now understood he didn't need that means to an end. However, he had needed her letters and she'd provided them out of kindness, nothing more. He had to respect that.

"Shall we see about a book for Nellie?" he asked, now experiencing a sense of guilt for asking her to help him.

"Yes, I think I know just the one, if they have it here. The library doesn't have it yet, and I'm sure Nellie would enjoy it."

There was excitement in her voice, or maybe he was just hoping that's what he heard. "What is it?" he asked as they walked around the end of the aisle and down the next one.

"It's called *Raggedy Ann Stories* and a rag doll is to be sold with each book as a package deal. I read about it in our book-ordering catalog at school."

"A package deal. I like the sound of that."

She giggled slightly and then hurried forward in front of him. "They are here. Right here. Isn't it cute?"

There was definite excitement in her voice and in her eyes as she lifted a rag doll with red-yarn hair off the shelf that had a large book tied to one arm. The front of the book was covered with red cloth and a picture of the doll was pasted to the cloth. "That is very cute," he said, referring the way her eyes shone more than the book or doll.

"I'm sure Nellie will like it." She ran a smoothing hand over the doll's hair. "Any young girl would."

An inner warmth filled him and he couldn't stop himself from reaching out and touching a tendril of her hair that was poking out beneath her white scarf near her cheek. "It looks like the perfect gift."

They stood there a moment, neither moving, neither speaking, just looking at each other, and once again the idea of kissing her became foremost in his mind. He couldn't do that here, in the middle of the store, but he could imagine how wonderful it would be.

She looked away and took a step back. "I—I think both children will be happy with what you're buying for them."

His fingers were tingling from touching her hair and he squeezed his hand into a ball to prolong the sensation, even as he chastised himself for his thoughts. Kissing her, no matter where they were, was not something he could do unless she wanted it to happen, and he had no reason to hope that was the case. He held up the box of toy logs in his hand. "Let's take these to be wrapped and I'll help you with your shopping. What are you looking for?"

"Oh, um, a sweater for my sister and a pair of gloves for my brother-in-law."

Steering her in the direction of the counter the clerk had pointed out, he said, "Well, I might not be much help with the sweater, but I know gloves. A pair with thick palms is the best if he does any amount of driving."

"He does drive," she said.

"The thicker palms will keep his hands from getting cold while holding on to the steering wheel. I'll ask the clerk where we will find them."

"I'm sure you have more important things to do than help me shop."

"No, I don't. Besides, I have others to buy for— my parents and Janice, her husband, Bill, my aunt and uncle—and I could use some more help." He quickly completed the last few steps to the counter and set down the toy box of logs.

She set the doll and book next to them and after asking to have the toys wrapped, he inquired about gloves and sweaters, then steered her in the direction indicated, which was back downstairs.

"I don't have ideas for any of them, so any suggestions you have will be appreciated," he said as they walked. "And as I said, I have plenty of time. I don't want to go home until the brunch is over and the house is cleared out."

"Why?"

"Because there are probably twenty ladies there and I have no desire to get caught up in whatever discussions they are having. I'm just hoping it's over by suppertime."

"It's to end at one."

He felt her go stiff and paused on the steps to gaze down at her. "How do you know that?"

She shrugged, then said, "Beverly is there."

That didn't surprise him. Once his mother proclaimed someone as a friend, they were invited to all sorts of gatherings. "Why aren't you?"

"Because I have shopping to do. I need to get the gifts in the post today. I may not have another chance this week."

They began walking down the stairs again and he asked, "How is the knitting coming along?"

"Good, but I still have several scarves to make before Christmas."

"I promise I won't keep you long today, and in exchange, I'll give you a ride to the post office and then home. That will save you some time." He lifted an eyebrow. "Deal?"

"You don't need to give me a ride, but I will help

you with your shopping." Stepping off the stairs, she gestured with her hand. "The gloves are over here— perhaps you'll find a pair for your father while I find a pair for Eddie."

He'd never liked shopping, but with her it was different. They talked about various subjects, besides their gift buying, and laughed about things they saw that were completely impractical or downright silly.

He found gloves—they both did—and he found other gifts for everyone in his family, including a pair of slippers for his mother. Emma found the gifts she was looking for, including a silk scarf for Beverly.

As their packages were being wrapped, he inquired about having hers wrapped a second time in brown paper, in preparation for mailing. The clerk went one step further by saying the store could mail the gifts if Emma knew the address of where to send them.

She provided the information, they both paid for their purchases and then they left the store.

"Thank you for thinking about the mailing paper," she said as they waited to cross the street to where his car was parked. "I had no idea the store offered mailing services."

"I didn't, either, and thank you for helping me. I'm sure everyone will like their gifts." He nodded for them to cross as a break in traffic occurred.

"I'm sure Nellie is going to love her doll and book," she said.

"I am, too." They arrived at his car and after piling everything in the trunk, he said, "I think I should have bought a packaged deal of doll and book for you, too."

"I'm too old for a doll."

He had questioned buying two of the dolls and books

just because of the delight holding that book and doll had put on her face. There was something about her that turned him inside out. Made him think in ways he never had before. "Who says?"

"I do."

He closed the trunk lid. "You're not too old for a bowl of soup, are you?"

"Why?"

Nodding to the nearby café, he reached over and wrapped his fingers around her hand. "Because I'm hungry." He saw her hesitancy, so he added, "And I don't want to eat alone. It won't take long, and we saved time by not having to go to the post office." Yes, he was cajoling her, and shouldn't be, but he didn't want their time to come to an end yet. While shopping, her quiet shyness had dissolved and they'd laughed and joked; he wanted to see more of her like that. While writing, it had seemed as if there had been nothing between them and he wanted to know what stood between them now. Between them being friends, for he understood that she didn't want anything more than that.

He didn't, either. But he had gotten used to sharing things with her via their letters and missed being able to do so.

It was a very long moment before she said, "All right."

"Excellent."

They entered the café and took a table in a quiet area near the back. She appeared to be pleased by that and that made him wonder if she was hiding from something. Someone. Yet, she had been out shopping on her own, so maybe it was him. That she didn't want to be seen with him. Because of who he was? Because of his broken engagement that she felt responsible for? He could ease her mind about that, even though it meant revealing things about himself that he'd never revealed to anyone.

When it came to her, that seemed like a very small price to pay.

After ordering the lunch special—though he hadn't paid enough attention to the waitress to know what they were serving—he leaned forward and rested his arms on the table. "Martha and I were never in love."

She looked at him, eyes wide.

"I didn't love her," he continued. "And she didn't love me."

Blinking several times, she looked away, then back at him with a frown. "Then why were you engaged?"

"Because a merger between Weston Lumber and North Country Logging would create the largest lumber company in the nation."

Puzzlement filled her face. "An arranged marriage?"

"You could call it that." He wasn't sure if he was defending the past arrangement or himself as he said, "They've been around for centuries." That sounded shallow, an excuse, and in truth, that's exactly what it had been. He'd been shallow and uncaring about that aspect of his life, and Martha's. He'd never dated anyone else, and as far as he knew, neither had Martha, until Delmar. How she'd eloped with the other man so quickly made sense. She had wanted out of Albany. Had told him that more than once and had encouraged him to consider it. He would never have considered it, though, because Weston Lumber was his life.

"What happens now?" Emma asked.

Oddly enough, even the broken engagement hadn't

changed his outlook. His focus was still on the company—however, now it included growing the entire industry. "I will still take over Weston Lumber when the time comes as there is no one else. I had an older brother, Robert. He died when I was seven."

"I'm sorry for your loss," she said quietly. "How did he die?"

"Cancer." No one, not even his parents, knew what he was about to tell her. "He was the one who taught me how to pitch rocks and play checkers. We played many games of checkers during his illness, before he died, and we talked. He was fourteen and had been going to work with my father for years. Learning the lumber business." His throat grew scratchy, as it always did when he spoke of Robert. He took a drink of water.

"He sounds like he was a wonderful brother."

"He was. I looked up to him like no other. When he told me that I'd be the one to take over the business, I promised him that I would. That I would make it the biggest lumber company in the nation. He also told me that everyone was going to be sad and hurt when he died, and that I should try and make Mom and Dad happy. 'Be real good so they're happy,' he said." George grinned, remembering his brother saying the words. "I promised him that I would. That I would never do anything to make them sad, anything to hurt them."

Her expression was soft, caring. "The promise you told me about on Thanksgiving Day."

He nodded. "By the time I was old enough to understand what I'd promised, I was well on my way to keeping it." Letting out the sigh in his chest, he added, "In several ways."

"What do you mean?"

After Robert had died, he'd told his mother that he was never going to let someone love him like he'd loved Robert, so they wouldn't hurt like he was. His mother had told him that was impossible because his family already loved him. He'd told her that he'd make sure no one else ever would then, and had taken that to heart.

He took a drink of water before explaining. "When I was about ten or so, I can't remember for sure, I was concentrating hard on how I was going to make Weston Lumber the largest in the nation and told my father that we should start our own logging company. North Country Logging has always logged our land—it's a partnership that goes way back—so when Jill King, who is Martha's mother, heard what I'd said, she told me that would never happen. Then, a couple of months or so later, she told me that if I truly wanted to create the largest lumber company in the nation, I had to marry Martha. I don't know if she convinced me of it, or if I just accepted it. I was young and at that point in my life, she scared the dickens out of me."

The color had drained from her face. He reached across the table, touched her hand. "Are you all right?"

Her head half nodded, half shook. "Au—Jill King decided the two of you should marry?"

"Yes. I remember she told me that's what Robert had planned on doing, merging the two companies into one. She convinced Martha, too, and from then on, the two of us knew we'd marry one day. As we got older, Martha never questioned the marriage, but would say that we'd find people to run the company and move to New York. I never questioned how unfair it was to either of us, until after she'd eloped. Now, as I look back, I don't think my parents had ever totally agreed to it. They'd insisted that I go to college before getting married, and then encouraged my enlistment in the army."

The waitress was walking toward their table, so he quickly, quietly, said, "You hold no responsibility in me and Martha not getting married. None."

Chapter Ten

Emma was trembling inside and out. She didn't dare pick up the spoon when the waitress set a bowl of soup in front of her. The door of the café was all the way across the crowded room. She had appreciated that when they'd sat down. It wasn't as if anyone would recognize her, but ever since he'd come home, she'd felt as if Aunt Jill would find her at some point. She'd felt that way at the store, too, but he'd made shopping so fun, she had momentarily forgotten her fears.

Not now.

They were back tenfold.

Aunt Jill was the one who'd wanted the marriage between Martha and George. That made what had happened even worse.

"Wh-what about North Country Logging?" she finally asked. "Who will take over there when the time comes?"

"I'm not sure, but Weston Lumber will continue working with them, do whatever we can to assist them now and when the time comes."

Now it gets even worse. It was more than just a broken engagement between him and Martha. Because of her, the future of North Country Logging—her mother's family's company—had been affected.

Emma glanced towards the door again, questioning if she could make an escape, but her thoughts momentarily shifted as she recognized a man walking towards their table.

"That's Willis," she said.

George turned and greeted the man as he arrived at their table. "Hello, Willis."

"Excuse me, sir," Willis said before he turned to her. "Miss." Addressing George again, the chauffeur continued, "Your attendance is requested at home immediately."

"Is there something wrong?" George asked.

"Is Beverly all right?" Emma asked. That's where her mind had gone when she'd recognized Willis.

"Mrs. Buttons is perfectly fine," Willis assured her. "Your attendance is required as well, miss."

"Me? Why?"

"I'm sure it's about the event my mother is planning," George said. He then nodded at Willis. "We'll be along shortly. Thank you."

"Very well, sir." Willis nodded at her again. "Miss." He then pivoted and walked away.

"What event?" Emma asked, trembling even harder. Aunt Jill could have been at the lunch and Beverly might have accidently said something.

"Remember the tree you wrote about in your letters last Christmas?" he asked.

She nodded. It had been a huge evergreen that had been set up in the park by the skating rink and people had tied ribbons with the names of soldiers on it as a signal of sending Christmas well-wishes overseas. She had written his name on one and tied it to a branch. So had Beverly.

"My mother arranged to have that tree set up and plans on having another one put up this year. That's what her brunch was about today. I told her last night that I'd go find a tree for her this weekend, and if I was to guess, I'd say that Beverly told her about your scarves and mittens, and Mother is interested in learning more. I'd also guess that Beverly informed Willis where he could find you. He knew I was going shopping this morning, too, and lucked out seeing my car out front and in finding us together." He nodded toward her bowl of soup. "We can finish our lunch before leaving."

She felt less like eating now but was able to eat enough soup to be polite before they left. There was no reason for Beverly to have told his mother about the scarves and mittens, or to have told Willis where he could find her.

It had to be something more than that.

A terrible feeling took over her entire body.

Though George tried to initiate conversation on the way to his house, she wasn't able to come up with more than one-word answers to any of his polite questions.

"There isn't anything to worry about," he said. "You'll see."

She'd see all right, and was sure there would be plenty to worry about.

He parked his car near the side of the house, and they used a door there to enter rather than one at the front of the house. James was at hand to take their coats as he had been on Thanksgiving Day, and he assured George he'd see to the packages in the car.

Emma could barely make her feet work as George held her arm and guided her down a long hallway, and then down another one that she recognized as leading to the front room, where she'd read to Nellie and Nathaniel.

The closer to that room they walked, the harder her heart pounded. As she stepped over the threshold, into the room, her heart sank clear to her ankles at the sight of one woman.

She'd known this wasn't going to be good.

"Emma Leigh Ellis!" Aunt Jill shrieked. "Let me tell you one thing, young lady! You are not going to get away with any of this!"

The room erupted with other people talking and Emma felt her legs giving out. If not for George's hold on her arm, she would have crumpled into a heap on the floor.

"Emily?" he asked.

She heard him only because he was next to her and had wrapped an arm around her waist, as if knowing she needed more help to remain standing.

"Emma Leigh," she said. "Two words. Not one."

"You are just like your father!" Aunt Jill shouted as she stormed closer. "You ruin everything you touch! Everything!"

Emma wasn't sure if George lifted her or not, but somehow, he moved her out of Aunt Jill's path and she ended up on the other side of the room, near Beverly, who wrapped an arm around her as she sank onto the sofa beside the older woman.

"What the hell is going on here?" George asked above Aunt Jill's shouts.

"She is what's going on here!" Aunt Jill pointed a finger at her. "She's just like her father. A good-for-nothing, no-good scoundrel who kills people!"

Other voices erupted again, including Beverly's.

Emma wanted to cover her ears with both hands, but Beverly had a strong hold on one of her arms. Unable to look at anyone, Emma closed her eyes and hung her head. So much for the miracle she'd begged to have happen. This was the nightmare she'd feared, and she'd brought everyone into it along with her.

A loud whistle split the air, and because of the sound's close proximity, she knew it came from George as he was standing next to where she sat.

When silence filled the room, he said, "Mother, what is going on here?"

"I'll tell you—"

"No, Jill, you won't," George interrupted calmly, but firmly. "Go ahead, Mother."

Emma couldn't contain the groan that rumbled in her throat.

"Well, dear," his mother said, "Emma is Jill's niece and—"

"She's not my niece!" Jill shouted. "Her mother is dead! Killed by her no-good father and I told her that I never wanted to see her again two years ago when she needed a reference to rent an apartment! She went behind my back and did it, anyway! And now she's trying to ruin everything. Everything! Just like her father!"

This was all so much more than she'd imagined. Unable to take any more, Emma shook off Beverly's hold and stood. "Stop. Please stop."

Aunt Jill didn't stop. She kept shouting nasty and mean things about Emma and her father, and tears sprang forth from Emma's eyes as George looked at her. "I'm sorry," she said, though no sound came out.

He shifted, twisted enough to face her and wrapped his arms around her shoulders.

Emma knew she shouldn't, but it was as if someone else living inside her took control of her actions and wrapped her arms around his waist and held on tightly as she buried her face into his chest.

She wasn't sure how long he held her, tightly, and softly kissed the top of her head. It might have only been a minute, but inside her, it felt like a lifetime. A wonderful lifetime where she was protected from the hate being fired at her. She quickly surmised that that was just her wishing. Wishing that something this comforting, this solid, could be real and could last a lifetime. Nothing could protect her from the real world or from what she'd done.

George could only think of one thing. How Emma was trembling in his arms. He had to get her out of here. Despite his parents' attempts, and his own, to stifle Jill, she continued her badgering. Her behavior was disgusting, but they'd all seen it before.

However, she'd gone too far, this time.

Emma's fears made perfect sense to him now, and he was guilt-ridden to know he was at the root of those fears. "Come," he whispered, easing his hold enough to steer her toward the door.

"Stop right there. She's not going anywhere," Jill insisted.

"Yes, we are," George said, guiding Emma across the room. "We aren't listening to any more of your insults."

"She belongs in the slums! Where the others like her live!" Jill shouted.

His anger was reaching a boiling point, but his first concern was Emma, and so he kept walking without saying a word.

That increased Jill's screeching. Her words were vile, and with the doorway right before them, George paused. He could protect Emma now, but what about tomorrow, or the next day? Jill wouldn't stop. She was like a cat stalking prey and wouldn't give up until something bigger scared her away.

That was him right now, and it needed to remain him. He turned and said the only thing that would provide Emma with lasting protection. "You should be happy, Jill. You are getting what you always wanted."

"What are you talking about?" Jill snapped.

"A merger between our families," he answered calmly, firmly. "Emma and I are engaged to be married."

The shocked silence that encompassed the room gave him a moment of satisfaction, until he felt Emma wobble. Afraid she was about to collapse, he tightened his hold on her waist until they were around the corner, then he caught her beneath the knees with his free arm and carried her down the hall.

She was light, weighing less than the heavy packs he'd carried in the army, and he didn't stop, didn't put her down until they'd entered the sitting room in the west wing of the house.

He slowly lowered her onto the gold-colored sofa and searched her face, her eyes, making sure she was coherent. Anger still coursed through his veins, but so did concern and compassion. Brushing hair away from her face, he said, "There now, there's nothing to be afraid of here."

Shaking her head, she closed her eyes. "I'm so sorry."

He brushed a tear off her cheek. "Don't be. You didn't do anything wrong."

She opened her eyes, shook her head. "I'd thought enough time had passed when I'd moved here. With both of my parents dead, I'd thought she wouldn't have a reason to hate me anymore."

The sorrow on her face, in her eyes, nearly gutted him. He wanted to hug her, hold her, promise her that Jill would never hurt her again, but how could he fulfill that promise? Stating they were engaged would work for a while, but not forever. She was still trembling, and he stood. "I'm going to get you something to drink."

"D-did you—" she bit down on her bottom lip "—tell her that we were engaged?"

At some point, he might regret that, but not right now. "Yes."

She covered her face with both hands. "Why would you say that?" she asked, through her hands.

He walked to the buffet table and cracked a smile while pouring a small amount of brandy into a glass. The look on Jill's face had been a sight to see, but it could also be costly. Very. "Because if there is one thing Jill hates, it's not being in control," he said.

Emma groaned louder than a man twice her size and three times her age.

He carried the glass to her. "Here. Sip on this, it will help with the shock."

She dropped her hands away from her face. "Will it help with the aftershocks?"

He grinned at her honesty. "It might."

She took the glass and downed it in one swallow, then coughed until her eyes watered.

He took the glass from her hand, quickly crossed the room and filled another one with water. Once her coughing subsided, he handed her the water. "I'd said to sip the brandy. Are you all right?"

Her one-shoulder shrug was adorable as she took a small drink of water. "My father used to give Sharon and I a small amount of brandy when we were sick, but it had been diluted with water. I didn't expect it to burn that bad." She leaned her head back on the sofa and let out a long sigh. "Oh, George. I don't know how to fix this. I truly don't."

"There is nothing for you to fix."

"Yes, there is."

He sat down next to her. "I now remember meeting you the day Jill refused to give you a reference for an apartment. I never made the connection because I thought Martha had called you Emily, not Emma Leigh." That and he'd never have any reason to think she was Martha's cousin. "Why didn't you tell me who you were?" The girl he'd met that day had looked so small and hurt that he'd instantly felt a powerful compassion toward her, but he had never imagined she was that girl.

"Because of what just happened," she said. "I knew it would be awful."

"Jill is who made it awful, just like she made that day awful."

"She told me to leave town that day, but I had already accepted the job, and I couldn't go back. I just couldn't."

"Nor was there any reason for you to. You have as much right to live in Albany as Jill does." He leaned back, rested a foot on his opposite knee. "I told Martha to give you the reference."

"You did?"

"Yes. She said Jill would be mad. I said that I didn't care. That she either gave you a reference or I would. She told me that she had a few days later."

"She had," Emma said. "She found me at the boarding house and gave me a letter for Mr. Allen—he and his wife live in the apartment below Beverly's—and then she came to the apartment a week or so after I'd moved in, to make sure that I'd gotten the apartment."

That had been shortly before he'd shipped out, when he'd requested that Martha confirm that the young girl—Emma, not Emily—had obtained her apartment. He'd wanted to make sure that had happened before he'd left town.

"That was the day she met Delmar," Emma said, her eyes full of remorse.

It had been a week later when Martha had suggested they wait to get married until he returned home from the war. He'd been fine with putting it off. Was fine that it had never happened. His train of thought shifted. "What was Delmar doing at your apartment?"

"He'd claimed that I owed him money for not completing my work, but I didn't. I'd completed everything. I hadn't owed any rent money, either, like he also claimed."

Fully comprehending that there was more to it than that, he asked, "And?"

She sighed. "He had suggested that we...that we date, when I'd been working for him, but I wasn't about to do that. Not while working for him, or later, when he found out where I'd moved to and came to my apartment."

That's what he thought. Delmar had had ulterior motives when it came to her, and he doubted it was just dating. "Because you didn't want to get married?"

"I'd decided long before then that I wouldn't get married."

"Why?"

"Because I didn't want to get stuck in that life. I saw that happen to others in my apartment building in New York City. They thought it was a way out, but before long they had babies, and..." She shook her head. "They are just stuck there. They'll never get out." Looking at him, with eyes full of compassion, she continued. "I never imagined that Martha would elope with him."

"There would have been no reason for you to have imagined that."

"He was so...dishonest. Shorting our pay and claiming things that weren't true, that cigars were missing or not rolled right. I don't know why Martha would marry him."

"Honest man or not, once Martha discovered Delmar was from New York City, she would have glued herself to him."

"But she was engaged to marry you."

"Because of her mother. Jill had run her life for years, and knowing Martha, she knew a dishonest man wouldn't mind if she was defying her parents." He would never say that he and Martha hadn't tried to fulfill their agreement. She had. They both had, and he didn't blame her for taking a way out when she'd found one.

Emma sighed. "I will tell them that it was my idea to say we were engaged and—"

"No, you won't," he said. "We need to take some time and think about this." He did for sure. Needed time to fully consider the consequences of announcing an engagement to her. He didn't regret it. Deep inside, it felt right.

"There's nothing to think about," she said.

"Yes, there is." He needed more information before he could figure out what to do. He didn't want her to feel stuck in anything, including an engagement. He'd been there himself and wouldn't do that to her, but she deserved his protection and he wanted to give her that. "Tell me about your mother and father."

"Why?"

"Because I want to know. I honestly do."

Frowning, she asked, "Aren't you mad at me for not telling you that I was Martha's cousin?"

"No. I've known the wrath of Jill and I don't blame you for wanting to avoid that. She's like a bag of hot air—it can only stretch so far before it explodes, and no one wants to be around when that happens." He winked at her. "Now, tell me about your father."

Emma had to fight to hold back a smile at his description of Aunt Jill, even though nothing about this was funny. It was horrifying. Everything about it. He just had a way of making it seem like it wasn't that bad. It was! And there was nothing to think about. They couldn't have people believing they were engaged.

He was looking at her, waiting, and she tried to clear her mind enough to answer his question. "My father wasn't anything like Aunt Jill said. He was a good man, a good father and a good husband."

"You're his daughter, so I believe he had to have been."

She always felt a special warmth when thinking about her father and leaned farther back on the sofa. "He truly was a good man. Kind and caring. My mother was ill for some time and he took care of her. He paid the neighbor woman, Mrs. Mills, to look after Mother while he was at work and Sharon and I were in school. We all looked forward to her getting better, but she didn't, and when she died, I think a part of him died right along with her. He was still good to Sharon and I—made sure we had everything we needed, and teased us, told us jokes—but there was a sadness about him that just never went away."

"How did he die?"

She'd never forget that day. "An accident. Something spooked the horses and his milk wagon overturned."

"When was that?"

"Six years ago. I was sixteen and Sharon was eighteen. That's when we started working for Delmar's family's company, rolling cigars. Sharon had graduated school, so she worked all day, every day. I did, too, but still went to school, until I graduated. Then, two years ago, when Eddie was done with college, he and Sharon got married. That's when he told me about the job here—he even loaned me the money for the train ticket to come and apply. He also loaned me enough money for rent. I could never have done it without his help, and I paid him back first thing."

"You should be very proud of what you've accomplished."

Implications of all the trouble she'd caused filled her. "I should never have moved here. Never have asked Aunt Jill for a reference. Beverly said she would have given me one, but I hadn't met her until after I'd asked Aunt Jill."

"I'm sure Beverly is as proud of you as I am, for all your accomplishments."

She had nothing to be proud of, nothing for him to be proud of for her.

"Tell me about your mother. When did she pass away?"

Emma understood what he was doing. Keeping the subject off what they needed to talk about—the big lie about them being engaged. She didn't know what to say about that, how to fix it, so she answered his question. "When I was nine. I think she'd been sick for longer than either Sharon or I knew, and she and father kept it from us, because she was at the doctor a lot. But she was always happy, and she and my father held hands all the time. Whenever we went someplace, they held hands, and I would hold his and she would hold Sharon's."

"That's a nice memory," he said.

She nodded because it was a nice memory. She had many good memories, but they were overshadowed by others. "She was happy except for when Aunt Jill would visit. Every year. Maybe it was more than that. I honestly don't know. I just remember walking downtown to the hotel, to visit her there. Aunt Jill would tell Mother how old she looked, how worn out, and that she needed to move back to Albany, without any of the rest of us. Mother said she'd never do that, never leave her family, and that would make Aunt Jill even madder, and she'd say awful things about my father."

Like the things she'd said about her earlier. How she needed to move back to the slums. Her face burned with embarrassment. His family had to think awfully of her, and he should, too. She *had* grown up in the slums and nothing would ever change that. A man like him wouldn't want anyone to think he was engaged to a woman from the slums.

"Did your mother inherit anything when your grandfather died?" he asked.

She shrugged, no longer able to keep her mind off what he'd said to Jill. "I don't know. I was just a baby when both of my grandparents died."

He was frowning, deeply, and her stomach sank. If anyone had reason to dislike her, hate her, it was him. Convinced that his frown was because he'd said they were engaged, she fought against the way her eyes burned. "I'm sorry. So very sorry. I know you wish you hadn't said that to Jill earlier, and I—"

"No, I'm not sorry." He grinned and took a hold of her hand. "I'm thinking that it was the perfect solution."

"Solution to what?"

"Everything."

The heat from his hand was moving up her arm, all the way to her heart. She cared about him. Had for a long time, and if there was any possible way that he'd want to be engaged to her, she'd be the happiest woman on earth. But there was no possibility of that, and she wasn't foolish enough to think there ever might be.

He released her hand and touched her cheek with the tip of one finger. It made her heart pound and she pinched her lips together to keep from saying that there was no solution to anything.

"I'm thinking our engagement is exactly what we need."

"No, it's not," she said. "It's most certainly not what you need. Or want. I will return to New York City. Right away. I already have a train ticket."

He frowned again. "Why do you have a train ticket to New York City?"

"I bought it for when my sister has her baby, so I can go see them." Sharon had been one of the lucky ones. Finding a husband who hadn't lived in the slums. She and Sharon had talked about that, about how they weren't going to get stuck in a life that kept them there forever. Ever since moving away, she'd been proud that it hadn't happened to either of them. She wouldn't go back there, refused to, but would have to leave Albany.

"I believe an engagement is what we both need right now, and I think we should make a deal."

"A deal?" She shook her head at the impossibility of that, even as her heart began to pound harder.

"Yes, a deal," he said. "You can't go back to New York right away. You have your job at the school. They'll need time to find a replacement, and there's your apartment, and lest we forget about the scarves you need to deliver for Christmas. That has to happen for sure."

A variety of emotions fluttered through her. She did have several scarves yet to knit, though Beverly would see that they were delivered to the orphanage, but the school would need time to replace her.

"I think we should make a deal to stay engaged until after Christmas, then you can decide what to do about your job and apartment."

She couldn't ask that of him. Wouldn't. "That wouldn't be fair to you."

"Yes, it would be."

"No, it wouldn't. Aunt Jill will…" She pinched her lips together. "It'll be awful."

He took a hold of her hand again, gently squeezed it. "Being engaged to me would give you protection from Jill."

"But who would protect you from her?" she asked.

One of his best-in-the-world smiles appeared on his face. "You."

Like always, his smile made her want to smile. It was that wonderful. That perfect. Yet, she said, "That doesn't make any sense."

"Oh, yes, it does." He took a hold of her other hand. "I like you, Emma."

Her heart pounded so hard that warmth rushed into her cheeks. "I like you, too, George."

"I've liked you since your first letter arrived," he said. "Those letters were like fuel for my soul. When I was tired, worn out, cold and hungry, I'd pull one of your letters out and the words you wrote, the idea of meeting the woman who smelled like warm vanilla, would give me the energy to keep going, despite all obstacles."

His letters had meant the world to her. Each time one had arrived, she'd read it over and over again.

"I owe you so much for that," he said. "More, because your letters didn't just do that for me. Other men would see me reading your letters and ask me to read parts to them, and that's where your jokes and riddles came in. The questions and answers would float up and down the trenches, making worn-out and tired men smile and laugh. Seeing how that happened is what made me decide to expand Weston Lumber. I saw how one person brought everyone together. We fought as a unit, for all of us to come through every battle together, and for everyone back home. People that we'd return to and those that we didn't even know. Now, I want to implement that unity into the lumber industry. Want to see everyone working together, providing for those we know and those we don't. I don't want to see just one company become the largest in America. I want to see our industry become the largest in the world."

"I can understand how you'd want to do all that. You're a leader and you care about others, but it was the army that brought you all together to fight as one," she said. "Not me."

"The army put us all together, but you made us into a unit who fought for everyone to get back to base to hear your next riddle."

"That's not why you fought to get back to your base."

"It was for me." He squeezed her hands. "I wanted to get back home, so I could meet the woman who wrote those letters in person."

She glanced around the room, everywhere but at him, because the way he was looking at her made her want things that she knew she could never have. Him. "I wanted to see you return home, safe and sound, more than I wanted anything else, but I still don't see how a pretend engagement would benefit you."

"It will benefit me in putting together a lumber-industry coalition."

"How?"

George's heart was thudding harder, faster, and it was from excitement. He had found a way to keep her protected from Jill, but Emma wasn't buying in to this easily. He respected that. She was smart. A lot smarter than her aunt gave her credit for. "I need a diversion, and our engagement would be perfect. Jill believes that Weston Lumber should work with no one but North Country Logging and attempting to convince her otherwise would be useless. She also has a one-track mind. With her attention on our engagement, my coalition will be in place before she can protest it. She wants to hold on to a large portion of the market, which hurts others, and I don't think that's fair to the men and women who work hard, very hard, but are hampered by the big companies in their way, which have been Weston Lumber and North Country Logging."

"Won't that hurt Weston Lumber?" she asked.

"No. My father and I agree that we—all of the companies in the industry—should work together. It's those standing in opposition that will hurt everyone."

"Aunt Jill."

"Yes."

She was contemplating everything. He could tell by the various expressions that tugged her eyebrows and twisted her lips.

He rubbed his thumb over the backs of her hands. "I swear to you that you will have my protection, and my family's protection. Jill will never treat you like she did today, and she will know that. Know that we won't stand for it."

"That will just make her angrier."

He was sure of that, and he was sure what Jill would do. She'd already told him to go find Martha, which he refused to do. "That anger will make her take action. My guess is that she'll go to New York City, try to convince Martha to return, but Martha hasn't been home since she eloped for a reason. She's enjoying her new life. Her freedom from her mother. Martha isn't going to give that up. I guarantee it."

"Then what?" she asked.

"Jill will have to accept that a merger between North Country Logging and Weston Lumber will never happen, and by then, you'll have had the time to complete your scarves, deliver them and decide what you want to do." He didn't like the idea of her leaving town, but would wait to see what he could do about that. "I'll assist you in whatever decision you make."

A knock sounded on the door, and he turned in that direction. "Come in."

James pushed open the door. "Forgive my interruption, but Mrs. Weston would like to know if there is anything Miss Ellis needs?"

George looked at Emma, waited until she shook her head. "No, thank you, James, we are fine, but you can tell Mother we'll be along shortly."

With a polite nod, James backed out of the room and pulled the door closed.

"We don't have to go talk to them until you're ready," he said.

She nodded but remained silent.

"And no one will know about this except for you and I."

She looked skeptical.

"Not even Beverly."

She grimaced.

He chuckled. "You don't think she's been outside the door this whole time, with a glass to her ear, do you?"

A smile slowly grew on her face. "If she knew what room we are in, she would have been."

He laughed louder. "My mother wouldn't have al-

lowed that. She can be a bit protective. I have to warn
you—that will include you."

"Warn me?"

"In a good way. She'll just be looking out for you.
Like Beverly. And me, and my father." Watching her
expression, he asked, "So are we going to do this? Remain engaged?"

She bit down on her bottom lip until it turned white
before she asked, "Until Christmas?"

He nodded.

Her cheeks puffed as she slowly huffed out a puff
of air. "All right."

"All right." He planted both feet on the floor and
tugged her off the sofa as he stood. "I have to get something—will you come with me? It's just upstairs."

She nodded.

The catch inside him told him he wasn't as indiffer-
ent to being engaged to her as he had been to Martha.
Not by a long shot. He would have to deal with that, but
that would happen in time. Right now, he was going to
enjoy her company, while having some questions answered. What he'd said about Jill standing in opposition
to his idea of bringing the industry together was true,
so were his other thoughts. The only thing Jill had ever
cared about was money, and somewhere along the line
there was a connection between that and her hatred of
Emma. He'd find it and expose it, and being engaged
to her gave him the opportunity to do just that.

They took the back stairway to the second floor,
and he stopped two doors from his bedroom. "This is
a powder room, if you'd care to use it."

"I would, thank you," she said.

"My room is at the end of the hall, but I should be back before you're done."

"All right."

As soon as she entered the room, he hurried to his bedroom, and to his top dresser drawer, from which he pulled out a box. They had been his grandmother's rings. One had a large ruby stone, surrounded by small diamonds, and the other was a simple gold band.

He took out the ruby ring and put the box holding the wedding band back in the drawer. People would expect her to have a ring, and this time around, he was going to meet expectations. Including his own.

Back in the hallway, he had one foot pressed against the wall behind him as he waited across from the bathroom door, and grinned when she opened it.

Smiling in return, she touched her hair. "I hope you don't mind that I used the brush in there."

"I don't mind." He liked the way her hair was hanging loose today. Had noticed that as soon as she'd removed her scarf inside the store. "Your hair looks beautiful. It's looked beautiful all day."

She pushed her hair off her shoulders. "I guess I'm just nervous."

He stepped forward, took a hold of her left hand. "Don't be. I'll be at your side the entire time, and I promise I won't let you down."

"And you keep your promises," she said.

"I do."

He lifted her hand. "Should we see if this fits?"

Her eyes widened at the sight of the ring. "Oh, George, I don't think—"

"I do. It was my grandmother's, and no one has worn it since she did." He slid the ring onto her finger, where it fit perfectly. "No one has actually even seen it since my father gave it to me years ago."

Glancing up from the ring, she asked, "Why not?"

"Because I never wanted anyone to wear it, but I do now."

"So everyone will think our engagement is real?"

It wasn't real, he knew that, but he was going to embrace it. Every part of it. "Yes. We want people to believe it's real. Very real. Does that make you want to change your mind?"

She looked into his eyes, searched his entire face. "Does it make you change your mind?"

"No."

She grinned. "Me, neither."

He laid a finger under her chin. "There's one more thing that I think we need to do."

"What's that?"

He'd been thinking about this for weeks, and though it might be considered taking advantage of the situation, he felt it necessary. Holding her face in place, deliberately, slowly, he leaned closer. "This."

Chapter Eleven

The moment George's lips brushed against hers, Emma's eyes fluttered shut of their own accord and a wave of something she'd never experienced washed over her. It was warm and soft, and so amazing that it was utterly indescribable.

Then his lips didn't just brush against hers, they met hers. Firmly. Warm and dry. With enough pressure that the wave washing over her increased. Spread faster and went deeper.

His hand cupped her cheek, making her head tilt into his palm, and his other hand pulled her closer. The kiss that followed was...

The kiss of a lifetime.

She couldn't even think. All she could do was feel. Feel as if she became weightless, floating on the air. She looped her arms around his neck to make sure that she wasn't lifted right off the ground by the sensations. She didn't want them to stop. Not ever. It was the most wonderful feeling in the world.

The other thing she had to do was to tell herself to breathe, to release the air she was holding in her lungs.

Her lips parted slightly as she did so, and George playfully nibbled on her bottom one before his lips, his mouth, met hers again, with that wonderful, perfect pressure that had her entire being feeling warm and fuzzy. Cozy, like she was enveloped in a warm blanket on a cold night.

The kiss ended as slowly and perfectly as it had started, with him kissing her cheek and the tip of her nose before he leaned back, looked down at her.

Feeling as if she needed to learn how to breathe all over again, Emma didn't move, just continued to stare back at him, as her lungs filled and emptied.

As reality gradually returned, she realized her arms were still looped around his neck. Slowly, not overly sure what to with them, she slid them across his shoulders and down his arms, before they fell to her sides.

"I thought we should do that in case we encounter mistletoe and others are around," he said. "We wouldn't want them to think it was our first kiss."

"Oh, no, we wouldn't," she said. Was that her voice? It sounded breathless. She was breathless. So, yes, that had been her. But why were they talking about mistletoe?

Her head was foggy. "Mistletoe?"

"Yes, you do know what that is?"

His eyes crinkled as he grinned at her. That was one of the ways his smile was the best in the world. The way it made tiny creases form around his eyes. "Yes."

"We might encounter some and need to kiss beneath it."

"Oh. Okay."

He winked at her. "Shall we go join the others?"

Her entire body froze, even her lungs, which she'd

just figured out how to use again. The only thing working, truly working, was her heart. It was pounding a hard, steady beat against her ribcage. "Wh—" She sucked in air. "What are we going to tell them?"

"The truth." He picked up her hand and kissed the beautiful ruby ring he'd slid on her finger a moment ago. "That we are engaged. That we fell in love through the letters we wrote to each other."

"Oh." That was hardly the truth, and things were now even more complicated than ever. Especially inside her. "They think Beverly wrote to you."

He folded his fingers through hers, so their palms touched as they had when he'd suggested they pretend to be engaged. Had she really agreed to that?

Yes, she had.

"I'm sure Beverly has told them the truth," he said. "If not, we'll just play it by ear."

"I don't think I know that game," she said, still afraid to move.

"Don't worry, I do, and I'm very good at it." Grasping her other hand, he walked backward and tugged her forward, down the hallway. "Besides, we won't be here long."

He was smiling, his eyes twinkling, and he looked extremely handsome, and happy. She had to focus on putting one foot in front of the other, because she knew why everything was so complicated inside her. It wasn't something she'd considered—perhaps because she'd known the truth for a long time—but had no choice but admit it now. To herself. No one else could ever know that she was in love with him. She'd fallen in love with him while writing to him and continued to love him, in a way she hadn't known she could love someone.

"Do others know that you don't want to get married?" she asked, and then bit her tongue for saying that aloud.

His smile never faltered. "Does anyone know that about you?"

"No." Not even Sharon. Her sister had thought marriage was the way out, and assumed she did, too.

"Then we're good."

"We are?"

"Yes." Then he asked, "Have you ever cut down a tree?"

He was still walking backward, pulling her along, and smiling, but a frown tugged at her lips, because she had no idea why he would ask that. "No."

"Do you want to?"

His enthusiasm was making a unique happiness swirl inside her, much like it had at the store earlier. Maybe this was a good plan. It would give her time to figure out what she needed to do. "Why?"

"Because that is what we are going to do, if you want to." He released one of her hands and fell in step beside her. "I couldn't do it this morning because the horses were being used—that's why I decided to go shopping—but they should be available now."

"Why do you need horses?"

"Because trucks get stuck in the woods."

That made sense, and it might be the only thing that did right now.

"Do you have pair of boots?" he asked.

"At my apartment."

"We'll stop there so you can change."

Despite knowing that their engagement was pretend, and that he was asking her to go with him to cut down a tree because of that pretend engagement, she had no control over the happiness swirling inside her. It could be because going to cut down a tree sounded fun, or simply the idea of spending more time with him. She had enjoyed every moment they'd spent together, even while trying hard not to and while telling herself that she shouldn't be with him or be having fun with him.

She contemplated that, and other things, as they walked down the hall, the stair steps and several other hallways before they finally arrived at the front room.

Her heart was once again pounding hard as they walked into the room. In spite of the fact he was still holding her hand, fear of facing the occupants of the room was erupting inside her.

She had a brief moment of relief seeing that Aunt Jill was no longer there, but his mother, father and Beverly were still in the room. All three of them had told Aunt Jill to calm down earlier, but nothing had done that. Not until George's announcement about their engagement.

Craig met them in the center of the room. His smile was almost as good as George's, with the way it filled his face.

"Allow me to be the first to congratulate the two of you." He shook George's hand and kissed her cheek. Then his face grew serious. "And please allow me to apologize for what happened earlier."

"Thank you." Knowing she had to accept the blame, she said, "But it was all my fault."

"Nonsense." Amy pushed her husband aside. "Absolutely none of that was your fault." She then wrapped her arms around Emma's shoulders. "And we are so happy for the two of you. Beverly told us that it was the two of you writing to each other, not her and George."

Still holding Emma's shoulders, Amy shook her head. "All because you didn't want your aunt to know. That's tragic in and of itself and the display she put on today will never be tolerated again."

Emma didn't know what to say to any of that. Even if she had, there wasn't time before Amy noticed the ring on her finger.

"Oh, Grandma's ring." Amy waved her hands in front of her face. "I'm so happy, I'm going to cry."

"I'm already crying," Beverly said. "I'm just so stinking happy. This is just how things should be. How they should be." She, too, gave them both hugs. "And how I knew it would be. Congratulations."

Having these people be so excited over an engagement that was fake caused Emma as much anxiety as writing to George had. She'd just gone from one mistake to another.

"Thank you, all of you," George said. "We are very happy, too." He squeezed her hand. "I do apologize for the manner in which you learned the news, but it couldn't be helped."

"You can blame me for that," his mother said. "When Beverly said she was helping a friend make gifts for the children at the orphanage, I'm the one who told everyone Emma's name and how she'd been here for Thanksgiving, and—"

"That's when all hell let loose," Beverly interrupted dryly. "You'd have thought the house was on fire the way this place cleared out when Jill blew her stack."

There was amusement in Beverly's eyes, and Emma could imagine that her friend hadn't stayed quiet, all in defense of her.

"We are glad the news is out," George said, "and

hope you will all excuse us. We have plans that were interrupted when we were called home." Grinning at her, he said, "We have a Christmas tree to cut down."

If anyone was disappointed that they were leaving, no one voiced it. Instead, they encouraged them to have fun, and his mother said they'd see them for the evening meal, as George whisked her out of the room and down the hallway.

He glanced down at her. "Having second thoughts?"

She studied his face, but there were no telltale signs that he was questioning their deal. His smile was the same familiar one. "Are you?"

"Not about our engagement, but I was asking about cutting down a tree."

She was having second thoughts about many things, including how she should feel.

He stopped in the hallway, faced her and placed both hands on her shoulders. "What's happened in the past is in the past. We can't change it. Nor can we know what will happen in the future, not with complete certainty. What we do have is today, and the choice of making it a memorable, wonderful day, or one filled with worries about the past or the future."

Her heart did a somersault. "You sound just like one of your letters."

"Those letters were in response to your letters, which were full of optimism, hope and joy. I clung to that and vowed to get home to meet the girl whose letters changed my life."

Attempting to justify her letters, she said, "I just wrote about what was happening here, in town."

He nodded. "Exactly. You didn't dwell on the past or question the future."

She hadn't, and since his return, she'd done nothing but dwell on both.

"For the rest of the day, I think we should forget everything else and have some fun," he said. "I think we both deserve that. Don't you?"

Even if she had the want to say no, she didn't have the will. He was right; after all he'd been through, he deserved to have fun. "Yes, I do."

He kissed her forehead, then twisted and opened a door that revealed a closet. After collecting her coat, he held it as she slipped in her arms, and then retrieved his coat.

Glancing at his shoes as they walked to the door at the side of the house that they had used earlier, she asked, "Won't you need boots, too?"

"They are in my car." He opened the door. "I'd planned on going to get the tree after I'd finished my shopping."

As her mind shifted into thinking about how much had happened since she'd left her apartment to go shopping this morning, she stopped it. In part. She'd never have imagined that what had happened would happen, but at the same time, she realized that she would never have the opportunity of going into the woods and cutting a tree down ever again and was going to enjoy it. Just as he'd suggested. "The tree last year was very large."

"Good thing I have you to help me." He gave her a wink and took a hold of her hand as they walked around the side of the house and along a shoveled roadway that led to large building, painted white with red trim.

"This used to be the stable when we had horses, but the stalls were all removed so we could park the autos inside," he said as they approached the building. "James pulled mine inside after we arrived."

If she was in the right state of mind, she might use how different their backgrounds were to convince herself that she shouldn't have agreed to a deal, but she didn't want to be in the right state of mind right now. She wanted to enjoy the rest of the day. "Did you have a horse?"

"I did—his name was Little Buck, and he liked to buck."

"Did he buck you off?"

He laughed. "Yes, but we eventually came to an understanding."

"What was that?"

"That I didn't want to walk home, and he didn't want me to."

She laughed. "That was a good understanding."

"Yes, it was. I suspect you didn't have a horse in New York City."

"No, but my father used the same team of horses to pull his milk wagon every day. Jack and Jenny. He talked about them like they were two of his best friends. My sister and I were always happy when he'd stop by and we'd get to pet them." She sighed, feeling a touch nostalgic. "You don't see many horses on the roads anymore."

He opened the building's door and gestured for her to enter. "That's true, but the streets are certainly clearer."

"That's true, too," she admitted.

"There were a lot of horses in the war. Work horses. They moved machinery, equipment, full camps through knee-high mud and across frozen grounds. They were true unsung heroes."

They stopped next to his car and a touch of the fear she'd known between each of his letters washed over her. "I'm so glad that you made it home."

He brushed the side of her face with a knuckle. "I am, too."

Her breath caught, and she considered stretching on her toes and kissing him. She couldn't do that, so she bit down on her bottom trembling lip and looked away.

"Do you want to see where we are going?"

Wondering if she'd been so foggy-headed earlier, after he'd kissed her, that she'd missed something he'd said, she asked, "I thought we were going to Weston Lumber."

"We are." Still holding her hand, he led her around the automobiles, toward a set of narrow stairs along one wall. As they climbed the steps, he explained, "This used to be the hayloft, but now it holds junk of all sorts."

Tires, cans and other automobile parts that she didn't know the names of, or what they were used for, as well as furniture and other items, were stacked along the walls as they walked to the far end, where he opened a door.

She gasped slightly at the sight before her. The door led outside, onto a small balcony of sorts, complete with a short roof and low side walls so the area was snow-free. This high up, she could see over the tops of the trees, to the river. "Oh, my." Stepping onto the balcony, she walked to the edge, where the wall came up to her waist. She rested her hands on the rail as she gazed at the pristine, snow-covered ground, the lush fir trees and the skeletons of those that had lost their leaves for the winter. "I can hear the water," she whispered, not wanting the sound of her voice to interrupt the serenity.

George nodded as he laid a hand atop hers.

They stood there for an extended length of time, simply admiring the sights and sounds.

"This was my favorite place while I was growing up," he said.

"I can see why."

"I slept out here many summer nights, right here on the balcony."

Twisting, she looked up at him. "Why?"

"Because I wanted to."

"Weren't you afraid?"

"Of what?"

She didn't know, but she'd never slept anywhere but behind a closed and locked door her entire life. Remembering Thanksgiving Day, she asked, "Bears?"

He laughed and leaned over the edge. "Look over there, downriver. See the tops of those buildings?"

Following the direction where he was pointing, she saw the rooftops. "Yes."

"That's Weston Lumber, but we have to go through town and use the bridge to cross the river to get there."

"That's where the woods are, too?"

"Yes, the acreage around it had been harvested in the past, but my grandfather replanted it."

"Do you do that everywhere? Replant trees after others have been harvested?"

"We do, but other companies don't. That's something else I want addressed by our coalition. Depending on the species, it can take a large number of years before a tree is mature enough to harvest, and without replanting, there won't be any to harvest in the future."

She didn't know much about the lumber industry but was interested in knowing more. "I never thought about that."

"Most people don't, but our families have known forever that our forests are not never-ending resources."

She glanced down at the ring on her finger, the fake engagement ring. Their ancestors had worked together in the lumber industry for years, but their work together, their history, had been lost on her. That saddened her.

"If you don't like it, I'll buy you a different one. One you pick out yourself."

Understanding that he was talking about the ring, she shook her head. "No. I like this one very much." Today was supposed to be about fun, and therefore she wasn't going to think about the past. Not at all. Grasping his hand, she tugged him to the door. "Let's go find a tree to cut down." It had been a long time since she hadn't worried about anything or anyone and she was going to make the most of it.

George didn't know what had happened to Emma on the balcony of the hayloft, but he liked it. She was full of life, smiles and laughter during the ride to her apartment.

There, when he opened the trunk to collect his warm clothes and boots, she said, "My present for Beverly isn't in here."

"James must have carried it in the house." He closed the trunk. "We can get it later. We have almost two weeks before Christmas."

"You're right," she agreed.

Would he be able to convince her to focus on having fun for the next several days, and beyond? Most likely not, because Jill was sure to retaliate, but he'd be there when that happened. He'd make sure of that.

Once in her apartment, he took a deep breath, loving

the smell of warm vanilla, as he sat down on the sofa to take off his shoes. "Do you have any wool pants?"

"Yes. I'll go put them on and my boots, unless you need to use the bedroom?"

"No. Go ahead."

She looked at the clothes he'd set down on the sofa beside him. "What about changing your pants?"

The blush on her face was adorable. "I can do that here."

With eyes as wide as silver dollars, she said, "Oh."

Figuring he'd shocked her enough, he stood and grasped his wool pants. "These go over the pants I have on. So does the shirt."

The look she leveled on him was meant to appear serious, to say that she wasn't impressed with his teasing, but she couldn't pull it off. She knew it, too, because she grinned and shook her head at him, then picked up the pillow off the sofa and threw it at him before making a dash into the bedroom.

He laughed as she closed the door. "Make sure you put on thick socks."

"I will," she replied through the closed door.

George was going to enjoy being engaged to her. Enjoy it very much.

He was tying his boots when she came out of the bedroom. Eyeing her closely, he said, "That's the same dress you were wearing when you went in there." She had put a sweater over the green dress, as well as her long, blue coat.

"I know." She lifted the hem of her skirt. "I put my wool pants on beneath it. I wear them while walking to school on cold days. And I put on my boots."

He patted his knee. "Put your foot here."

"Why?"

Eyebrows lifted, he looked at her, but didn't answer.

She stepped closer and carefully set her foot on his knee. He lifted the hem of her dress and felt the thickness of her pants. They were thicker than they looked, and lined—he could feel the two layers separating as he rubbed them between his fingers.

"They are very warm." She lifted her foot off his knee. "I bought them from Mrs. Martin, next door, at the laundry. And I'm wearing a pair of socks that Beverly knit for me. They'll keep my feet very warm."

"She gave them to you for your birthday," he said, recalling one of her letters. "January nineteenth. Perhaps I'll ask her to knit me a pair."

"Your birthday is July nineteenth. I highly doubt you'd need heavy socks on your birthday."

He stood, stepped forward so there were only inches separating them. "Maybe not, but if your feet are warmer than mine after we are done with the tree, then I'll ask her and I'll save them for winter."

She didn't move, just stared up at him, smiling. "She will make you a pair, you know that."

"I do know that."

"Unless I ask her not to."

The challenge in her eyes excited him. "Now, why would you do that? Or is that the kind of wife you plan on being, one who wants to see her husband cold and miserable?"

Her face fell. "No, that's—"

He laughed and kissed the tip of her nose. "Or one who doesn't know when her husband is teasing her?"

"You aren't my husband."

No, he wasn't, but he wasn't averse to the idea. Why

was that? Because her letters had filled him with optimism and hope, or did it go deeper than that? Her letters had also filled him with desires and a longing he'd never known. They were still there, had taken root inside him, but that would mean he wanted her to love him, and he didn't want that for anyone. His only desires, wants and goals were focused on Weston Lumber. Neither he nor his father had mentioned his coalition to anyone at North Country Logging because Jill would be in opposition to it—that was a given. She'd always been opposed to anything that didn't benefit her directly.

He would have to contemplate that, and other things, but today, he'd promised Emma fun, and that's what he would provide. He tapped the tip of her nose with one finger. "Time to find a tree ready to be cut down."

It took a brief moment before her smile returned. "Ready to be cut down? I don't think any tree is ready to be cut down."

"You are going to be surprised because you'll soon see a tree and it will whisper to you, telling you that it's the one."

"Trees whisper?"

He opened the door to leave her apartment. "Yes. Only you will be able to hear it, and me. I've heard it before."

Her face was once again alive, shimmering with happiness. "Have you?"

"Yes, I have."

Their back-and-forth banter continued about trees and several other subjects that kept the mood light and fun as they drove across town.

The lumberyard was a busy place, with men processing logs into lumber, and he answered her questions about the process as they made their way to the stable. He also explained how logging was a major industry across the entire United States, how wood from as far away as Michigan was marketed through Albany, and that from here, lumber had been shipped around the world for years.

When he'd stopped by before going shopping, he'd told Wayne MacDonald that he'd need a team-and-two sled this afternoon. The stable man had waved at him when he'd parked the car and by the time he and Emma arrived at the huge stable, the man already had two horses hitched to the long sled.

"Those are the biggest horses I've ever seen," Emma said. "And the longest sled."

"They are draft horses and can pull a sled of logs that will fill a train car." He winked at her. "The downside of that is they have one speed. Slow." That wasn't completely true. The horses could move as fast as some of their smaller counterparts, if they chose to, which wasn't very often. "They are Belgians. As are all the horses we use here."

"Was Little Buck a Belgian?" she asked as he helped her up and onto the seat that was just wide enough for the two of them to sit.

"No, Little Buck was a Morgan."

She asked other questions about the horses and the sled, and listened intently as he explained how the double set of runners beneath the sled was needed for the weight, and how the road they traversed had been sprayed with water to form a thick sheet of ice, making it easier for the horses to pull the sleds and about the spiked ice shoes that the horses wore during the winter.

He'd lived and breathed the lumber industry his entire life, and enjoyed sharing that expertise with her. She was truly interested, and her questions were thoughtful as they made their way through the stacks of timber covered in snow, and then into the snow as the road ended.

"I've never seen anything so pretty," she said as the horses treaded along the edge of the trees.

He agreed, but he was looking at her, not the snow-covered ground and the massive pines. She wore a blue knitted hat, pulled down over her ears and forehead. It enhanced the delicateness of her features and the darkness of her brown eyes and lashes.

"How will we get one of these trees onto the sled?" she asked. "They are too big for the two of us to carry."

"They are?"

She laughed and bumped his shoulder with hers. "Yes. Not even you are that strong."

"Are you sure?"

"Very."

"So you think I'm a weakling?"

She laughed. "No, I think those trees are huge."

He nodded to the flatbed of the sled. "We have a rope hoist to load it on the sled, and the horses to pull it out of the woods."

"That sounds like a lot of work."

"Scared?" he asked her.

"No."

He laughed, fully believing her.

Chapter Twelve

The sun reflecting off the snow made everything look bright, white and glorious, and Emma was glad that she'd put her wool pants on beneath her dress and for the sweater she'd added beneath her coat. However, the chilly air didn't hamper her enjoyment as she wandered from tree to tree, looking for the one that would be perfect for the city park.

The untouched snow came to the tops of her boots and was deeper than that in areas where it had drifted. George had left the horses and sled in an open area, and he, too, was walking from tree to tree, waiting for one to whisper to him. The idea of that made her giggle.

"What's so funny over there?" he asked.

He looked very handsome and rugged in his red-and-black plaid shirt. Then again, he looked handsome no matter what he was wearing, and he fit in no matter what he was wearing. When he'd been wearing his uniform, he'd fit the role of a captain, and in his suit coat, he fit the part of businessman, and now, he fit the part of a lumberman.

There were no parts that she fit in, never had been.

She'd always just been her. Emma Leigh Ellis, no one special, no one unique. A girl from the slums of New York.

"Not going to tell me?"

He sauntered closer, giving her one of his teasing grins. She liked the teasing and grinned in return. "I was just wondering if a tree had whispered to you yet."

"Has one whispered to you?"

She walked toward him. "No."

They stopped, inches apart from each other, surrounded by tall pine trees. The air was chilly, the ground snow-coated, but she was warm, almost hot, and it wasn't because of the layers of clothing. It was her, all of her. Her body felt alive.

"You must not be doing it right," he said.

"Oh? What should I be doing?"

"Turn around."

She pivoted so her back was to him. "Now what?"

"Lean back."

She glanced over her shoulder. "Lean back?"

"Yes. I'm here. I won't let you fall."

He was standing behind her, but he could move, and then she would fall. Not that she had reason to believe that he would move, but he could. "Why do I have to lean back?"

"Because you have to trust. You have to trust that you won't fall, then you'll be able to trust yourself to hear."

Nervous, because she didn't want to fall, she rocked onto her heels, but stopped before actually leaning backward.

His hands settled on her upper arms. "Try again. I'm right here. Won't let you fall."

She closed her eyes, telling herself she could lean

back, that he was there, but couldn't. "What if I knock you over?"

"You won't. I promise."

Remembering how she'd feared her legs would give out earlier today, at his house, and how he'd kept her upright, she drew in a deep breath and pushed past the fear, leaning back.

The moment she leaned back enough that her balance threatened to slip away, panic filled her, but it was at that exact same moment that his arms folded around her from behind. He stepped closer, bringing her body back into balance, but she didn't need it, because his body, firm and solid behind her, was letting her know she was safe.

"Now, close your eyes," he whispered next to her ear. "And don't listen."

"Don't listen?" she whispered.

That was one of her problems—she listened to her own thoughts too much sometimes.

As if he knew what she was thinking, his arms tightened around her. "Don't think. Just feel."

She could feel. Feel his arms around her. His body pressed against her back, his chin resting on the top of her head. She could hear, too. Hear her heart thudding, her blood pounding at specific pulse points. Even as all that was happening, she also felt herself relaxing, as if her body was being absorbed by his, or maybe just merging with his.

A tension that she hadn't realized was there eased from her shoulders, her neck, her spine, and a soft, encompassing sense of well-being washed over her.

Then, almost as if out of nowhere, she had to open her eyes and turn slightly to the left—just her head, her neck. There it stood. A tree. The tree. Similar to all the others surrounding it, but somehow more beautiful. It would be the perfect tree to stand downtown, wishing everyone a merry Christmas.

"That's the one," she whispered.

He lifted one hand and pointed at the very tree she was looking at. "That one?"

His chin was still resting on the top of her head, and there were so many trees, he couldn't know exactly which one she'd chosen. Yet, he did.

She turned around, to face him, and with his arms still around her, they were so close she rested her forearms on his chest, her fingers on his shoulders. "How did you know which one I was looking at?"

"Because I knew which one it was. I saw it before we climbed off the sled. It's the perfect tree for the park." He leaned close enough so the tips of their noses briefly touched. "I knew you'd see it, too—you just needed to trust yourself. But you couldn't do that until you trusted me that the tree would pick itself."

Her insides were speaking to her again, but this time, they were focused on him. Specifically, they were telling her to kiss him. Her stomach fluttered. All she would have to do was stretch up onto her toes and their lips would be aligned. Tiny tremors rippled through her body.

Slowly, then faster, her hands inched upward. They looped around his neck and then she was kissing him.

And he was kissing her.

His lips were chilly at first, but quickly warmed, and the inner workings of his mouth were hot when their lips parted and so their tongues could play a game of hide-and-seek.

They would pause briefly, to breathe, to switch the positions of their heads, their hands, and then kiss again, and again.

When the kissing ended, she was light-headed and had to lean against him, fully trusting that he would hold her upright.

He held her until she felt able to stand on her own, and as if knowing exactly when that was, he leaned back and kissed the tip of her nose. "We better get that tree cut down or we are going to be stuck in the woods after dark."

She stepped backward and turned to look at the tree. It truly was the most beautiful one around. "What do we do first?"

"First we need to decide where we want it to fall, so it doesn't damage any branches or any other trees."

She asked how they would do that and listened intently to his answers. He was so knowledgeable about every aspect of the lumber industry. She couldn't imagine there would be a better person to lead a coalition supporting it.

Doing what she could to help, and standing out of the way when directed, she was in utter amazement when he felled the tree, hitched a horse to it with a heavy rope, pulled it out to the sled and winched it aboard the large flatbed. They had laughed nearly the entire time. Certain parts of what he'd done had been dangerous, and he'd been careful, but he'd also been playful and fun. He'd also been patient in explaining everything, like he had been when teaching Nathaniel how to play checkers.

It was nearly dark by the time they climbed into the small seat, and though there was enough fading sunlight to see, the absence of the bright rays made the air much colder.

"Snuggle close," George said. "It's going to be a cold ride."

He didn't have to suggest that twice. She could see his breath, and her own, and nearly glued herself against his side. "Will we take the tree to the park tonight?"

"No, just the lumberyard. I'll build a frame for the trunk so it can't tip over and then deliver it to the park tomorrow. Mother has it arranged with the city."

"I didn't see it stood up last year, but I tied a ribbon to it with your name on it."

"Thank you." He winked at her. "You'll see this one stood up. You have to. You helped cut it down."

"I watched it being cut down," she corrected.

"You handed me the saw."

She laid her head on his shoulder. "Because you wanted me to feel like I was helping."

"You were helping. It would have taken me longer by myself."

She doubted that but had truly enjoyed the entire event. "Thank you for letting me help you today. It was fun."

"I'm glad you enjoyed it because we'll be repeating it next weekend."

She sat up and leaned forward to see his face. "Why?"

He smiled. "A tree for the house, and one for your apartment, and Beverly's, if she wants one."

She'd had Christmas trees when her parents were alive, but after their father died, she and Sharon couldn't afford one, and since then, with it just being her, she didn't see the need, but might this year.

"Are you freezing yet?" he asked.

"No." She wiggled against him and laid her head on his shoulder again. "Are you?"

"No." George figured he could be dropped into the ice-cold Mohawk River right now and still be warm because of the way his blood was pounding through his body due to her being cuddled up to his side. An electric thrill had shot through him when she'd initiated their kissing earlier. He'd still be kissing her if he hadn't had to worry that they'd end up in the woods after dark.

Alone, he wouldn't have worried, but he wanted her to know she could trust him. Her aunt would not hurt her again, not under his watch. In fact, the more time he spent with her, the more the idea of retribution grew inside him. Emma should never have had to borrow money in order to move to Albany. She should never have had to roll cigars. Her mother should have inherited a goodly sum when Emma's grandfather died. Jill certainly had. She'd sold the family home, then she and Roy had built a new house on the south side of town.

"What will happen to the tree after it's taken down from the city park?" she asked.

He smiled. Of course, she would worry about that. "Do you want something special made out of it?"

"Made out of it?"

"Yes, it's big enough to be turned into lumber. Not a lot, but enough to make a small piece of furniture. A chair or side table, or a small chest. Would you like a chest, or maybe a jewelry box?"

"I don't have any jewelry."

"You will someday."

She lifted her head off his shoulder, and looked behind them, at the tree. "I like the idea that it will be made into something."

He made a mental note to have the lumber from the tree sent to Jepson's Woodworking. Joel Jepson did amazing work and would come up with a unique item for her. "It will be," he said.

A jewelry box is what he'd ask Joel to make, and he'd buy her jewelry for Christmas, so she'd have something to put in it.

They arrived at the stables a short time later, and Wayne was waiting for them. George turned over the horses and sled to the man and hurried Emma to the car. Someday, car manufactures would figure out a way for vehicles to have heaters, but this wasn't someday and the heat coming from the motor wasn't enough to chase the chill away as he drove to his house.

If she'd been a man, he would have stopped at the pub that the lumbermen often visited on cold days for a hot toddy. He'd see she got one as soon as they arrived home, or some hot mulled cider if she preferred.

As he'd assumed, Beverly was still at the house, and all smiles when they arrived. So were his parents, and upon saying hello, he excused himself, and Emma, so they could go upstairs and shed their wool clothes.

She used the hallway powder room, while he used the bathroom in his bedroom suite, and they once again met up in the hallway.

"We can go sit by the fireplace and warm up," he said. "Have some hot cider."

Her cheeks puffed as she glanced down the hallway, nodding.

He reached for her hand, entwined their fingers. Her

hand was warm, and small, delicate, next to his. He could tell her there was nothing to be nervous about, but that wouldn't ease her doubts. "The entire time I believed that I needed to marry Martha, my parents never once questioned her about our decision. They were never anything but respectful to her, and if I thought it would be different for you, we wouldn't be here right now. I promised you my protection, and you have it."

She looked down to the floor. "That's not a very kind position to put you in."

He lifted her chin with one finger. "I like the position that I'm in." It was hers that concerned him. "We have been given an opportunity, each of us. You can decide if you want to move, or if you want to continue living the life you've come to enjoy here in Albany, and I'll be able to put my plan for the lumber industry in place."

Her smile was gentle yet strained. "You don't need me for that. You just cut down a huge tree by yourself."

"It wasn't that big of a tree. Little more than thirty feet. I've cut down much bigger ones, and you helped me."

She shook her head while her teeth sunk into her bottom lip.

He weighed his options and came up with the only right thing to do. "There is another reason."

She looked at him and the way her hand tensed, he wondered if she was considering pulling it from his hold. He tightened it, so she couldn't. "I believe you've been wronged, Emma. Not just today, by your aunt, or the day she refused to give you a recommendation, and not just you, but your entire family."

Her sigh echoed in the hallway.

"When your grandfather died, your mother should have received an inheritance."

A frown formed.

"I don't know what was in his will, but he only had the two children, your mother and Jill. I can't believe he left everything to Jill and nothing to your mother."

Her frown grew. "I remember Aunt Jill saying that if mother left us, she'd have money. Money to pay for better doctors. My mother said she didn't need better doctors, and that no amount of money would make her leave her family."

"It would have been more than enough to pay for better doctors. Furthermore, your mother should have received the money when your grandfather died. You would have only been a baby then, or not even born. I don't remember him, but I know he died when Martha was a small child."

"There's nothing we could do about it now."

"I think there is, and I think it's worth investigating."

She was staring at him as if he'd lost his mind. "Aunt Jill would be furious."

"I'll protect you."

"Why?"

"Because I like you, and you don't deserve to be treated the way you've been treated." It might be more than liking her, but he wasn't ready to admit that. Couldn't, because he didn't know what it would mean. "This is your family legacy. You and your sister deserve to know the truth. To receive an inheritance that you should have received years ago."

"Sharon." Her voice was barely a whisper.

"Yes," he replied. Then, he suddenly realized something about her. She wasn't one to fight against something, but she would fight for something. That's why she was knitting scarves. She understood that's how to make an impact, how change was made. "You've already accomplished so much, and could do more if we find out the truth." He rubbed her hand. "Engaged to me, you have nothing to fear—I won't let anyone hurt you."

There was more confusion inside Emma than ever before, except for one thing. She touched George's cheek. "It's you that I don't want to see hurt. You and your family."

He stood still for a moment, looking at her. "Then let me help you. Let me stand bedside you, because not doing that is what will hurt me."

Her heart tumbled inside her chest and her eyes stung. He was so kind, so special.

George pulled her into a hug. A tight hug. She wrapped her arms around him and held on tight. It was impossible for her to not love him, and that was so frightening. So very frightening. Her parents had loved each other, but that love hadn't protected them from Aunt Jill's hatred. Hadn't protected any of them.

Her mother hadn't wanted money, and she didn't, either, but was George right? That it wouldn't end until she got to the truth—the reason behind Aunt Jill's hatred?

It was hard to explain, to anyone, but she'd once read a story about a garden of love. It had been full of flowers and then hatred had planted seeds that became weeds, and those weeds grew around the stems of all the flowers, strangling them. She'd never been able to forget that, never been able to not compare the story to her life.

His hold eased enough for him to lean down and kiss her, a soft, gentle kiss that melted her insides. She didn't want him to be hurt. Not by anyone, including her. She didn't want his garden to be taken over by weeds.

She was going to have to do this. There was no escape, and it would take more than begging for miracles.

"Ready to go downstairs?" he asked.

She took a moment to stare at him. She'd written that first letter to him because she'd wanted to help him, and if in some small way she could help him with his coalition, she would do it. Even if it meant facing her greatest fear. She now knew that it wasn't Aunt Jill that she feared the most. It was love. It was having to fight against the weeds that would always try to strangle it.

The air she drew in felt as if it rattled in her lungs, but she nodded. "Yes."

A few moments later, hand in hand, they entered the front room. His parents and Beverly were there, and Emma concluded that she not only had to convince these people that the engagement was real, but also couldn't let them think she was a coward.

"Thank you, Emma, for helping George get the tree for the park," his mother said. "I'm so excited we're able to provide it again, and I hope you'll be excited about who we are dedicating the tree to this year."

Emma accepted the cup of warm cider from George as he sat down beside her on the sofa. "I'm sure I will be," she said.

"It's the children," Beverly said excitedly. "Every child in the city."

"Yes," Amy said. "Children will be able to write their own name on a ribbon and tie it to the tree."

Emma stole a glance at George and took his slight shrug to say he hadn't known about that.

"There's more," Beverly said. "Women from across the city are going to collect gifts for children, and not just those we know about at the orphanage, but any child who needs a gift will get one this Christmas. Isn't that wonderful?"

"Yes, it is," Emma answered, feeling tears prick the backs of her eyes. Many more children had been affected than the ones she knew, but she'd known what she could do for them had been limited.

Between Beverly and Amy, Emma soon learned that the two women had been working on the project all afternoon, calling those who had left the meeting earlier, and all had agreed to help.

Amy explained that once the tree was up, even more people were sure to want to help, and the discussion about that continued until it was announced that dinner was ready to be served.

After they'd been seated, and the conversation had briefly bounced to a few subjects as they ate, his father said, "We, Amy and I, are sorry to hear that both of your parents have passed away, Emma. We hadn't known that."

Emma patted her lips with her napkin before acknowledging his statement. "Thank you."

"We are very sorry for your losses." Amy's voice and face held sincerity. "We knew them. Your mother and your father."

Learning they'd known her mother wasn't a surprise, but her father had never mentioned living in Albany. "You did? You knew my father?"

"Yes, he worked at North Country Logging," Craig said.

"That's how he met your mother," Amy said. "I remember when they eloped."

That was something else that Emma hadn't known. Perhaps that's what had started the bad feelings toward her father. "Did that upset my mother's family?"

"No, not that I recall." Amy shook her head. "Other than Jill, but she was always high-strung."

Chapter Thirteen

Hours later, Emma was lying in her bed, twisting the ring on her finger and thinking about the day and all that had happened. Craig and Amy had talked more about her family during dinner, including how they'd all been at her grandmother and grandfather's funerals—her, Sharon and their mother and father. She couldn't remember any of that and wasn't dwelling on it.

Instead, her thoughts were on George. He would be picking up her and Beverly tomorrow morning so they could help get everything ready for the tree ceremony. The idea of helping so many children filled her with joy. Almost as much joy as George did. She was in love with him, and though that scared her, she couldn't help but imagine how wonderful it would be if he loved her in return.

She would never expect him to do that, wasn't even certain she wanted it, but it sure was a wonderful thing to imagine.

Until she'd think about weeds and flowers and all sorts of other things.

So many things that she had a hard time falling

asleep and the following morning she was both apprehensive and excited for George to arrive. Excited to be helping with the tree and an event that so many children would benefit from, and apprehensive because every moment she spent with George could very well cause her to fall more in love with him.

The knock on her door sent her heart into a frenzy and it calmed considerably when she opened it to reveal Beverly, coat and purse in hand, standing there.

"Good morning, dear. George will be here shortly, and since we didn't have a chance to talk last night, I thought we could this morning," Beverly said all in one breath. "I'm dying, simply dying to know the details of him asking you to marry him. That certainly knocked the wind out of your aunt. I nearly peed myself with laughter. I truly did."

Emma had known this was coming and had lucked out last night because it had been well past Beverly's bedtime when George had brought them home. "I need to finish getting ready first." Emma closed the door. "Would you like a cup of tea?"

"No, thank you, I'll help you get ready." Beverly walked toward the bedroom. "That maroon dress is very becoming on you. I knew once you told George it had been you writing to him that everything would work out exactly as it should. I wish you could have seen Jill's face when Amy said you and I had been at their house for Thanksgiving. Jill looked like she'd seen a ghost, then turned beet-red and went off on a tangent that cleared the house."

They were in the bedroom and Emma walked to the mirror to check her hair, something she'd already done ten times this morning, but it made her look busy.

"Tell me, dear, when are the nuptials?"

Emma turned away from the mirror. She wanted to say "don't start looking at dress patterns," but couldn't because no one could know the truth about the engagement. "We haven't decided yet."

"Why not?"

Emma picked up the lint brush, then ran it over the front of her blue coat, which was hanging on the back of the bathroom door—it was something else she'd already done several times this morning. "We are taking time to get to know each other."

"What more is there to know? You've been writing to each other for a year and a half."

"He's only been home a short time."

"What aren't you telling me?" Beverly asked.

"We just aren't rushing anything." Emma took down her coat and carried it out to the other room, where her boots and wool pants were already sitting on the desk.

"Not rushing or avoiding?" Beverly's sigh echoed in the room. "Darling, this is your chance at happiness, don't let the past keep that from you. Don't let anything or anyone keep that from you."

She didn't want to, but there was more to it than that. She'd never been as happy as she had been living here, in this apartment, working at the school every day. She liked her independence, and even though there had always been the chance that she'd run into Aunt Jill at some point, she hadn't worried about it or the consequences, because she'd lived with that her entire life.

All of that had changed since George returned home, and her life could never go back to that happiness now, not here.

She was saved from accidently saying any of that

by a knock on the door. Wrenching the door open, she greeted George with her best false smile. "Good morning."

He glanced from her to Beverly with a single raised eyebrow. "Good morning." He dropped a quick kiss on her cheek. "Ready to go?"

She nodded.

"Yes, we are," Beverly said, and continued to chat all the way to the car, and then all through the drive to his house.

There, they separated briefly, for Emma to put her wool pants and boots on beneath her dress. It was another sunny day, and she was looking forward to helping him with the tree. She knew she wouldn't be able to avoid Beverly's questions the entire length of their fake engagement, but she would take every hour she could get of not having that conversation. Which made her feel guilty. Beverly was a dear friend, her only friend, and if the engagement was real, she would be revealing all the details to her. Just as she had read every letter he'd written to Beverly.

Once in the car, he said, "Beverly cornered you for answers this morning."

It was a statement, not a question, yet she answered, "Yes."

"Wanted to know when the wedding is?"

His profile even had a charming smile. "How did you know?"

"My mother asked me the same question."

"What did you say?"

"That we aren't rushing anything."

"That was my answer."

He glanced her way. "Forgive me, I didn't know some-one could own an answer."

She slapped his shoulder. "You know what I mean."

He not only had the best smile, he also had the best laugh, one that encouraged her to laugh along with him. Afterward, they talked about all sorts of things. That was so easy to do with him.

George purposefully kept the conversation light, afraid to say anything that might lessen her cheerful-ness. He'd imagined that Beverly did have questions, just as he'd known his parents would. They'd asked those questions this morning.

They weren't upset, just concerned that after all his years of insisting he and Martha would marry, merge the companies and create the largest lumber conglom-erate in the nation, that he'd chosen Emma to marry. His father had pointed out that even if she was due an inheritance, it wouldn't give her controlling interest in the company for a merger to happen—if that had been what George was still set upon doing.

That idea had never entered his mind, but should it have? Was that behind his interest in her? Did he see her as a means to an end?

If it was, it was sure to do just the opposite.

It would take months, perhaps years if there were legal issues, for her to get what was coming to her, if there was any inheritance, and in the meantime, North Country Logging could cut all ties with Weston Lum-ber.

Jill was ruthless enough to do that, but her hatred toward Emma aside, just as Weston Lumber had the choice to work with others, so did North Country. However, neither were currently doing that. North Country was logging Weston land right now and could stop, which would halt lumber production. It would take time to get other loggers onto their land and logs to the mill. Instead of creating the biggest company, his actions might send it spiraling downward.

He hadn't thought of any of that because when he was with Emma, he wasn't thinking about anything but her and him. With her he felt things he'd never felt before.

Their engagement was simply an arrangement, not a real promise of marriage, but either—a fake engagement or a real marriage to her—could ruin Weston Lumber. That was the exact opposite of what he'd always wanted. Of what he'd promised he'd do.

He'd just been a kid when he'd made that promise, and a kid when he'd vowed to wed Martha, and though he was a grown man now, and understood the immaturity of those initial promises, his actions held consequences that affected more than just him.

Weston was one of the largest employers in the county. Men—families—depended on their jobs. Other companies depended upon the wood Weston Lumber milled.

It was a doubled-edged sword because he'd made a promise to Emma, too. Not the engagement, but to help discover the truth, and he wanted to keep that promise. She had been hurt, mistreated, and that wasn't right, yet, in keeping his promise to her, others could get hurt.

He'd thought he understood the complexities of life. Instead, he'd created one that was too complex for clear understanding.

Bottom line was, people didn't need to love in order

to get hurt, and he wasn't sure what that meant for him. For his reasons to never get married. Not that it truly mattered. Emma didn't want to get married. She didn't want to get stuck in that life.

Weston Lumber was as quiet as a ghost town this morning. Unlike logging camps, it was closed on Sundays. He pulled his car into the parking area, and warned as they exited the car, "Be careful where you step. Frozen ground or not, the sun has a way of making mud."

"I wore my boots again today." She lifted a foot to show him.

He'd already noticed her boots. Noticed everything about her the moment she'd opened her apartment door. He'd also noticed Beverly, and if the older woman hadn't been standing right behind Emma, he would have done more than just kiss her cheek.

He should never have given in to that first kiss. It had made him want more, and the second one had increased that want tenfold. Never had a kiss consumed him. Nothing had ever consumed him except for Weston Lumber.

"We'll be over there." He pointed to the workshop building, one of the numerous buildings, sheds and work areas. "We'll build the frame in there and then carry it out and attach it to the tree." Then, because his thoughts could ruin the day if he didn't let them go, he shot her a grin. "Bet you always wanted to be a carpenter, didn't you?"

"I've never built anything." Her smile lit up her face. "Except for a gingerbread house. I made one of those last year, but I don't think that qualifies."

"Why not? All it takes to make anything is the right tools and ingredients."

"Is that so?"

He draped an arm around her shoulders and tugged her closer. "Yes."

She looped her arm around his back. "Just so you know, the icing didn't stick and my gingerbread house collapsed."

He laughed.

They continued to laugh through the morning of building the base from rough milled lumber, carrying it outside and attaching it to the base of the tree that was still on the flatbed sled.

"Do we take it to the park now?" she asked, swiping her gloves together to knock off lingering sawdust.

He dropped the hammer into the toolbox and picked it up by the handle. "No, Wayne and a couple other men will do that, and help set it up." In jest, he reached out and gave her upper arm a squeeze. "I need more help than these puny arms to do that."

Her appalled look was fake. The twinkle in her eyes gave it away. "I'll have you know, these puny arms helped carry that frame out here."

"That's how I know I'll need more help to set up the tree."

Quite adorably, she planted her hands on her hips. "I didn't hear you complaining."

"Because I couldn't talk," he teased. "It was taking all I had to carry the frame."

She slapped his arm and then squeezed his bicep. "Maybe you're the weakling."

"I was the one carrying the bulk of the weight."

"Oh, stop." She let out an exaggerated sigh while biting back the grin that was making her eyes twinkle even more. "Quit picking on me."

He wasn't picking on her, he was flirting, and she was flirting with him. Good thing this engagement was fake, because if it was real, he'd have to marry her before Christmas. It would be either that, or ravish that perfect little body of hers out of wedlock.

It would be incredible. He didn't need any convincing to know that. Nor did he need to never have craved a woman before to know that's exactly what he was doing right now.

He craved her.

Craved her company.

Craved her attention.

Craved her kisses.

And more. Far more. Not just her body. Her. All of her. Body and soul.

Those were things he'd never have imagined he'd one day want, and those were things that didn't fit into his life, the one he'd set up for himself. It would be like trying to fit a square peg in a round hole.

That was an image he didn't need in his mind right now.

Worse yet, none of that was what she wanted.

"You're grinning. Thinking about picking on me some more?" she said.

He set the toolbox back on the sled. "I'm not thinking about picking on you."

Tilting her head sideways, she looked into his eyes as if searching for her own answer. "Then what are you thinking about?"

He had a choice, but right now, it was between slim

pickings and next to nothing that he'd change his mind about what he was about to do. Still, he gave himself a moment as he asked, "Do you really want to know?"

Her answer was little more than a whispered "Yes," and a nod.

"This," he said as his lips met hers.

The kiss was one he'd been thinking about all morning. Not quick, or a slow, exploring one. It was the type of kiss a man gave a woman when he craved her.

All of her.

Their bodies were pressed together, and he wished that there were no heavy coats between them. No layers of material at all. He could feel her breathing. It was as fast as his. As hot as his.

Sharing the same air with her was extraordinary. He couldn't remember a single moment in time that compared to how he felt. To the life she breathed into him.

A portion of her breath was still in his lungs when the kiss ended, and she looked up at him. Smiled.

"Well," she said. "That certainly was something to be thinking about."

He couldn't feel happier, but did as he agreed, "It was."

Emma's heart would never be the same. Something had happened to it during their kissing. Something as real as the air they breathed, as bright as the sun shining down upon them and as beautiful as the smile on his face.

And she didn't have the slightest idea what to do about any of that.

As luck would have it, she didn't need to figure that out right now because a truck entered the lot and drove all the way to where they were standing near the sled. She recognized the driver as Wayne, the stableman from yesterday, but had never met the passenger.

"Rex and I shoveled the spot at the city park." Wayne climbed out of the truck and then lifted a big shovel out of the back. "Borrowed the scoop shovels out of the stables."

"This looks good," the other guy said, walking over to look closer at the frame on the tree.

"Emma, this is Rex McKay," George said. "Rex, this is Emma, who helped me build the frame."

Tall, with a face full of gray whiskers, Rex made a show of touching the short brim of his knitted hat. "It's nice to meet you, Emma, and now I know why the frame turned out so well."

"Thank you." Glancing up at George, she added, "It's all in getting the angles right." He'd told her that, and many other things that she'd found interesting, but right now she was teasing him as he had her.

Rex laughed, so did Wayne, and George, while shaking his head at her.

He knew she was teasing, just as she'd known when he'd been teasing her, and that connection to him was special. Made her feel special.

She'd never felt special, not ever.

That wasn't true. She'd started feeling special while writing to him—being with him in person just made it more real.

It was more than that. He made life more real, and that made her wonder if she'd been living it wrong.

Chapter Fourteen

If she had been living life wrong, Emma was living it right today. She'd never participated in something as wonderful as the tree ceremony. Children were skating on the pond, warming their hands over the fire in a big barrel that had been cut in half, and eating the cookies that had been supplied by women of the committee.

Nearly, if not more, than half the city had to be in attendance, excited to tie a ribbon on the tree and pledging to provide gifts for children and drop them off at Weston Lumber.

George seemed to know everyone, or they knew him. He held her hand as they mingled through the crowds, where she encountered many children from school, and met their parents, and said hello to several teachers that she recognized, but had never befriended.

The park was downtown and took up several blocks, which meant there were several streets leading to it, and each one was lined with parked cars. Yet, people continued to arrive as the afternoon slowly slipped into evening. The entire lower part of the tree, every branch within reach, was covered with ribbons of all colors.

It truly was the perfect tree, and she would never have imagined that her desire to knit scarves for a few children would have turned into so many other children receiving gifts for Christmas.

That was the topic of discussion around the table later that evening at George's house, where she and Beverly once again joined his family—the gifts and how to get them to the children. It was determined that having them delivered on Christmas Eve would be best and Craig said that he was sure he had employees who wouldn't mind delivering gifts rather than working in the yard that day.

The main dilemma was finding where all the children lived. There were so many throughout the city who had lost fathers to the war or mothers to the pandemic who might not have gifts for Christmas.

Emma suggested the schools, and everyone agreed that was an excellent idea. She had never been so proud, so connected with other people. Especially George. She couldn't help but smile every time she looked at him, and when their eyes met, it felt as if her entire being smiled.

The week that followed was so busy with collecting names and sorting gifts, which filled one entire room at Weston Lumber, that Emma barely had time to think. The only time she and George had alone was when he would drive her back and forth to school.

When he'd been outside her apartment on Monday morning, she'd questioned why, and he'd explained that he was driving that way, anyway, and might as well give her a ride to school. The same had happened when he'd been outside of the school building that afternoon, and proclaimed she had to see the number of gifts that had been dropped off at the lumberyard that day.

On Saturday, they went into the woods to cut down a tree for his home and brought Nellie and Nathaniel with them so they could pick out the tree for their house.

George dropped her off at her apartment afterward so she could get ready for a Christmas party his mother was hosting, which was to be at the hotel again.

Beverly stepped out of her apartment as Emma reached the top of the stairs.

"I've been watching for you," Beverly said. "Come see what I have for you."

"For me?" Emma asked. "Why?"

Beverly merely smiled and waved her into the apartment.

Emma had been busy each evening lately, but so had Beverly. It was as if she'd become a member of the Weston family. She was often already at the lumberyard when Emma arrived and stayed until George gave them both either a ride home, or a ride to his house, where they'd eat supper.

Stepping into the apartment, Emma gasped at the gown hanging on the back of the bedroom door. Deep red and made of velvet, with white lace on the scalloped neckline, cuffs and hem, the dress was stunning. There was also a row of silk-covered buttons down the front and a tufted waist.

"It's for you," Beverly said.

Emma moved closer, examining the dress and the silk underskirt. "It's gorgeous. Mrs. Martin outdid herself on this one." The party was sure to be as big as George's welcome-home party and she'd been wondering about what to wear. In the end, she'd planned on wearing the same dress she'd worn to George's party. Turning to Beverly, she asked, "When did you have time to see if she had anything available? You've been helping with the gifts all week."

Beverly shrugged. "While you were at work. I got a new one, too, but neither of them came from Mrs. Martin. George bought them."

"George?"

"Yes, he asked me to go shopping with him the other morning, to get the size right, and insisted upon buying mine, too, for helping him." Beverly walked over and unhooked the hanger of the red dress from the top of the door. "Go, now, take your bath and get ready. He'll be here to pick you up again before you know it. I won't be riding with you. Willis is coming for me. I've been like a built-in chaperone for you two lately, but not tonight."

A thrill shot through Emma. She never minded having Beverly with her and George, nor had she minded having Nellie and Nathaniel with them today. It was just that since the day of the tree celebration, she and George had only been alone long enough for quick kisses, and she was longing for another one like the one that they'd shared while building the tree frame.

The other thing that hadn't yet happened was that they hadn't talked about how all of this would end. Their engagement. At night, when she'd lie down, she'd think about that, about how it wouldn't last much longer, but was always so tired, she fell asleep before any answers would come to her.

Even now, as the thoughts formed, she shoved them aside in order to get ready for the party.

He arrived at her door with a red-rose corsage that he pinned to her dress, and then, as if wishes could come true, he kissed her.

A long, wonderful kiss that heated her so thoroughly, she considered leaving her coat behind.

That would have been foolish, and she slipped her arms into her coat as George held it for her, and they left.

"I've missed you," he said as they drove to the hotel.

"You've seen me every day," she reminded him.

"But we've barely had a moment alone, and I'm afraid we won't tonight, either. Or tomorrow." He gave her hand a squeeze. "I'll be glad when Christmas is over."

That gave her an opening to ask what would happen then, but she chose not to take it. She was doing that a lot more lately—making a choice to not think about what would happen when Christmas was over. It was as if she was having a wonderful dream and didn't want to wake up from it.

"I've arranged a truck for you and I to use on Christmas Eve," he said. "To deliver the gifts to the children at the orphanage."

"You have?"

"Yes. I thought it fitting that you deliver those gifts."

She leaned over and kissed his cheek. "Thank you."

Her heart was so full of happiness, she didn't think anything could hamper it…until several hours later, when she exited the powder room and came face-to-face with her Aunt Jill.

Arms crossed over her bosom, with her lips pursed and icy eyes staring at her like they always had—like she wanted to spit on her—Aunt Jill said, "You think you have this all figured out, don't you? How long did you and your father plot this?" Her sneer increased.

"And your sister. I'm sure she has something to do with this, too, because Lord knows you aren't smart enough to come up with it on your own."

A thousand thoughts rushed through Emma's mind like a flock of birds leaving a tree at the same time. "My father—"

"Don't even mention him!" Jill hissed. "He's like a disease that won't go away!" She stepped closer. "So are you. You're nothing but scum. Everyone will see that soon, then you'll know that I'm the one in charge. I'm the one who's always been in charge." Pointing a finger, she went on. "You will never see a dime. Not one dime of my father's money. What you will see is the ruin of Weston Lumber."

Emma shivered as if a draft of ice-cold air had just struck.

"You'll ruin him, just like your father ruined your mother." Jill's waggling finger came closer. "Listen and listen well. You either take your claws out of George, or I'll see his company run into the ground. Don't think his little idea of working with other companies will save it, either. I've been in this business a lot longer than him. Without my company logging Weston property, they won't have any lumber to sell. Don't think for a moment that I haven't researched all of my options and that I won't do whatever it takes to get rid of you once and for all."

The moment George stepped into the hall, he cursed and rushed forward. It had been the first time all night that he'd let Emma out of eyesight, and he shouldn't have done that. Jill had her cornered outside the powder room.

Her aunt moved past Emma, entering the powder room before he got there.

Grasping Emma's shoulders, he asked, "Are you all right?"

No, he could see she wasn't. She was ashen and trembling, and he wanted to knock down the powder-room door, give Jill the same type of tongue-lashing that she liked to deliver. There was no doubt she'd just delivered one.

"Yes," Emma said. "I'm fine."

She didn't sound fine. He pulled her into his arms. Held her tight. "I'm sorry, honey. So sorry. I—"

"It's fine," Emma said, her voice sounding shaky. "She just said some things about my father again. That he's a disease that won't go away."

He kissed her forehead. "I didn't know she was here." He hadn't seen Jill or Roy tonight, but hadn't looked for them, either, and the hotel was as packed as the tree ceremony had been. It was of little consolation, yet he repeated, "I'm sorry."

She stiffened and pushed against his chest to separate them. "It's fine. I—I think I'd like a glass of wine."

"All right." He searched her face. Color was returning, but the shine was gone from her eyes. "Or we can leave."

She shook her head. "No."

Stepping from his hold, she began walking away and he could have sworn he heard her say "the damage is done."

George caught up to her in a single stride. "What?"

"Nothing." With a heavy sigh, she added, "She had her say. That's what she'd wanted."

He wanted to know more. He wanted to know every

word Jill had said. He'd promised to protect Emma, and he'd failed.

He'd failed in other ways, too. The fake engagement had become real to him.

They entered the ballroom and he flagged down a waiter, ordered Emma a glass of wine and then escorted her to their table, where others were taking a break from dancing and visiting.

Keeping his anger at Jill contained was killing him, and it grew as he watched Emma sip her wine and smile, and talk with Janice about the tree the children had picked out this morning.

The only thing that saved his anger from totally consuming him was his attraction to Emma. That consumed him so fully, there wasn't room for anything else to completely take over. What he felt for her was everywhere. From his head to his toes, but mostly in his heart. That's where he felt her.

He wondered what she would say when he told her that he wanted the engagement to continue beyond Christmas. That is what he wanted. He wanted it to continue right up to their wedding day. But was afraid. He might have changed his mind about marriage, but there was no guarantee that she had.

She kissed him like she might be open to the idea, and that was the only reason why he'd yet to mention it. That and the fact they'd barely had two minutes alone the last week. He'd wait until after Christmas, when things slowed down, to mention any of it.

Wait until after he repaired his mistake—that of failing her.

He had to make that right before asking her anything.

She'd trusted him and he had to prove that he wouldn't do that again. Would never fail her again.

George didn't need to question what that meant. He knew. He'd fallen in love with Emma.

He'd loved before—his family, his brother—and still loved them, but loving her was different. It had been so new and unfamiliar at first that he hadn't wanted to acknowledge it. Hadn't wanted to think about what it would do to his life.

Now he knew. It was wonderful. It would make his life wonderful. His only question was if it would make her life wonderful, too.

It hadn't so far, and he had to change that.

George set his plan into place the next morning. Emma, Beverly, his mother, aunt, cousin and several other women were packing gifts in crates and bags, and creating delivery routes for the drivers to use on Tuesday. His mother insisted everything be completed today, leaving tomorrow for last-minute additions that would still allow the drivers to set out first thing Tuesday morning.

His father was standing near the doorway of the huge room in their office building, which had been completely taken over by the project. "This has become bigger than some companies in this city."

George nodded as he stepped up next to his father. "It has."

"And I have a feeling it's going to be repeated in future years," his father said.

George agreed and wasn't opposed to helping each and every year, but that wasn't what he needed to speak to his father about. "I need to tell you something."

His father nodded and waved a hand toward the hallway.

Upon climbing the stairway and entering his father's office, George closed the door behind him. "Taking over this company was always my goal. Managing it, growing it…" He shrugged. "Living it."

Arms crossed and leaning against the front of his desk, his father nodded. "I know."

With no regrets or second thoughts, George stated, "If I have to make a choice between Emma and Weston Lumber, I choose Emma."

"Why would you have to make a choice?"

"North Country Logging, namely Jill."

His father nodded. "You've heard what she's been saying."

Anger flashed through George. "What has she been saying?"

"She claims Fred, her father, disowned Ruth, Emma's mother, when she eloped with William, and that Emma, along with her father, when he'd been alive, had been plotting to get their hands on North Country Logging ever since Ruth died."

Instantly defensive, George said, "That's not true! When did she tell you that? Why didn't you tell me? Her hatred—"

"I know, son. I know." Shaking his head, he continued, "Jill didn't tell me. Roy did, last night, and he's worried that Jill is out of control. He hadn't known that either Ruth or William had passed away. What he has discovered since learning that is that Jill never dispersed the inheritance, and she wanted the marriage between you and Martha in order to merge the companies, because that meant there would be no monies exchanged. North Country Logging would be dissolved, no longer exist."

"So there would be nothing for Emma or her sister to ever inherit," George said. Understanding more, he said, "Jill's been planning this since Ruth died, and before that, she spent years trying to break up Emma's family."

His father lifted an eyebrow.

"Emma told me that Jill visited them yearly and tried to convince Ruth to leave her family and return to Albany."

His father shook his head as he pushed off his desk and walked to the window. "When Fred and my father started these companies, it was a true partnership. They shared everything. Their employees would cut lumber all winter, and mill it all summer. It wasn't until my father married my mother that the companies made a formal separation. My father said he was staying here, in Albany, year-round, with his family."

Turning about, his father continued, "My father made a choice—his family over the company—so what you said about choosing Emma is nothing new. It's how it should be. When a man loves a woman, has a family, they come first. It sounds like Ruth chose that, too."

George nodded, yet he admitted, "I wanted you to know so you wouldn't be disappointed."

"You've never disappointed me."

"My choice could cause North Country to cut all ties with us."

"Business—life, for that matter—is full of risks." His father shrugged. "The best advice I can give on that is sometimes you go by your gut, sometimes by your heart." He scratched the side of his face in front of one ear. "Your mother and I had to do that, with you. We were never an opponent of you and Martha marrying. She's a nice enough girl and I wish her all the best. At first, we thought it was just two young children with unrealistic expectations, but when that never changed as you grew up, we became concerned, but ultimately had to go with our hearts and believe that you'd make the right decision for your life."

Reading between the lines, George said, "You knew Jill was behind it."

"Yes, and if you recall, anytime I brought it up, you became more determined, so I bit my tongue and your mother gnawed off her fingernails as we waited for you to figure out you had choices."

Embarrassed to admit it, George said, "I would have done it, Dad. I would have married Martha if she hadn't called off the wedding."

"And you would have accepted the consequences," his father said. "Because that's who you are. You've never shied away from responsibilities. But I'm glad that didn't happen, and so is your mother."

"I am, too. Very glad, but what should we do about Jill? About North Country?"

His father shook his head. "You've already done it. You've put the wheels in motion. Come spring, we'll be accepting delivery of logs from other loggers. If North Country defaults or pulls their contracts, we'll go out on the market and buy more logs. We can afford it."

"And the family alliance?" George asked.

"I'll leave that up to you and Emma," his father said with a grin. "She is Jill's niece, but she'll be your wife and therefore our daughter-in-law, the only one we'll ever have, and we'll always support the two of you, in every decision you make."

George smiled sadly. Emma would be the only daughter-in-law his parents would ever have, but only if he could change her mind about marriage.

His father squeezed his shoulder. "In my opinion, we better hold on to our hats."

"Why?"

"Emma had the idea to help children, and your mother bought in hook, line and sinker. Look what they created. Trust me, this won't be the last thing those two come up with."

"Probably not," George agreed, laughing.

"We should go see if we can help get things wrapped up here. Otherwise, we'll be decorating a tree at midnight. It's on your mother's list of things to be completed today."

George knew that, and he knew exactly when he'd ask Emma to make their engagement real. Tuesday. While delivering gifts to the orphanage.

Chapter Fifteen

Emma had been at school for less than an hour Monday morning when she was asked to report to the principal's office by the school secretary. That had never happened before, and she assumed it had to do with the gift-giving program. Perhaps Mr. Segal had a family that he wanted to include on the list. The teachers had all been more than willing to help and had expressed gratefulness on behalf of the children they knew the program would benefit.

The number of gifts that had come in was shocking, but Amy was so good at organizing and planning things that even with a few additions, everything would be delivered to the children tomorrow. On Christmas Eve.

Emma was overjoyed with the entire program and was looking forward to seeing the children at the orphanage tomorrow.

With happiness filling her, she entered the school office and crossed the room to the door of the principal's office.

Mr. Segal was a large man, with a ring of black hair around his otherwise bald head and black-rimmed glasses that sat low on his nose. His deep voice could be considered intimidating to both children and adults.

"Miss Ellis," he said, gesturing to a chair near the door of his rather small office, compared to his size, upon her entrance.

George was taller than Mr. Segal, and his shoulders broader, but Mr. Segal was certainly broader in all other areas.

She found herself doing that all the time—comparing George to every other man she encountered—and tried to clear her mind as she sat and folded her hands on her lap.

"It's been brought to my attention," Mr. Segal said, looking at her over the rim of his glasses, "that your position here is no longer needed. Your final pay will be mailed to you at the end of the month."

Emma was too stunned to speak. To think. It took several seconds before she was able to say anything. "No longer needed?"

"That's what I said." He waved at the door. "My secretary has collected your coat and whatever else. You can get it from her."

Overwhelmed with shock, confusion and questions, Emma didn't move. Couldn't. This didn't make any sense. Mrs. Davis, the librarian, had praised her work the entire time she'd been here. Needing some sort of clarity, she asked, "Excuse me, Mr. Segal, but I have done something wrong?"

"Please don't insult neither mine nor your intelligence with unnecessary questions. I said your position is no longer needed."

Other questions formed, but she accepted he wouldn't answer them, so she stood, on weak, trembling legs, and walked out of his office. His secretary, Miss Wallace, was standing there, with Emma's blue coat and purse in hand.

"I'm sorry, Miss Ellis," the woman whispered, shaking her head so hard that her red curls bobbed. "So sorry. You've been wonderful. Mrs. Davis is beside herself at the news."

Mrs. Davis was a dear. Working with her had been wonderful. And the children… Emma shook her head, trying to keep the tears at bay. "Thank you," she said, taking her coat and purse.

"I wish I knew why he was doing this," Miss Wallace said. "I truly do."

So did Emma, but voicing it was impossible. Barely managing to get the word out, she whispered, "Goodbye."

The principal's office was near the front door, and she grasped ahold of the banister as she maneuvered down the outside steps of the building. Without the banister, she may not have been able to walk without falling. She couldn't imagine this was because of the gift program, and Mrs. Davis had never suggested she'd done anything wrong.

It was so shocking. So confusing.

George had given her a ride to school, so she wasn't wearing her wool pants or boots, but was too numb to notice the cold as she began the walk home. Still holding back tears, she purposefully didn't look behind her, at the school. If she did, the tears would start rolling.

She hadn't yet reached the end of the block, when the *ahooga* of a horn honking sounded behind her. It couldn't be George, yet she turned to look because she certainly could use his comforting arms around her right now.

It wasn't his black-and-red car; instead, it was a bright blue one, driving slowly.

Emma's entire being turned colder than the air as the car rolled up next to her, with the woman driving it showing a grin so evil the devil would be frightened.

"I told you to heed my warnings," Aunt Jill said. Then, she sped up and drove away, her cackling laugh echoing in the car's wake.

At that moment, it felt as if a hole had opened in the ground beneath Emma's feet and sucked her into it.

She hadn't truly disappeared, but it felt as if her entire world had.

She should have expected something like this to happen. She'd known the life she'd been living couldn't last. She should have imagined that her aunt would do just as she'd said. Ruin everything. But the ultimate truth was it was never real, and could never have lasted. George could never be engaged to, let alone marry, a girl like her. Why, when had she let herself believe that?

The tears could no longer be contained because she understood exactly what this meant.

By the time she got home, she was stiff from the cold, and her face numb from the tears that had fallen for several blocks. She could no longer feel her heart beating, either—it was as if it had frozen, too. Either that, or she was so full of anxiety, of worry, that she couldn't feel anything. Her entire being had turned to ice. The panic that had overtaken her at times had gone from ragged and wild, to suffocating. At the moment, she just felt exhausted, like there wasn't a single part of her that could go on, could function.

She sat on the sofa, head in her hands, as all sorts of thoughts swam about in all directions.

One stuck out. Aunt Jill would ruin Weston Lumber. Run it into the ground. She'd gotten her fired from the school to prove she could do anything.

Anything.

Emma rubbed her forehead, hating the thought that came next. The life she'd been living here was over. Over.

And she had no one to blame but herself.

Feeling came back to her body with stabbing, burning jolts of pain, and her thoughts faded as if she was awakening from a dream.

All except for one.

She had to leave. Now.

Leaping to her feet, she paced the floor, looking around at all the things she'd acquired since moving here. Dishes and rugs, the picture of a ballerina, the vase with the rose painted on it, the books stacked on the desk and the lamp with the fringes on the shade.

They were little things, replaceable things, but she loved them. Bought them with money she'd earned. It was as if they were proof that she hadn't gotten stuck in the slums.

It was the things that she couldn't see that were really breaking her heart.

The children at school.

Beverly.

George.

Her heart felt as if it was breaking in two and her

lungs forgot to breathe, sending her body into mini spasms of panic as she tried to gulp for air. She clung to the back of a kitchen chair until air finally filled her lungs.

After that, reality came in flashes. There were moments she knew what she was doing, and moments when the fog in her mind was so thick that she just moved, making decisions that moments later she'd change, question why she'd put something in her suitcase, take it out and replace it with something that couldn't be left behind.

She couldn't say if reality ever truly returned while she was at her apartment. At some point, a strange hollowness had filled her, and it was still there when the taxi dropped her off at the train station. It remained as she stood in line and eventually showed her ticket to the man inside the caged booth.

It was the one she'd bought to go to New York City after Sharon's baby arrived. She wouldn't stay there long. Just long enough to figure out a place where no one would find her.

Not ever.

"Your train won't leave for an hour," the man said, sliding the ticket back under the bars. "The porter will validate it after you board. Next!"

"Thank you." She took the ticket and stepped aside, moving automatically and without feeling. The station was full of people, but there were open spaces on the benches in the center of the large depot. She remembered admiring the beauty of the building when she'd first arrived in Albany, but now it was all just a blur.

She found a spot to sit, set her one and only suitcase

on the floor by her feet, her purse on the bench beside her, and tried not to think.

Not think about all she was leaving behind. She'd long ago learned that her feelings didn't matter and it was foolish to believe that they did this time.

George used the key Beverly had given him to enter her apartment, and upon closing the door, he saw the bags of scarves, hats and mittens that she'd described. She had forgotten them this morning when Willis had picked her up to finish the preparations for distributing the gifts. She'd been beside herself at her forgetfulness and he'd offered to drive over and pick them up for her.

He chuckled when he saw the hat hanging on the hook above the bags. The one with the daisy pinned to it. A lot had changed since the day he'd met her at the train station.

George then turned to the table, to look for the gloves that Beverly had also forgotten and asked him to retrieve. They were there, but as he approached the table, he noticed a key lying there, identical to the one in his hand, and a ring.

His ring.

The one he'd given Emma.

There was also a note, with handwriting that he instantly recognized.

A shiver rippled over him as he stared at the cream-colored paper. Images of letters flashed through his mind. Every letter that Emma had written him.

On their own accord, his eyes scanned the first line, then he grabbed the note off the table, read it completely, with his heart pounding the entire time.

Dearest Beverly,

I'm already missing you and haven't even left yet, but I must, and I must hurry. I'll write when I can. Please give George the ring and tell him I'm sorry. So very sorry.

Please tell Mr. Allen that whoever rents my apartment can have everything I left behind, unless there are things you want. Perhaps the vase with the flower painted on it that you admired? There will be a letter arriving for me from the school, please forward it to Sharon's address in New York.

Thank you.

I'm going to miss you very much.

Love,

Emma

Her sister's address was written beneath her name.

He flipped the note over, searched the table for something, anything, that might tell him more, but there was nothing.

Nothing to tell him what the hell was going on, what any of this meant.

His throat burned as he read the note again. The penmanship was the same, yet it wasn't as smooth as usual, as if she'd been shaking while writing.

Something stronger than fear and rawer than anger rose in him. It was pain. That of losing someone he loved. She was gone and had no intention of returning. Ever.

Why?

He knew the answer to that.

He'd trapped her. The one thing that she hadn't wanted.

Sick to his stomach, he leaned over the table, staring at the ring and breathing through the pain.

Then he grabbed the ring and shoved it in his pocket, along with the letter.

The engagement had been fake, a deal they'd struck, but he'd made it real, and in doing so had scared her off.

She'd even quit her job. A job she'd loved. All because of him.

Marriage hadn't been something she'd wanted. She'd told him that the first time they'd met. He'd told her the same thing.

Because he'd known marriage wasn't for him.

That it would never be for him.

Nor was love. It only caused pain. Raw, hot, searing pain.

Furious at himself, he grabbed Beverly's gloves and threw the door open. Taking one step over the threshold, he remembered the bags he'd been sent there to retrieve. He walked back inside, grabbed the bags and left.

After locking the door, he realized the white hat with the daisy pinned to it had fallen into one of the bags. So be it. He wasn't unlocking the door to put it back. He'd deliver the stuff to Beverly, and then he was leaving.

It didn't matter where he went, just out of here.

Out of town.

If Emma wasn't here, he didn't want to be, either.

At his car, he threw the bags on the seat beside him, started the engine and laid his foot hard on the gas accelerator as he pulled away from the curb. His anger was rising. At how foolish he'd been.

Why hadn't he talked to her? Asked her why she

felt trapped and what he could do about that? Tell her that he'd choose her above all else, and always would?

He'd told his father that, so why hadn't he told Emma? Instead, he kept making excuses that he'd wait, claiming in his own mind that there hadn't been time.

But there had been time. Every night when he walked her to her door, every morning when he'd picked her up. Damn it! He could have made time. She was more important than anything else.

Blinded by the anger filling him, he had to slam on the brake pedal to keep from hitting the car ahead of him. Taking his fury out on the other driver, he squeezed the bulb on the horn, then swerved, shot around the car and barely missed colliding with an oncoming truck.

That's when it struck him, when he was back in his own lane, with the collision avoided.

He hadn't told Emma, he hadn't done anything, because he'd been afraid of the risk. Afraid of saying anything for fear of what her answer might have been.

That seemed inconceivable. He'd taken risks every day while in the army. As their captain, he'd led his entire unit through peril regularly, and there had been no sure outcome with any of their missions. Except the desire to return home. For all of them. Including him. His goal had been to meet the woman writing him letters.

Emma had been his reason for taking risks overseas.

Then, after meeting her, falling deeper in love with her, he'd feared that he had a reason to love her, but she hadn't had a reason to love him. Because he didn't want her to love him. Because he was afraid of getting hurt. Afraid of her getting hurt.

He convinced himself that he'd come up with the fake engagement to get back at Jill King, for how she'd treated Emma—a means to an end. But that wasn't completely true. He'd already been in love with Emma and was afraid to admit it.

Damn it! He'd returned home and put himself right back in the role he'd always had as the man who would ensure Weston Lumber continued to prosper.

He hadn't been that man in the service. There, he'd put everything on the line to complete a mission.

What had happened to that man? To Captain Weston? He was using the skill, training and knowledge he'd gained to secure a future for more than one company, because he knew there was more to life than a company, any company.

Why hadn't he realized there was more to life than the past, too? He'd been seven when Robert had died, and, yes, it had changed his life. Changed who he would become, but he'd always had a say in his future. He'd chosen not to say it. His fear of people being hurt had caused more hurt, more pain, and he was solely to blame for that.

Tears blurred her vision as Emma stared at the letter in hand. She'd read all of George's letters while sitting in the crowded station, waiting for the train, and each one made the pain inside her grow. The thought of never seeing him again was worse than anything she could imagine.

Far worse than losing her job, or her apartment, or anything that Aunt Jill could do, and far more painful. It hurt to even breathe.

An announcement of the next train departure echoed through the depot.

Her train.

She wiped the tears from her cheeks with her hand, then carefully slid the letter back in the envelope and replaced it in her purse, where all the other letters from George were tied together. They were her most prized possessions. Each one of them was special, not only in what he'd written, but also because of the joy she'd felt upon receiving each one.

Those letters had changed her life. Changed her.

"Excuse me, miss. Would you care for your suitcase to be put in the baggage car?"

Emma glanced up at the porter, but it wasn't his face that she noticed. It was his dark blue uniform with shining brass buttons.

It wasn't that of an army man, most certainly not that of a captain, but it reminded her of George. As did everything else.

There wasn't a thing on this earth that didn't remind her of him. Could she live with that the rest of her life?

Live with nothing but memories?

Once again, she thought of the letter she'd just returned to her purse. The story he'd shared with her in that letter.

"Miss?"

She shook her head. "No, thank you. I'll keep it with me. It'll fit under the seat."

"Very well," the porter said. "Boarding is at gate three."

She nodded, stood, put on her coat, but as her gaze landed on the porter again, his back as he walked away, she sat down.

The answer was no.

No, she couldn't live the rest of her life with nothing but memories.

She had been living life wrong. Instead of begging for miracles and wishes, she should have been creating her own and making them come true. Instead of fearing that weeds were growing in her garden, she should have been plucking them out, not giving them a chance to take root and grow.

Aunt Jill wasn't in control of her life. Not unless she let her.

The past wasn't in control of her life, either. She may have grown up in the slums, but that's not who she was now. She'd escaped. Hadn't allowed herself to become trapped in that life. Instead, she'd made a new life for herself, one she loved, one she was proud of and didn't want to lose.

Foremost, that new life included George.

She could get on the train, see Sharon, then leave New York City, move somewhere else, but that wasn't what she wanted. She wanted George. She wanted the life she'd known since meeting him, writing to him, and especially since becoming engaged to him.

He was behind so many good things that had happened to her. Her apartment, the children's gift program, her happiness. She had been happy, truly happy, since he'd announced their engagement.

It wasn't real, that had been their deal, but if she left now, there was no chance that their engagement ever could become real. That was what she wanted—for their engagement to be real—but she hadn't believed that could ever happen.

Her heart tumbled slightly. That hadn't been what George wanted. He didn't want it to be real because he didn't want to get married. She hadn't wanted that, either, but that had been before she'd realized how wrong she'd been about so many things.

She loved him, had loved him for a long time, and leaving wasn't going to change that. Nothing would.

Boarding for her train was announced again, and she drew in a deep breath.

Just because she'd changed her mind didn't mean that George had. Nor did she expect him to.

She reached down, grasped the handle of her suitcase, but then released it. Nor could she let Aunt Jill believe that she was in charge, or that she'd won.

There was no sense in begging for a miracle. If she wanted one, she was going to have to make it happen.

George wasn't a pair of dove-gray slippers, but he was her Christmas wish.

Still mad at how he'd behaved, at how foolish he'd been, George sharply steered the car around a corner. So sharply, one of the bags on the seat tipped over.

The white hat, with the daisy pinned to it, rolled onto his lap. He grasped it, was about to toss it back in the bag, but tightened his hold on it instead.

He had returned home wanting the love of a woman. One woman.

The confidence he'd had in the war, that of knowing what needed to be done, and of doing it, was still there, inside him—he just had to use it.

His own common sense was there, too.

To love or not to love couldn't be controlled, or defined by a reason. Any reason.

Love is a gift. A miracle. To not embrace it, to not share it, took away the reason for living.

He'd give Emma a reason to love him.

Love him like he loved her.

The car tires squealed against the pavement as he turned the car around and headed toward the train station. If her train had already left, he'd drive all the way to New York City.

The bags tumbled and the tires squealed again a short time later, when he pulled into the train station. He threw open his door, leaped out and ran, pushing his way through the people making their way into the depot.

Flustered by every person blocking his route, he continued pushing his way to the front of the line, where he asked, "Train to New York City, where? When?"

"The eleven o'clock just left. The next one is in three hours."

He slapped the counter and spun around.

The line was long and wide. George pivoted to run around the benches that filled the center of the room. It would be quicker than pushing his way back through the crowd to the door.

That's when he saw her.

Sitting on the end of a bench.

There was no mistaking her beautiful chestnut-colored hair, her blue coat.

He skidded to a stop, dropped on one knee next to the bench. "Emma."

She looked at him, closed her eyes and shook her head.

Words eluded him. There was plenty he wanted to say, but the single tear that slid down her cheek left him feeling frozen. Like time had stopped. Like his life had stopped.

"I couldn't do it, George," she whispered. "I tried, but couldn't do it."

He laid a hand on her knee. "Couldn't do what?"

She opened her eyes. "Get on the train. Leave you."

Relief flooded his system. "I'm glad."

She pressed a hand over her mouth for a moment. "I read your letters while waiting, and remember the one where you told me about the little dog you found? Where it was stuck in the mud and you rescued it, then gave it to a little girl who loves it very much?"

There had been a lot more to that story than he'd written. The dog had been in one of the trenches. He'd thought it was a rat and would have shot it if it hadn't barked at him. He'd cleaned it up, and it had followed him through the trenches and fields on its short little legs for over a month, until their mission had been completed. Once at the base, he had given Dog, as he'd called it, to a local man for his daughter, who had become smitten with the animal. "Yes, I remember that letter," he replied.

"I loved that letter. Loved how an army captain, risking his own life every day, saved a dog, and sitting here, I thought about that dog. How you'd saved it, gave it a new life, and how if it had run away from you, tried to escape, it probably would have died and would never have known a life with a little girl who loved him."

"That might have happened, but it didn't attempt to run away."

She nodded, looked at him with puffy eyes. "I did. I thought I had to, because..." She pinched her lips together.

He touched her cheek, wiped away a tear with the pad of his thumb.

"Then I thought of my mother, and how, no matter what Aunt Jill said, she wouldn't leave us. Wouldn't leave my father because she loved him. Loved us. Me and Sharon. She'd tell us that while we walked home, and that nothing Aunt Jill could ever say or do would ever change her mind."

He could say things about Jill and Weston Lumber, but the only thing that mattered right now was her. "Nothing could ever change my mind about you, Emma," he said, slightly hoarse by the emotions filling him. "I love you. I fell in love with you through our letters and have grown to love you more each day since we met."

She tilted her head so her cheek filled his palm. "Oh, George, I love you, too. So very much. I dreamed of you loving me in return, but I knew that's not what you want and—"

"Yes, it is," he interjected. "I want to love you, and I do. So very so much that there's no room for anything else." That was true, yet he understood her fears. "I was afraid to tell you how I felt, because you didn't have a reason to love me."

"I have a thousand reasons to love you."

"And I have a thousand reasons to love you, but the main one is love. Love *is* a reason. Love is why I want to spend the rest of my life with you." He slid his hand off her cheek, into her hair. "No one will ever love you like I do, because I know I'll never love anything the way I love you. It's with every part of my being, and nothing, not a single thing, means more to me than you."

"Nothing means more to me than you," she whispered. "That's why I couldn't leave. Because I refuse to let anything keep me from having what I want. You.

I'd thought I'd needed a miracle, but all I'd needed was a wish and to find a way to make it come it true."

He'd never granted someone a wish before and was excited to do just that. He slipped his hand out of her hair, touched her cheek, then reached in his pocket, pulled out the ring. Holding it before her face, he asked, "Emma Leigh Ellis, will you marry me?"

She pressed a hand over her mouth.

"Soon," he continued. "Today, tomorrow, because I can't wait any longer than that for you to become my wife. I swear I'll show you how much I love you every single day."

While nodding, she held her hand out to him. "Yes, I will marry you. Whenever you want. I'll show you how much I love you every day, too. Every day."

He slid the ring on her finger, then kissed her. An all-consuming, fully engrossing kiss. So engrossing that he had no idea why the depot erupted into a roar of cheering and clapping. So engrossing that when he lifted his head, to look around, he wasn't sure how he and Emma had ended up standing, arms around each other and bodies pressed tightly together.

Realization made him smile. The need to be closer, as close as possible, is what had brought them to their feet, and the crowd was cheering for them. Nearly every person in the depot was looking at them, clapping, cheering and shouting congratulations.

"Evidently," he told Emma, "people noticed that I was down on one knee."

Her eyes were sparkling, her smile big and bright. "I guess so."

He lifted her off her feet and spun in a circle, kissing her again as the crowd continued to cheer.

Chapter Sixteen

If she wasn't so happy, Emma might have been embarrassed by having become such a spectacle, but there was nothing—absolutely nothing—about marrying George that was embarrassing. It was her greatest wish come true.

Filled with happiness, all she could do was laugh, smile at those cheering and clapping, and when George made a show of taking a bow before the onlookers, she curtsied beside him.

With shouts of congratulations and waves, the crowd dispersed, went back about their business, but they left behind a joyfulness that filled the air. It filled her, too, and she looked at the ring on her finger. She had done that many times the last couple of weeks, however, this time, as the ruby glistened back at her, nothing other than elation filled her.

Then, she frowned. "How did you know I was here?"

"I found the letter you left for Beverly. She forgot the bags of hats, scarves and mittens at her apartment this morning," he replied. "I offered to pick them up for her."

"I set the bags by the door so she wouldn't forget

them." Due to everything else that had been keeping her busy, she'd just finished the last scarf last night, and Beverly was to take them to the lumberyard this morning, to be boxed up for delivery.

"*Behind* the door," he said. "That's why she forgot them. She opened the door for Willis when he arrived to give her a ride and the bag was hidden behind the door."

Emma loved that dear old woman. "I put it there because that's where she hangs her coat."

"I know. That's also where she hangs this." He pulled Beverly's white crocheted hat with the silk daisy on the brim out of his pocket, and then tugged on the brim, trying to straighten the creases that had formed from being in his pocket.

She giggled. "What are you doing with that?"

He put the hat on her head. "There." Grinning, he adjusted the flower on the brim. "You're the woman who should have been waiting for me, wearing that hat, the day I returned home. The woman I'd fallen in love with through pen and paper."

She made a show of adjusting the hat, then looked at him and smiled. "Hello, Captain Weston. I'm so happy you're home."

"Me, too," he whispered, then kissed her.

It wasn't a long, drawn-out kiss, just a short, sweet one, that was full of promises.

As it ended, he flicked the end of her nose with his finger and then, laughing, picked up her suitcase. "Let's get out of here."

She wrapped her hands around his arm, hugged it as they walked through the depot and outside, all the way to the parking area. Seeing his car, she looked up at him. "I don't think that's a place people are supposed to park."

Cars were having to drive around his car to get in and out of the parking area because it sat in the middle of the driving lane.

He shrugged. "I was in a hurry. If your train had already left, I planned on driving to New York City."

"You did?"

"Yes, I did." He opened the passenger door for her but stopped her to plant a fast kiss on her lips. "I'm glad I didn't have to do that."

"Me, too."

He winked at her, then grabbed the bags off the seat so she could climb in. He then deposited her suitcase and the bags in the trunk before climbing in through the driver's door. "You look cute in that hat."

"Thank you," she said, "but don't get attached to it. Beverly loves this hat."

"That's all right, I'd rather be attached to you."

Happiness bubbled inside her and she scooted closer to him so she could rest her head against his shoulder.

"Where to?" he asked. "Your apartment to unpack, or Weston Lumber to drop off the bags for Beverly?"

She wanted to spend every moment with him, just him, but knew that Beverly would be worried about the scarves, hats and mittens. "Weston Lumber." Many things had weighed heavy on her since making her decision to leave and she'd done a lot of thinking at the depot, but other than knowing she wouldn't run away this time because George meant too much to her, she hadn't found any answers as to what to do about certain things.

"How can Aunt Jill ruin Weston Lumber?" she asked.

"She can't."

She lifted her head and took the hat off so she could see his face. "Are you sure? Because she's awfully convinced that she can."

"I'm sure." He glanced at her. "Is that what she told you? When? This morning?"

"She told me that on Saturday, at the Christmas party."

"Did she tell you to leave town?"

"No, I decided to do after I no longer had a job."

"Why did you quit?"

Despite her happiness, which was still alive inside her, there was sadness, too, because of many things, including not working with the children any longer. "I didn't. I got fired this morning."

"Fired?"

"Mr. Segal didn't use that word. He said that my position was no longer needed."

"Why?"

"I don't know. He told me to not insult his or my intelligence by asking questions." She pushed the air out of her lungs. The whole event was now making her mad rather than sad. "It was Aunt Jill. When I walked out of the school, she was there, in her car. She honked at me and told me to heed her warnings."

He stiffened and was staring straight ahead. "She did, did she?"

"Yes. And you know what I'm going to do?" She answered before he could. "I'm going to get my job back." That sounded good, and it felt good to say it, but she wasn't sure she could do it. Yet, she had to try because she refused to let Aunt Jill to win. Her mother had never let her win and she wouldn't, either.

George smiled at her. "I'm sure you will. You are very good at that job." He reached over and took a hold of her hand. "Though once we are married, you won't need a job."

"You don't want me to have a job?" She hadn't thought of that but realized now that his mother didn't have a job.

"I just mean that you don't have to if you don't want to. I want you to be happy, and I know working at the school made you happy. If that's what you want, I'm fine with it. Just know that I will never do anything to make you feel trapped, I promise."

Kissing his cheek, she said, "I like the idea of being trapped by you. More than like it."

He laughed, then lifted her hand, kissed it. "Then when am I going to trap you into marrying me? It needs to be soon. I've waited long enough already."

"Whenever you want."

"Tomorrow?"

She laughed. "Tomorrow is Christmas Eve, and we are supposed to be delivering gifts." She hadn't forgotten that while sitting at the train station. Hadn't forgotten a lot of things. Was that truly only an hour ago? That seemed impossible, but the happiness inside her said it was true. All of it. She'd soon be married to him.

"We aren't busy tomorrow evening," he said.

He'd had to return his hand to the steering wheel in order to take a corner, and she snuggled closer to his side, wrapped her hands around his arm. "You want to get married on Christmas Eve?"

"I want to marry you as soon as possible. I don't care what day it is."

She didn't, either, but knew from Sharon's wedding

that some planning was needed. "I suppose I could ask your mother to help and Beverly, and—"

"Me," he said. "The courthouse is open. We'll tell everyone our plans, and while they are helping you, I'll go get the license."

She closed her eyes, half wondering if she was dreaming all this.

"I'm rushing you," he said after a moment.

She opened her eyes. "No. I want to marry you as soon as possible. I love you. Nothing will ever change that."

"I love you, too, and I feel as if I wasted time in not telling you that."

"You didn't waste time. Before today, I was too afraid to admit that I'd fallen in love with you." Before today, she'd been too focused on other things to fully understand that she'd found life-altering love. Because that's exactly what had happened. He'd altered her life.

He steered around another corner, onto the road that led to the lumberyard. She could see the large buildings. They both remained quiet during the distance to the parking area, then, as he turned off the car, he asked, "What's wrong?"

"Nothing is wrong." Huffing out a sigh, she shook her head. "It's just Aunt Jill."

He took a hold of her hand. "I wish I could change the past for you. Make it so you'd never been hurt. I can't. I can't even promise that you won't get hurt in the future, because parts of life are painful. What I can promise you is that Jill can't hurt you anymore. She has no control over us."

Emma wished that was true, but she'd just lost her job because of her aunt. However, she had made a choice to not run away, and to marry him, because that was what she wanted above all else. To be with him, no matter what. "You're right. She doesn't have control over us."

He slid his hand up her arm, over her shoulder and cupped the back of her neck while leaning closer. "I love you."

She melted into his kiss as their lips met. This was what she wanted with her whole heart. If it meant she'd have to fight Aunt Jill in order to have it, so be it.

Minutes later, the gift room was filled with as much cheering and clapping as the train depot had been. Amy insisted a Christmas Eve wedding would be perfect, and instantly began making the arrangements, which included sending George off to get the license.

He'd only been gone a short time when the door opened and another man walked through it. Dressed in a uniform, Emma didn't recognize him, but the squeal that Janice let out made it clear that her husband, Bill, had finally returned home.

Almost as tall as George, and almost as broad, Bill was from whom Nellie and Nathaniel had inherited their copper-colored hair.

"I told you I'd be home in time for Christmas," Bill said, with Janice still in his arms.

"Why didn't you call?" Janice asked him. "I would have met you at the station."

"I called your father." Bill waved toward the door, where Walt stood. "Had him pick me up so I could surprise you."

Emma was so happy for Janice, and for Nathaniel and Nellie.

"This is Emma and Beverly," Janice said. "Emma and George are getting married tomorrow."

"No kidding?" Bill greeted both she and Beverly, and then explained, "While I was on the phone at the depot, a man asked a woman to marry him. I didn't see the couple, but the entire depot was cheering for them."

A blush heated Emma's cheeks.

Even more as she felt Beverly's eyes on her.

"Oh, is that so?" Beverly asked.

George's first stop was the courthouse. That didn't take long, though, as he'd gone to school with Nancy, the clerk who waited on him. From there, he drove to the school.

"I'm here to see Mr. Segal," he told the woman sitting at the desk as he walked past it to the door labeled Principal's Office.

He opened the door, closed it behind him and, arms folded, leaned back against it. "You eliminated a position in the library today."

Instantly on the defense, Segal stood, puffed out his barrel chest. "What concern is that of yours?"

George merely stared back at the man. Waited.

Segal shifted from foot to foot, then, gave a nod. "It was brought to my attention that an employee was stealing."

With his jaw growing tighter, George asked, "Stealing what?"

"Money from her aunt. The young woman lived with her."

"Emma Ellis," George said.

Segal's Adam's apple bobbed above the collar of his shirt.

"My name is George Weston, and—"

"Oh, Mr. Weston," Segal interrupted, looking almost relieved. "George. Welcome home. Mrs. King informed me that Miss Ellis has also been pilfering money from the children's gift program that your mother created. I fired her immediately. Couldn't have someone of such low morals working here, at the school. I assure you, no one else in this building would ever do such a thing. I hope you understand that. Understand that I took care of the issue posthaste."

Steaming, George moved forward and slapped both hands on the desk. "What I understand is that you listened to a conniving woman, and rather than seeking the truth, you made yourself judge, jury and executioner without giving Miss Ellis the opportunity to defend herself."

Segal took a step back, bumping into the chair behind him and almost toppling, but managed to stay upright by grasping ahold of the chair.

George leaned farther across the desk. "What you don't understand is that the woman you fired has never lived with Jill King, that Miss Ellis is the woman who created the children's gift-giving program in the first place and that she has never stolen anything her entire life. She is also the woman who will become my wife tomorrow."

"Your wife?" Segal asked while stepping behind the chair as if it could offer protection.

It couldn't, but George had already decided that punching this man wouldn't give him the results he wanted. "Yes, my wife. And she is very dedicated to the gift program she created. So dedicated, she walked the woods until she found the perfect tree for the city park, which is now covered with ribbons." He could go on about all the good things that Emma had done, but that would take all day and he had more stops to make. "She is also the woman that you will write a formal letter of apology to."

"Yes, yes, of course. I'll do it right away. Today even."

George slapped the desk one last time before he straightened and turned about.

"She can return to her job after Christmas break," Mr. Segal said.

George paused with his hand on the doorknob, looked over his shoulder. "That will be her decision. If she wants to work with a man who has such low intelligence, I won't stop her, but if she does I will expect that she is treated with the utmost respect."

"Oh, yes, of course. The utmost."

George pulled open the door, nodded to the woman at the desk on his way out, but then stopped, walked back to her desk and spoke with her for a moment. Then, satisfied with their agreement, he left the school.

His next stop was on the south side of town.

Oliver, the stooped butler that had been working at the King residence for years, greeted him with a smile. "George—Mr. Weston—I was happy to hear you'd returned from the war."

"Thank you, Oliver, I'm here to see Mrs. King." Due to the terseness of his tone, George wasn't surprised by Oliver's disappearing smile.

"Yes, sir. Right this way."

George knew the house well but followed the man along the hallway—the very hallway where he'd first met Emma—and then made two turns before entering the living room. There had been no expense spared during the building and furnishing of this house, and the contrast of it to the small apartment that Emma lived in was fuel for the fire of anger already flaming inside him. It infuriated him that Emma had struggled her entire life, yet had found a job that she'd love, only to have Jill take that away from her, too.

"George," Roy greeted, rising from his chair.

Jill sat on a white velvet sofa, smirking like a cat that just knocked a fish out of its bowl and was about to eat it.

She'd soon be eating crow, and best get used to it, because as long as there was a chance that she'd interfere in Emma's happiness, he wouldn't let up.

"Roy," he said with a nod.

"I'm assuming you're here because… Well, allow me to apologize for the things Jill said about Emma." Roy turned to Jill. "We've discussed it intently."

A quiet man who often looked the other way when it came to his wife's behavior, Roy might think a discussion would make a difference, but George knew better and held his gaze on Jill. "Before or after she had Emma fired from the school?"

"Fired?" Roy asked.

Jill gave a slight shrug with one shoulder as she tapped her long fingernails on the wood of the sofa arm.

Twisting one curled edge of his mustache, as he often did when flustered, Roy walked to the sofa. "I said it was over, Jill. Over."

She didn't so much as glance at her husband. "She'll ruin you, just like her father did her mother."

"No, she won't ruin anything," George replied. "But I will."

"You." Jill cackled. "You don't have the authority to do anything." She stood and pointed to herself. "But I do. One word from me and every North Country logger will stop cutting timber for Weston Lumber."

"You mean stop cutting Weston timber," George said. "It's Weston land, we own the timber, and that's exactly what I am here to discuss. By January first, every North Country logger needs to have vacated Weston property, or you'll be fined every day thereafter, per day, per man."

Jill laughed. "You don't have the authority to do that."

"Yes, he does," Roy said, twisting harder on his mustache, loosening gray hairs. "Craig will stand behind any decision George makes. You know that as well as I do." Turning to him, he asked, "George, can't we discuss this?"

George shook his head. Just like while in the army, he was here to do a job and exit.

"There's nothing to discuss," Jill said. "He's only bluffing."

"I'm not bluffing," George said. "Unlike some, I only *heed warnings* that I believe are genuine."

Her eyes narrowed, knowing Emma had told him everything.

"We have over a hundred loggers in the woods right now," Roy said. "Men who need jobs. We have no other property to harvest. That will take time and—"

"And Weston won't have any lumber to mill," Jill interrupted, obviously still believing she had the upper hand. "His employees won't have any work."

"I have loggers ready to pull onto Weston land all the way into Pennsylvania," George replied. "If they can't get in the woods this winter for a full harvest, we'll go on the market and buy logs to process. Our millworkers will remain working. Every last one of them."

Jill's face was red, her eyes glaring. "You'd risk your family's business over a conniving little simpleton of a girl?"

George had to rock on his heels to keep from advancing on her. The heat of his breath burned his nostrils as he pushed out the air in his lungs, attempting to remain calm. "The question is, are you willing to risk yours?"

Jill's hands were balled into fists as she crossed her arms, stared at him.

"It's simple enough," George said. "Weston Lumber will fulfill our contracts with North Country this year, so your men will all have jobs, for one thing in exchange."

"What?" Jill snapped.

"An apology," he replied.

"I won't apologize to that little—"

"I won't let you near Emma," George said. "The apology is to Mr. Segal. The principal at the school. You will apologize to him for lying about Emma. Tell him that you lied about her living with you, lied that she stole from you and lied that she was pilfering money from the children's gift program."

"Jill!" Roy said. "You didn't."

"The apology will take place in front of Mr. Segal's secretary, who will contact me and let me know that each offense has been included in the apology," George added.

"She'll do it," Roy answered.

Jill hadn't agreed, and George wasn't worried if she

would or not. He was prepared to fulfill his warning to the fullest.

"I will not," she shouted. "Absolutely, will not."

"Very well." George gave her a nod of finality. "January first, it is."

Chapter Seventeen

"Nervous?"

Emma didn't turn from the window, but her smile grew "Not at all. I'm just admiring the view. It's snowing." Huge flakes were gently floating to the ground, adding to the beauty of the yard that sloped down to the river.

"It is." An arm fell around her shoulders. "It's beautiful. Everything about this home is beautiful, and I'm so happy for you."

Emma looked at her sister. "I'm so happy for me, too, and I'm so happy that you are here."

"Me, too," Sharon said. "I was shocked when Eddie came home yesterday and said to pack our bags, that we were going to Albany for your wedding."

Emma hugged her sister. "I was shocked when I walked in the house and saw you." That had happened a few hours ago, after she and George had spent the morning delivering gifts to the orphanage. While she'd distributed the hats, mittens and scarves, George had carried a tree in through a back door for the children to decorate tonight, and crates of gifts that the children would find under the tree tomorrow morning.

Not only had he done all of that, but he'd also done this. Called Eddie and asked them to come to Albany for their wedding.

For her.

He truly was the most wonderful man on earth.

Sharon released her, stepped back. "Let me have a final look."

Emma slowly turned in a complete circle so Sharon could see all sides of the lovely light gold-colored dress made of floral lace and satin, with a silk underskirt. It had short, flutter sleeves, a tufted waist with an attached thick ribbon of shimmering gold and a fishtail hem that started at the knees. Amy had taken her shopping yesterday afternoon, stating that once the dress was purchased, everything else would fall into place.

It had.

In a few minutes, she'd be marrying George.

A moment of nervousness struck then, and she faced her sister. "You like him, don't you?"

"George?" Sharon asked, then laughed. "I've liked him since your first letter about him. I could tell how happy writing to him made you." Sharon hugged her again. "It's obvious how much you love each other."

"I do love him. So very much." While getting dressed, she'd told Sharon everything that she hadn't mentioned in her letters, about why she'd started to write to George and about everything that had happened since his return home.

Biting back her smile, Sharon whispered, "And I love how it all turned out, not just for you, but for us."

"Us?" Emma asked, confused.

Holding up both hands, Sharon said, "I know Mother always told us to forgive Aunt Jill, or to ignore her, but that had been impossible with the way she'd treated us. How she always looked down on us as if we were the scum of the earth." Sharon laughed. "As Dad always said, we reap what we sow."

Emma stood silent. Their father had always said that, and Aunt Jill had certainly sowed hatred. Like weeds in a garden of flowers.

"You've proven that we aren't the scum of the earth," Sharon said. "We never have been. It doesn't take money to make good people. It just takes a good heart. That's something Mother would say, and I'd think to myself that a good heart was something that Aunt Jill didn't have."

Emma nodded. "I remember Mother saying that, and thinking the same thing." She glanced out the window again. The flowerbeds were covered with a blanket of white snow, but that didn't change the fact that the only way to not have weeds was to pluck them.

"I never could figure out how they could be sisters, and be so different, especially when I have the best sister in the world."

"So do I." Emma turned about and held her hands up at her sides as she teasingly asked, "How can that be?"

They were laughing, and hugging, when a knock sounded on the door.

A moment later, Beverly stuck her head in around the door. "Just me, and it's time. Your groom is waiting."

Emma wasn't nervous or apprehensive. There was no room inside her for anything but excitement, and love. Eddie waited with her in the hall as Sharon walked into the living room and took a spot next to the beautifully decorated Christmas tree.

The pastor stood there, too, and so did Bill, right beside George, who never took his eyes off her as Eddie took her arm, walked her into the room and handed her over to her soon-to-be husband.

She couldn't think of anyone else, anything else, except for him as they looked into each other's eyes and exchanged vows, pledging to love and cherish each other. She already did love and cherish him and knew she would for an eternity, but hearing him make those promises to her, an amazing warmth filled her entire being because George kept his promises. She knew that.

The kiss they shared at the end of the ceremony was more than a touching of lips. It made her think of their letter writing, of how she'd kissed each envelope after sealing it. That's what this kiss was like. Full of emotion, hope and promises. It was as if the two of them were being sealed together with their love locked inside. Forever.

Champagne came next, and hugs and laughter with their family. They were all family now. His parents, aunt and uncle, Janice and Bill, Nathaniel and Nellie, Beverly, and Sharon and Eddie.

More toasts, more fun and laughter continued through dinner. They'd just finished eating and had made their way back into the front room when James announced there was a visitor to see her.

Emma looked at George, wondering who it could be. Beside her on the sofa, he shrugged, and informed James to show them into the front room.

A moment later, upon seeing Uncle Roy walk into

the room, her breath stalled in her lungs, waiting for Aunt Jill to appear next.

But that didn't happen.

It was just Roy.

George stood. She rose to her feet, too, and hadn't realized how quiet the room had become until she heard Roy clear his throat.

"Excuse me for interrupting," he said, looking at her. "This will only take a moment. There were things that I never knew, never questioned, and I should have. I just thought—" He shook his head, walked forward and handed her a large envelope.

"It's your grandfather's will." Roy bowed his head slightly. "It was never followed." He then looked at George. "She'll need an attorney. Jill will contest it."

Emma pressed a hand to her heart at how Roy closed his eyes. He looked so sad, so lost. Stepping forward, she laid a hand on his arm.

He patted her hand. "I thought I could make her forget him. Even thought I had, but…" He shook his head again.

"Forget who?" Emma asked. "Her father?"

"No, dear, your father." Roy's sigh sounded shaky. "Jill was in love with him but he never had eyes for anyone but your mother. That infuriated Jill and when your parents eloped—" he shrugged "—I was there. Comforted her. Because I was in love with her. Still am. I don't know why, but I am." He pulled up a half smile and pointed at the envelope. "Your grandfather wanted everything split equally between his two daughters. It's all there."

"Can I get you a drink, Roy?" George asked.

"No, thank you. I'm leaving for New York City on the

next train. Going to spend Christmas Day with Martha and Delmar. They are expecting a baby soon."

"Tell her—them—congratulations," George said. "From all of us."

"I will."

Emma wasn't exactly sure what made up her mind. Perhaps it was the love she'd found, or perhaps it was knowing the reason behind Aunt Jill's behavior. Either way, she held on tighter to Roy's arm as she glanced at George, then her sister.

It was as if she read their minds, both of them. This was her decision, and they'd back her on whatever she decided.

She didn't want any weeds in her garden, and smiled at both of them, then at Uncle Roy. "Thank you. Thank you for coming here, for giving me this, but I don't need it," she said, handing him the envelope. "*We* don't need it," she added, once again glancing at George and then Sharon.

Roy didn't take the envelope, merely looked at her with confusion. "It's the only way Jill will—"

"I don't care." Her mother had asked her to forgive Aunt Jill many times and she never had. It was time she did. She had a new life. A wonderful life. One that had no room in it for anything except love. "I have no desire to fight Aunt Jill, not over an inheritance or anything else." She rubbed his arm. "I do wish she would see the love that she does have. Has had for a very long time. If there is anything I can do to help you, to help her, I will do it." She pushed the envelope toward him again, encouraging him to take it. "But I won't do this."

Roy took the envelope at the exact same moment

the slam of a door echoed from the hallway, along with clicking of hard steps on the floor.

George stepped forward, but Emma laid a hand on his arm as Jill entered the room, lips pursed and eyes glaring.

Memories flashed in Emma's mind of the last time Jill had been in this room, when she'd needed George's hold to keep her upright. She didn't this time. She had his love, and that love gave her strength.

She crossed the silent room and stopped before Jill. There was no fear inside her, but her heart was pounding, because in the past, she had been afraid of this woman. That was sad, because the woman standing before her didn't look like some kind of fairy-tale monster. She just looked old, tired. With sympathy, Emma shook her head. "I have no control over the past. None of us do. But I think we've all suffered enough. And needlessly, because it hasn't changed anything. Nor will it."

Jill's eyes narrowed and her breasts heaved as she drew in air.

Emma held firm and she felt even stronger when hands settled on her shoulders. Her entire being felt George standing behind her. It made her pulse race, but more than that, it confirmed she would never face anything alone again.

"You, along with Uncle Roy," she said, "have managed North Country Logging for many years, and there is no reason for that to change. No reason that the company can't continue to grow. But in order for that to happen, we all have to choose to put the past where it belongs and look toward the future, considering the impact of how our decisions will affect the next generation."

Jill lifted her chin a bit higher, shifted her stance slightly.

Emma wasn't going to beg or grovel. No matter what happened in the future, she had George's love and that would carry her through good times and bad. She laid a hand atop one of his on her shoulder and turned to look up at him.

He kissed her temple as he turned her about and they walked back toward the sofa.

"I—" Jill cleared her throat. "I've decided to go to New York City with you, Roy. Our train leaves soon." She then turned and walked out of the room.

Roy bid farewell and in doing so, kissed Emma's cheek. "You are more like your mother than you'll ever know," he whispered.

Honored, she whispered, "Thank you."

As he left the room, which was still heavy with silence, Emma turned to Nathaniel and Nellie. The past was in the past, and this was Christmas Eve. "I do believe that there are some presents under that tree that people need to open."

Gaiety soon filled the room again and lasted for hours.

Many, many hours.

The first light of dawn was filtering through the curtains when Emma opened her eyes, and sleepily closed them again. She was tired, but it was a wonderful tired. Neither she nor George had drifted off to sleep until the wee hours of the morning.

Memories of the shared intimacy of their wedding night released a tiny sigh from her.

So did the way George kissed the side of her neck

now. His body was pressed against her back, their legs were entangled and one of his hands caressed her stomach. It was all dreamlike, yet very real at the same time.

"Merry Christmas," he whispered.

She rolled over so they faced each other and dropped a tiny kiss in the hollow of his throat. "Merry Christmas."

He rolled onto his back and brought her with him, so she was lying atop him. As he adjusted the covers, pulling them up over her back and tucking them around her shoulders, he said, "Children across the city are waking up this morning to gifts under their tree because of you, but I'm the one who received the best gift of all."

Kissing his chin, she teasingly said, "I knew you'd like the book I bought for you." It was one that he'd never read—she knew that from their letters and had bought it for him before he'd returned home.

She felt his chuckle, and other things about his body. Wonderful things that made her so glad they were married and could share their love in every way.

"I do like the book." His hands roamed up and down her back. "But it's the gift I'm holding right now that I'm referring to. It's the best gift I've ever received, and it's a lifelong one."

She looked deep into his eyes, saw the love, felt it, too, and knew one thing for sure. Every time she'd written a letter to him, addressed the letter to Captain George Weston, she'd wished for one thing. "I received more than a gift this Christmas. I received a miracle. A true miracle." Then she kissed that miracle.

Epilogue

Four years later...

Emma pointed to the tiny green sprout growing among the flowers. "That one, Ruth, right there."

"Dat a weed?" Ruth asked, in her tiny two-year-old voice that was delightful to everyone's ears.

"Yes," Emma answered her daughter. "That's a weed."

"No weeds," Ruth said, tugging out the sprout. "Eberly like flowers."

"That's correct," Emma said. "Beverly likes flowers."

"I pick Eberly?"

"Yes, you can pick one for Beverly." Though Beverly still had her apartment, she also had her bedroom here at the house, and stayed in it far more nights than she stayed in her apartment.

"And Drama?"

"Yes, you can pick one for Grandma, too," Emma assured her.

It went on like that, with Ruth asking to pick flowers for everyone in the family before the two of them walked up the lush, green hill, with Ruth holding yellow-and-white daises tightly in both hands.

Once Ruth had distributed the flowers to Beverly and Amy, who were sitting in lawn chairs, enjoying the warm summer air, she busied herself by showing the remaining flowers to her Raggedy Ann doll.

"How are you feeling, dear?" Amy asked. "I remember when I was carrying each of the boys that the hill seemed to get bigger as my stomach grew."

"It does seem that way," Emma agreed, rubbing her stomach as she sat down. Although the next Weston wouldn't make his or her debut for a couple of months, everyone was anxiously awaiting the event.

The sound of a door opening and closing behind her made Emma's smile widen. She didn't need to turn around. The increase of her heart rate told her that it was George.

A moment later, he kissed the side of her face, and both of his hands caressed her stomach from where he stood behind her chair.

"How's Momma today?" he asked.

"Wonderful. How was your day?"

"Good." He didn't have time to say more because Ruth had noticed his arrival and was running toward him.

"Daddy home!"

"Yes, I am." He scooped their daughter off the ground and gave her kisses and tummy tickles at the same time. Then, holding Ruth in one arm, he laid his other hand on Emma's shoulder. "You have company."

"I do?" She twisted to look around him and began to rise at the same time.

"Don't get up," Aunt Jill said as she walked around George. "I just wanted to drop these off." She set a bag on the ground. "I was visiting Martha and the children in the city and picked up a few books for your library."

"Thank you," Emma said. "That was very thoughtful. I can always use new books." Years ago, Mr. Segal had sent her an apology and had encouraged her to return working at the school, but she had declined. Instead, with support from her husband, she'd started a mobile library so she could visit the orphanages and share books with the children who lived in them. George had purchased her a lovely truck—which meant he'd also taught her how to drive it—and had overseen the installation of numerous shelves in an enclosed box on the back. Within no time, she was not only visiting orphanages, but also neighborhoods and small nearby towns that didn't have access to books, and expanded her library to include offerings for all ages. She loved it even more than she'd loved working at the school.

"Yes, well, it's just a few, but have George carry them inside for you," Jill said. "The bag could be too heavy for you in your condition."

"Thank you, I will," Emma assured her, glancing up at George.

He winked at her as he set Ruth on the ground.

No one would claim that Aunt Jill had changed one hundred percent, but the changes in her were certainly noticeable. She had apologized years ago, too, and had joined the lumber coalition. George had been right about so many things within the industry. Lumber was in high demand, and with the booming economy, Weston Lumber and North Country Logging, as well as many other companies, were thriving.

After looking inside the bag, Ruth ran over to her doll, collected a flower and hurried back to hand it to Jill.

Jill pressed two fingers to her lips and glanced around as if nervous as she kneeled and accepted the flower. "Thank you, Ruthie."

"You welcome," Ruth said, toddling off toward her doll again.

Jill looked at the flower for several seconds before she rose and nodded at them. "I need to get home. Roy's been home alone for almost a week, and I'm sure he's waiting for me."

"I'm sure he is," Emma said as she stood.

"I'll see you to the door," George offered.

"No, that's all right." Jill looked at the flower in her hand again. Sniffed it, and nodded, with what might be glistening eyes.

That could be caused by the sunlight, but Emma doubted it. "Thank you, again."

Jill nodded, waved and walked toward the house, glancing at the flower in her hand every so often.

There was a moment of silence until Jill disappeared around the side of the house, then George chuckled.

"What do you find funny?" Emma asked, stepping closer and resting her hands on his chest.

He looped his arms around her, pulled her closer. "The proof is in the pudding, my dear."

"Proof of what?"

"That our daughter will be as much of a miracle maker as her mother."

He kissed her then, and she kissed him back, because she liked what he'd said, and because she loved him. Had loved him before she'd even known him. And would love him forever.

* * * * *

*If you enjoyed this story, why not try
Lauri Robinson's other great reads*

The Return of His Promised Duchess
A Family for the Titanic Survivor
Diary of a War Bride

*And be sure to read her miniseries
The Osterlund Saga*

Marriage or Ruin for the Heiress
The Heiress and the Baby Boom

Love Harlequin romance?

DISCOVER.

Be the first to find out about promotions, news and exclusive content!

Facebook.com/HarlequinBooks

Twitter.com/HarlequinBooks

Instagram.com/HarlequinBooks

Pinterest.com/HarlequinBooks

YouTube.com/HarlequinBooks

ReaderService.com

EXPLORE.

Sign up for the Harlequin e-newsletter and download a free book from any series at **TryHarlequin.com**

CONNECT.

Join our Harlequin community to share your thoughts and connect with other romance readers! **Facebook.com/groups/HarlequinConnection**

HARLEQUIN

Heartfelt or thrilling, passionate or uplifting—Harlequin is more than just happily-ever-after.

With twelve different series to choose from and new books available every month, you are sure to find stories that will move you, uplift you, inspire and delight you.

HNEWS2021

Get 4 FREE REWARDS!

We'll send you 2 FREE Books plus 2 FREE Mystery Gifts.

FREE Value Over **$20**

Both the **Harlequin®** **Historical** and **Harlequin®** **Romance** series feature compelling novels filled with emotion and simmering romance.

HARLEQUIN
PLUS

Announcing a **BRAND-NEW**
multimedia subscription service
for romance fans like you!

Read, Watch and Play.

Experience the easiest way to get
the romance content you crave.

Start your **FREE 7 DAY TRIAL** at
<u>www.harlequinplus.com/freetrial</u>.